A NOSE
FOR
MURDER
A SYLVIE
BROADSTAIRS
MYSTERY
M.S.SAXON

A Nose for Murder – A Sylvie Broadstairs mystery by M.S. Saxon

She's the psychic Geordie pensioner who tells it straight and suffers no fools. So when Sylvie's estranged drag queen husband is murdered, closely followed by a second family member, she can't help but get stuck in. Even when it looks like Sylvie herself may be the killer's next victim.

D.C.I. Seymour Witless is clueless and wifeless. Can he afford to refuse the psychic's help in both of these matters?

With side-kicks Bobs, Hoggy, Reverend Norris and a few more, the clues begin to stack up. And with an abundance of

suspects, what's a performing psychic to do other than to *stage* a confrontation?

'A Nose for Murder' is a *not-so-cosy* mystery, so described because it *does* contain a number of expletives, though not in excess and the 'f' word is used only once. The humour however is more freely scattered, for which I make no apology. So get comfortable and prepare to be entertained.

STATEMENT OF COPYRIGHT

Printed in the United Kingdom.

Book design by M.S. Sanderson

Illustrations by M.S. Sanderson

A Nose for Murder – M.S. Saxon
This publication available in ebook format.

First edition : September 2023

Website : www.mssaxonbooks.co.uk

There's a fine line between saying too much and saying too little. I walk that line like a drunken clown at the circus. – unknown.

TABLE OF CONTENTS

CONTENTS

Statement of copyright....4

Table of Contents....7

Prologue : June 1926....9

Chapter 1 : The Shoreline club - 1986....15

Chapter 2 : Cleaning up in ICU....19

Chapter 3 : Suspicion....27

Chapter 4 : The post mortem....39

Chapter 5 : The gig : St Martin-in-the-fields church hall....51

Chapter 6 : An inspector calls....75

Chapter 7 : The runaways....91

Chapter 8 : Finding where to start....105

Chapter 9 : The backstabber....115

Chapter 10 : The investigation deepens....125

Chapter 11 :The rejects hang out....135

Chapter 12 : The warbling witch....143

Chapter 13 : Hoggy & the Great North Run....155

Chapter 14 : The unofficial murder team....165

Chapter 15 : Clarabelle goes missing....187

Chapter 16 : A visit for Mr.Tracey senior....197

Chapter 17 : A new way in....205

Chapter 18 : Coffee Joe's....217

Chapter 19 : It's all about the keys....223

Chapter 20 : The flat search....245

Chapter 21 : Hoggy's nicked....253

Chapter 22 : The line-up....263

Chapter 23 : The Gucci handbag....271

Chapter 24 : Norris is exposed....281

Chapter 25 : Hoggy gets a grilling....291

Chapter 26 : An act of Sabotage....305

Chapter 27 : Back to the shoreline....313

Chapter 28 : When Mohawk met Crystal....323

Chapter 29 : Charlie's mystery illness & Royston's mystery girlfriend.....333

Chapter 30 : Brothers at war....347

Chapter 31 : An unexpected hitch....351

Chapter 32 : Preparations are underway....359

Chapter 33 : Gig number two....373

Chapter 34 : Winding up....399

Note from the author & acknowledgements....407

Other books by M.S. Saxon....408

A Nose for Murder

Prologue : June 1926

Sylvie glared at the second hand as it juddered towards the twelve, willing it to go faster. Squashed up against Stinky Simon in the tiniest classroom of Bessie Street Juniors was not the way she planned on spending another minute. The parting between her pig tails burned as the sun fired its rays mercilessly through the single sash window. And then of all things, Polly pee pants had a nosebleed, wailing like a banshee as it dripped onto the desk before her. *'**No, not now!**'* Sylvie whispered to herself.

Horror took over Miss Fletcher's eyebrows as she leaped forward, grabbing the blackboard duster en route to Polly's desk.

'Don't panic, Polly. Press this against your nose and lean your head back.'

But Polly wailed even more and began to sneeze violently.

'It's the chalk dust, Miss! You've killed me!'

'Don't be ridiculous, Polly. It'll stop in a minute. Just do as I'm telling you.'

Sylvie squeezed her eyes tight shut and held her breath while she waited. And then it came – the rhythmic clanging of the head's brass bell, followed by the scraping back of chairs announcing home time. She snatched up her satchel and darted for the door.

'No running!' shouted Fletcher, still dabbing chalk dust all over Polly's blood-streaked face. Sylvie disappeared into the corridor with twenty-five classmates hot on her heels, as Polly wet her pants for the second time that day.

Out in the yard she spotted him waiting in his cloth cap, shirt sleeves rolled to the elbows and his braces, hoisting baggy corduroys up to his armpits. Always with that grin, straining to reach beyond his enormous ears.

'Dad!' she shrieked, running towards him, arms extended. He snatched her up and swung her around.

'Oof lass, you're gettin' too heavy for me!' he gasped, returning her sandaled feet to the ground and grabbing hold of her outstretched hand. Sylvie dragged him towards the school gates with impatience, pig tails bouncing in rhythm with her feet.

'Can we go by the pond Dad? Can we throw stones in the water?'

'Course we can, love. Work up an appetite, eh?'

Minutes later, they swept onto Lizard Lane and Sylvie ran ahead towards the garden gate. The back door was ajar, and she burst into the kitchen searching for human life.

'Mam, we're home. Where are you?' She found her mother rocking baby Millicent back and forth by the sitting room window. Her cheeks were wet, despite a hasty wipe with the back of her hand.

'What's wrong, Mam?' said Sylvie. 'Is our Millie not well?'

Her mother stopped rocking. 'Your father's left us, Sylvie. He's gone.'

Sylvie's brow furrowed. 'Don't be daft. He just walked me home. He's right behind me.'

'No, he's not love,' her mother answered firmly. 'No matter how much you want him to be, he's not coming back, ever.'

Sylvie ran out of the room and back the way the way she'd come. Stretched over the garden gate she peered down the street but couldn't spot him. Racing back into the house she rushed upstairs.

'Dad? Where are you hiding?' Her folks' bedroom doorknob banged into the wall as she burst her way through. Then she stopped with a jolt. Laid out on the bed in a posh two-piece suit, shirt and tie, all of which rarely saw the light of day, was her father. She leaned across and took his hand. The warmth had gone out of him, and his skin had turned a weird blue grey. 'Dad, what just happened? I don't understand how …. Is this a game? Wake up please Dad. ***Please? For your Sylvie.'***

Her mother watched in silence from the doorway, tears flooding her eyes and still holding baby Millicent close.

'Your father came home from night shift this morning, fell asleep in the chair and never woke up. The funeral's on Friday.' She turned to leave the room, then paused. 'Whatever you think you saw, Sylvie, didn't happen. Unless of course you've inherited Great Aunt Sabrina's gift.'

Sylvie puzzled. 'Gift? What gift?'

'Didn't you know? Aunt Sabrina could communicate with the dead…'

And so the seed was planted in a very fertile corner of Sylvie's mind. She thought about the events of that day for many years to come; expected follow-up episodes to confirm her extraordinary inheritance. The fact that nothing more of a psychic nature occurred did nothing to deter her. So much so, that six decades on and being short of a few bob, she set herself up as the performing psychic, Crystal Gazer, touring pubs and clubs in her own locale. Little did she know that by bluffing her way through it all, she would eventually receive two 'follow-ups' in one evening that would begin a whole new chapter in her life.

Chapter 1 : The Shoreline club - 1986

Ernie Winters plopped his weary buttocks onto the worn velvet stool that remembered his shape so well and stared at his reflection. The dresser top between himself and the mirror offered every repair kit imaginable for a hung-over face. He selected a pair of eyelashes, smeared each with adhesive, took aim with one and missed.

'Bollocks!' he said, peeling the thing from his cheek as Nelson woke from his slumber and gave Ernie his coldest stare with the one remaining eye he still possessed.

'It's all right for you,' said Ernie, clocking the disapproval on Nelson's face. 'No-one's expecting ***you*** to sing for your supper dressed up like a tart.'

An urgent tap at the door offered more than just a time call for Ernie.

'Your five-minute call Mister Winters…?'

'Thanks, Prudence. You couldn't help me with these lashes, could you? They won't stay where I want them tonight.'

The door cracked open and the stage manager squeezed her ample form through the gap. Prudence wore a troubled face topped with a comical red ribbon bow. She snatched the offending eyelash from Ernie's fingers, tested the stickiness, and applied more adhesive.

'I don't know why you leave these things 'til the last minute,' she said, grasping hold of his stubbled chin, applying the lash with precision, and repeating with the second. '***And*** you've got a five o'clock shadow. No time for a shave either?'

'You ***are*** a nag, Prudence,' he answered with a squeeze of her bottom. She scuttled away, glancing at the sleeping cat.

'I suppose Nelson hasn't been fed either?'

Ernie stood up and swung a handbag over one shoulder, smoothing his attire with shaky palms. 'Just see to it will you, Pru? I'll be forever in your debt.' He opened the dresser drawer and took out a half bottle of vodka, unscrewed the top and gave Prudence a wink as he took several gulps. Replacing the bottle, he then belched, strode towards the open door and made his way to the concert stage, whistling his lucky tune, The Sailor's Hornpipe.

Marty was almost finished his stand-up routine as Ernie waited in the wings. If only he'd brought the vodka with him for another quick swig before he went on. The shakes were still very much present, and he took a few deep breaths to try and settle himself. Then suddenly, with a loud crash, the club doors burst open and a swarm of uniformed officers spilled onto the foyer.

'Everyone stay where you are!' yelled the sarge out in front. 'No-one is to leave.'

'Holy buggery, not again,' said Ernie, retreating the way he'd come, tottering on high heels past his dressing room as Prudence and Nelson appeared in the corridor. 'It's another bloody raid, Pru. Make yerself scarce!'

At the end of the corridor the fire escape beckoned. Ernie tugged on the locking bar but it wouldn't budge. He stepped back, took aim and fired with his foot, then remembered the ridiculous shoes he was wearing.

'Shite almighty!' he cried out as a flash of serious pain shot into his ankle and the door magically opened. Limping his way through to the top of the fire escape, he looked down the open weave stairway. It was raining. He slipped off one shoe, but as he went for the other, a dark, cloaked figure loomed from the shadows and gave a lunge towards him, speeding up his descent. With a short cry, he toppled, bounced and rolled comically down the spiral staircase for a full two floors, landing awkwardly at the bottom. The figure, with billowing cape, pursued him with lightness of foot as Nelson brushed past in his own dash for freedom.

Reaching the bottom and with a nudge of the foot, the mystery figure tilted Ernie's body from the wet cobbles as blood pooled around his head. Nelson looked up with his dependable eye and mewed loudly, his ginger fur glistening with fresh raindrops under the moonlight. The figure stepped away and Ernie's body rolled back to its face down position. A noise at the top of the stairwell hastened the figure to lean across, snatch Ernie's handbag from his iron grip and make a quick search of the contents before discarding. Then it fled across the cobbles towards the street and disappeared into the darkness.

Chapter 2 : Cleaning up in ICU

Monica and Joe had almost reached the end of a tiring night shift at Harton General, their tea break long since missed. With a firm twist of the handle, Monica squeezed out her mop against the metal bucket cone and sighed heavily.

'Joe, you do realize you've already wiped those locker tops. What's up with you this morning?'

Joe paused his cleaning. 'These night shifts kill me, Monica. It's hard enough trying to sleep with the sun poking through the curtains, never mind that hairy lump sticking its backside in my face.'

Monica grinned. 'The missus wouldn't be happy you're talking about her that way.'

Joe scoffed. 'We're ten years married, Monica. Afternoon ***lurve*** is well off the cards. It's that flaming dog who shall be referred to as King. Not my choice of name, I can tell you.'

'You're dying for a fag, aren't you?' said Monica. 'That's the proper reason you're so grumpy.'

Joe stroked his nicotine patch defensively. 'Maybe arms aren't the best place for these. I'm not getting the proper hit.'

'I don't know about that mate, but maybe a sticky bun will help.'

Joe was a stringy young man, swamped by the standard-sized blue overall he wore for the job, yet he could eat for England. Dragging his fingers through a blonde quiff, he glanced at the wall clock, then at the patients. It was still only 6 am and two of the geriatrics slept on.

'Come on then,' he said. 'These two have missed the tea round so it's just hard cheese. Our shift's over.'

Monica shoved her bucket into a corner and propped the mop shank against a wall. 'Right then, let's go. I'm gasping myself.'

They left the ward of patients mostly slurping their teas and swept onto the long corridor leading towards the refectory. Joe massaged the nicotine patch at the top of his arm again and Monica threw him an exasperated look.

'You won't squeeze any more out of it by doing that you know. I reckon you should just have a fag and be done with.'

'I am ***not***… repeat, ***not*** goin' back to those coffin nails ever again. Other people manage to quit and so will I. Anyway, how was it in I.C.U? All quiet?' he said.

'Oh, I meant to tell you. There was an admission last night. You know that old fella who does the drag act down at The Shoreline Club? Calls himself Ophelia, but his real name's Ernie?'

Joe sniggered. 'Everyone in Shields knows Ernie, for one reason or another. Our Sandra went to see him last weekend. He uses the ladies' toilets you know? Claims it's because the fellas won't let him into the gents when he's in drag. But it's just an excuse, because he cornered our Sandra in one of the cubicles. Hands everywhere …. filthy bastard.'

'That's disgusting.' said Monica.

'After she told me I was itching to go and sort him out, but the wife wouldn't let me. Bit of a stale act too, according to our Sandra. So, it ***was*** him?'

'Oh, yeah. He must have thrown himself down the fire escape by all accounts, judging by the state of him. They had to cut his frock off. I stuffed his wig and what was left of his clothes in the locker. He's wired up to all kinds. I don't know if he'll last the day.'

'Bloody hell. Whatever will The Shoreline do without him?'

'Rejoice and get itself a decent bloody act hopefully.'

They reached the refectory's swing doors and pushed them wide, one each.

'Could you manage a raisin croissant, Monica? My nose is picking up a light whiff of cinnamon this morning.' Joe grinned.

'Oh, go on then. What's another inch on the hips?'

∞∞∞

Twelve hours later, Joe was back on duty. On his way to the utility room to collect his cleaning trolley, staff nurse Brenda Cole stopped him in the corridor. Brenda managed to fill most of the space she occupied with little room to spare, and Joe steered his trolley to the wall to allow a safe pass.

'Joseph, my good man, can you cover for Monica? Just for an hour? She'll be a bit late…little one has a tooth abscess or something.'

Joe nodded. 'I can do that. Where do you want me to start?'

'Sure, so can you give I.C.U. the once over? Monica should be here by the time you're done with that. We've only got two in there.' The staff nurse glanced at her watch. 'I'd best get back, Joe. See you later.' With a squeak of shoe rubber against linoleum, she turned and was gone.

'Good old dependable Joe,' he said to himself.

Joe dragged his trolley to the doors of I.C.U. and peered through the porthole windows. Only two beds occupied as far as he could see, just as Brenda had said. A male clinician in green scrubs scribbled something on Ernie's chart, replaced the cap on his pen, slotted it behind his ear and hooked the chart over the bed frame. Joe used the keypad on the wall, listened for the tone and entered.

A brief nod was exchanged between the two men, and then Joe was alone on the near silent ward apart from the two inanimate patients. Regular beeps and whirrs from the machines interrupted the silence, but Joe always liked hearing those; they were an assurance that everything and everybody was functioning. He padded across to the foot of Ernie's bed, checked once more he was alone, then unhooked the chart. A radio played softly and there was a shuffling of papers from the office. Someone spoke on the telephone as Joe replaced Ernie's medications chart. With a curl of his lip, he gave Ernie the perfect scowl, then moved towards his bedside locker.

∞∞∞

Monica only just caught the elevator before the doors closed on her. Safely inside, she blew a tendril of dark hair away from her eyes with a thankful exhale of breath. She'd had the worst of days, ferrying all three kids to the pharmacy to have one of them looked at, then to discover a slow puncture on her way back. Begging the loan of her ex's car to get her to work on time had been the ultimate humiliation - which no doubt had delighted him.

Monica tried to put the day behind her as she hurried from the lift towards the utility room. Passing the I.C.U., she stopped for a snoop through the porthole windows. Joe was on his haunches, having a rummage about inside Ernie's bedside locker. She scanned the rest of the ward, smiled to herself and carried on down the corridor to hang up her coat and collect her cleaning trolley.

Just after midnight, Joe was back in the refectory embracing a large cappuccino and scouring the classifieds in the Evening Chronicle.

'So here you are, Joe Parker.' By using his surname, Joe knew she was trying to make a point.

He looked up. 'What have I forgotten to do now? I know I put fresh bin liners in all the bins like you keep reminding me ***and*** I used the polisher on the floor in ICU, just to keep you happy…'

Monica cocked an eyebrow, sat down opposite and placed her coffee mug on the table.

'No, that's all fine. I just spotted you rifling through that Ernie Winters' locker earlier. What were you looking for? Fancied borrowing his lipstick did you, or what?'

'Don't be soft. That sparkly dress of his was hanging out that's all. Being the kind soul that I am, I tucked it inside. …and of course I didn't happen to notice that he's got a Gucci handbag in there too. I must be in the wrong job. Anyway, how's your shift been so far, apart from short?' he chastised with a smile.

Monica sighed. 'Twinkle toes over on geriatrics got out of bed and scared the shit out of me while I was doing the sink. She had me down on all fours lookin' for her teeth, at stupid o'clock.'

'What for? After light out?'

'She said her Frannie had brought some Garibaldis at visiting time and she fancied one.'

'This Frannie she keeps on talking about …. doesn't exist, you know?'

'And as I discovered, neither do the Garibaldis,' laughed Monica.

'I'd have my doubts about the teeth too…..'

'What are you two giggling about?' Crusty Boniface cocked a leg over the last remaining empty chair, gave his usual snort of amusement and parked his plate of mixed grill followed by his butt. Crusty was so named because of his unstoppable acne and its inability to heal. But no-one called him that to his face.

'Oh, you know, just taking the ***pee*** out of the patients as per. So what's new with you?' asked Joe.

Crusty looked around furtively, then back again. 'You'll never guess….but you know that drag queen who was admitted yesterday to I.C.U?' He paused to pick up a sausage between his fingers, while he waited for an answer.

Monica and Joe exchanged a brief glance, then Monica said, 'Yes of course we do. So what's the latest?'

Crusty finished chewing his sausage and swallowed. 'He's just croaked it,' he said.

Chapter 3 : Suspicion

D.C.I. Seymour Witless marched into Accident and Emergency flashing his warrant card at the receptionist from several feet away. 'Witless!' he announced with authority from behind two old ladies blocking his path. One of the tiny old dears raised a pair of yellowing eyes in a scowl.

'No-one cares what you're suffering from young man, you still have to mind your place in the queue!'

Witless stepped impatiently with his size elevens from one side of the blockage to the other, desperately trying to attract the receptionist's attention. Slowly, she raised her head and peered over her spectacles with boredom.

'I'm here on important police business.' said Witless. 'Can you direct me to I.C.U. please?'

The receptionist stabbed a biro towards the elevator. 'You see those two plain clothes officers you came in with? ***They*** seem to know the way.'

Witless huffed, followed the biro's trajectory and spotted his D.S. and D.C. entering the lift. He managed to jump aboard before the doors closed, leaving the old ladies' disapproval behind him.

Outside I.C.U., D.S. Judy Conway and D.C. Richard Tracey had successfully kitted themselves out in SOCO's protective gear while Witless still hopped about on one foot attempting to apply a second shoe covering.

'Sit down sir,' said Conway, pulling up a chair from the open corridor.

With a wry smile, Witless sat, while Conway finished dressing him.

'Once we're in there,' he said, 'leave me to ask the questions. If I need your input I'll ask for it. But keep your eyes, ears and nose peeled for all things untoward.'

'Of course sir,' said Tracey, 'but I just wanted to ask before we go in there....will there be time to pop in and see my dad after? He's on men's surgical having a knee replacement tomorrow and I just wanted to wish him luck.'

'I thought you said last week he'd had a twenty to one win at Gosforth Park?'

'Well, yes he did sir.' Tracey lowered his gaze.

'Then he's already had his fair share of luck, wouldn't you say?'

'But sir…I could just…'

A masked nurse then arrived to open the I.C.U. doors. With a hand on the half open door, Witless grimaced at his D.C. 'The answer's ***no,*** Tracey, of course you bloody can't!'

Conway cast a smirk in Tracey's direction and followed them inside.

Scene of Crime Officers bustled around the ward, dusting, swabbing and bagging items of interest. Ernie Winters' lifeless body remained uncovered. An attempt by staff to remove his face make up on admission had not been entirely successful, and a single eyelash still remained attached to one eyelid. His canular was open, and on the floor beside his bed lay an empty syringe. Staff nurse Brenda Cole greeted the officers with a degree of embarrassment.

'Good evening … or rather, good morning, officers,' she said, with a glance at her watch to verify and a disappointed shake of the head. 'Can I say first off that there has ***never*** been a murder enquiry at this hospital in the two decades I have worked here…and that ***all*** my staff are devastated at what has happened to a patient in our care...' Although she stood almost eighteen inches from

Witless, her bosom gave a warm greeting through the upper quarter of his SOCO suit. He averted his eyes, not without some effort and cleared his throat.

'No speeches required at the present time thank you nurse. We'll be asking questions when we collect your statements….you just have to give us the appropriate answers,' said Witless, attempting a smile. 'Oh, and I'll be needing a list of all the staff, shift timings, contact details, medications and their schedules, etcetera, and visitors to this ward in the last week.'

'For sure, Inspector, I'll crack on with that. Can I make you a nice cup of tea?'

'Later, perhaps, thank you.'

The staff nurse gave a hip wiggle and returned to her office.

D.S. Judy Conway and D.C. Richard Tracey circled the crime scene from opposite ends, pointing out additional items to be bagged. The lights remained dimmed in respect of the remaining patient, still unconscious. Conway bent down and shone a flashlight under Ernie's bed. 'There's something under here sir,' she said.

'What is it?' said Witless.

With a gloved hand, she pulled out an evidence bag from her pocket and crawled under the bed, emerging with a newly bagged item of interest.

'Some sort of sticking plaster perhaps?'

'Well that's not unexpected in a place like this,' Witless remarked.

Tracey looked over Conway's shoulder as she held up the item, and she cringed.

'Looks more like a nicotine patch to me, sir,' said Tracey.

'How on earth can you know?' said Conway.

'It's those two faint letters in the right hand corner. They're the same brand my brother uses.'

Conway and Tracey exchanged glances. Hers was one of annoyance and his was smug.

∞∞∞

Back at H.Q., D.C.I. Witless strode into the incident room and slapped a thin paper file on the front desk. A sleeping bulldog beneath it opened one eye with the impact and snorted. Some of the team sat, but D.C Richard Tracey stood next to the radiator with the sole of his shoeless foot pressed against it and his head stooped beneath one of the ceiling lights. Sniggers from officers standing close made him aware his Mickey Mouse socks were on display. He grimaced, returning the foot to its shoe.

'Right, you lot!' said Witless, tugging at the cap on his whiteboard marker pen. 'We have a suspicious death on our hands.' He spoke as he wrote. 'Ernest Winters – well known drag artist at the Shoreline night club, stage name Ophelia Ass.' A faint chuckle erupted from the team and Witless turned in puzzlement as his comb-over flopped forward, revealing a bald patch of scalp. He sucked air between his teeth, dragging the rogue length of hair back to its intended position. 'Anyway, Ernie Winters was found at the bottom of the Shoreline's fire escape during a police raid the night before last. He was taken to Harton General but suffered a subsequent cardiac arrest the following night. C.P.R. was administered, and he did not survive.'

'I thought you said this was a suspicious death, Guv?' said a chinless officer holding a morning newspaper.

Witless waved his marker pen in the air. 'Yes...I'm getting to that bit…There was evidence that an unprescribed medication had been used. Also, Winters' cannula had been interfered with after the last check on him at 10 pm. And a nicotine patch was found under Winters' bed. Another interesting fact we've just learned from uniform, is that Winters' place of residence was turned over the same night of the Shoreline's police raid and Winters' fall down the fire escape.'

'Sir, so is it possible that the fall wasn't accidental?' Conway interjected from her front row seat.

'Absolutely, D.S. Conway. There's a team over at both places right now, and we'll just have to hope the two day delay hasn't enabled any scene contamination.' A satisfied smile crept across Conway's face as she crossed her legs and lowered her eyes to write something in her notes.

In the absence of photographs, Witless attempted to sketch the main suspects with his marker pen, each inside a rectangular box as vital parts of a link chart diagram.

'Did the budget not run to a photographer, sir?' sniggered Conway.

'Only just,' said Witless, 'but I think it was the caretaker with his Polaroid ….' He turned towards her, making direct eye contact. 'So why don't you run down to that hangout of his and offer to do him a trade-in?'

Conway frowned. 'What sort of trade-in … sir?'

'I usually find a bacon sandwich works quite well,' A tiny rumble of chauvanistic laughter came from the team, and Witless smirked. At the words 'bacon sandwich,' the bulldog raised his enormous head and snorted demandingly at Witless. 'Alright greedy, I haven't forgotten you,' said Witless, distracted for a moment before scribbling more portraits at random on the evidence board. 'People … or shall we say persons of interest.' He snapped the cap back onto the marker pen and used it as a pointer. 'Joe Parker – night shift cleaner was working in ICU the night of the murder. Monica Woodhouse – also night shift cleaner, came in late for shift, or at least that's when staff laid eyes on her. Staff nurse Brenda Cole – working in the office adjacent, checking on the patients every 30 minutes. Anesthetist Rory Buchanan came onto the ward briefly to prep for Winters' surgery the following day, which of course didn't happen. Winters also had some ex partners who may have had a grievance – apparently he had it away with many ladies and we're currently putting a list together….and I warn you, it's quite a long one.

'Now I know some of you will be as knackered as I am after last night, but every one of you has a list of duties - who they're speaking to today and where to find them. We're waiting for lab results on all the items of interest collected, and as soon as we know what's what we'll have another briefing. Oh, er, better just mention,' Witless indicated the impartial animal beneath the desk. 'This is Rambo, in case you were all wondering. Can't be left alone as he likes to eat sofas. So you may have to get used to his unusual habits until I can sort out a dog sitter.'

Rambo returned his massive head to its resting position and farted. Several officers groaned and chinless wafted his newspaper.

'....and let's hope that won't be too long.'

Outside the incident room, Judy Conway strode towards the exit and Richard Tracey ran behind her waving a sheet of paper. 'D.S. Conway....'

Conway rolled her eyes but didn't turn.

'D.S. Conway...' he'd now reached her side. 'It says here that I'm with you today?'

She kept her eyes forward and quickened her pace. 'Does it now?'

'Erm...so how do you want to do this? We can take my car if you like?'

She kept walking. 'I think it best we go separately, and I'll see you at the hospital.'

Rambo's nasal snorting seemed to get louder the further they distanced themselves from the room. In fact it was almost like he was right behind them.

'Wait up you two,' said D.C.I. Witless, clutching Rambo's lead as the dog dragged him towards the exit. 'We'll be going in my car, you'll both be delighted to know.'

Conway protested. 'But sir, you can't take a dog inside the hospital.'

'Then we'll have to think of something, won't we?' said Witless. 'Someone will have to wait outside with him, or check on him from time to time. You can take turns.'

Tracey and Conway exchanged looks but said nothing. Until they realized the problem of all four being squashed up inside Witless's soft-topped Morris Minor.

Rambo was first to the car, offering Tracey one of his pleading looks.

'Seems like you're the chosen one,' said Witless, unlocking the doors.

'Me, sir? For what, sir?'

'Well, look at his little legs, Tracey. He can't get inside on his own, can he?'

Tracey took a sharp breath in before bending, and encircled the dog's body with two exceptionally long arms. Once on a level, he met with Rambo's bloodshot but soulful eyes.

'He won't bite me, will he?'

'Only if you annoy him....and you wouldn't dream of doing that Tracey, would you?'

'Absolutely not, sir.'

Conway stood impatiently rocking from one foot to the other with arms crossed in front of her, shoulder bag swinging. Tracey eyeballed her reaction as he lifted the dog inside and placed him on the back seat, then stood back, dusting himself down. Conway didn't waste a second and jumped into the passenger seat next to Witless, leaving the smelly seat for Tracey.

'Right!' said Witless, doing up his seat belt. 'Are we all set?'

'Permission to open the window sir?' said Conway, crinkling her nose.

'Too cold for that, Conway. Just breathe through your mouth; you'll never notice the smell.'

Chapter 4 : The post mortem

The morgue was situated in the bleakest, coldest part of the hospital - the basement. It was completely windowless, with an air conditioning system that rattled like a witch's tongue and sucked in air directly from the rubbish bins outside. Tiled top to bottom in a sickly shade of yellow with a putrid smell of raw meat and disinfectant, the ambience did little to flatter the occupants within, dead or alive. A metal bucket of green liquid stood in one corner, with a blood stained mop beside it.

Conway raised a gloved hand to her masked face. 'Oh God,' she said, 'This stinks more than the dog.'

The Medical Examiner raised his head slightly from a stooped over position. 'Ah, Good Morning,' he said. 'Forgive me if I don't shake hands ….. rather bloody at the moment as you can see.' Sir Hugo's face mask and scrubs were splattered with fresh bodily fluids. Tufts of thick white hair poked from the outer edges of both cap and mask, similarly stained. He straightened up, resting knuckles on hips. 'You're D.C.I. Shitless, I presume?'

'Erm, it's Witless, actually Sir Hugo, Seymour Witless.' The D.C.I. scanned his team's faces. Conway's eyes were clearly laughing above the face mask, and Tracey's eyes popped.

'And this is D.S. Conway and D.C. Tracey,' Witless completed his introductions.

'Jolly nice to meet you, Shitless,' said Sir Hugo, 'and your delightful entourage....What do you think of my gaff? Rather splendid, hmm? Just got my new wellingtons this morning.' He thrust a foot forward, with toes aloft. 'God only knows who chose the white ones, silly bastards. There are some spares in that cupboard in the corner if you plan to get down and dirty with me?' he continued, shaking a bloody finger in the general direction.

Witless attempted a smile. 'There'll be no need for that, Sir Hugo, we'll just stay at the fresh end, if that's all right by you.'

'Wouldn't call it ***fresh*** at all sir,' said Conway softly.

'I wouldn't mind donning a pair of wellies to get close, sir, if that's okay?' Tracey chipped in.

Witless's heavy black brows leapt in surprise. 'Certainly Tracey, go fill your boots, pardon the pun, if that's what you want.'

The torso of Ernie Winters lay open and splayed on the examination table. Specimen dishes containing various body parts littered the surrounding surfaces. There were sets of scales, and an extendable mirror that sprang from the wall with a tilt facility, providing an extra angle of focus on the gore. The Medical Examiner, Sir Hugo Stubbs snipped away the last tissue strands attaching the liver, removed it from the torso and placed it respectfully on the scales. Tracey returned, wellington clad.

'Right, gentlemen....and lady,' Sir Hugo nodded in Conway's direction. 'This chap, for his age, has rather indulged himself. Arteries have enough plaque to fill every pothole on the Jarrow Road, kidneys not far from being shot altogether, courtesy of .... I'd say alcohol abuse. And the liver ... by George, what a whopper!' Tracey moved closer.

'So what do we deduce from a large liver, Sir Hugo?' said Witless.

Sir Hugo tossed Witless a look of disdain. 'It's diseased, Shitless. Just look at the texture. Lumps and bumps, ***even holes.*** Complete disrespect, that's what it is. This man knew he was dying. I'd stake my career on it. Plus, he's had gonorrhea at least once from the scars inside his….'

Witless raised a hand. 'Yes, yes we know he was a ladies' man by all accounts. What about all the bruising?'

'All conducive to a fall, I'm afraid. If he was pushed, that's impossible to prove in a case like this. But I've taken blood samples for toxicology, so those results should be with you in a day or two.'

Tracey remained suspended over a specimen dish, studying the organ inside. 'Sir Hugo, can I just ask….'

Witless was chomping at the bit to get away. 'I think we're all done here, Tracey. I'll let you see the Medical Examiner's report later, if you're a good boy.'

Sir Hugo beamed, and his voice boomed. 'Let the lad ask his question, Shitless. That's what he's here for, ***to learn,*** is he not?'

'Ask away, Tracey.' Witless conceded, checking his watch. 'But we do have other places to go, people to see.'

Tracey continued. 'It's this lung, Sir Hugo. It has the same appearance as a calf's lungs, after it's been euthanized.'

'Well that's interesting isn't it D.C. Tracey?' said Sir Hugo. 'Are you experienced in animal euthanasia at all?'

Tracey became animated. 'My brother's a country vet, sir. I worked as his assistant for a spell before joining the force.'

'How bloody marvelous! As you've just pointed out, there's a presence of blood-tinged froth in the tracheo-bronchial tree attached to this lung. Now just watch what happens when I pierce this rather swollen lung … just about … here.' Sir Hugo pointed with a finger, then picked up a knife from a nearby tray and made a centimeter long cut in one of the lungs. It hissed, oozing a frothy pink liquid.

'Oh, wow!' said Tracey with a grin.

'Wow indeed, young fellow. It appears you have the perfect grounding for a career in pathology.'

'Now just a moment, Sir Hugo,' said Witless with a tiny laugh. 'Don't go poaching my staff before I've had a chance to get them trained, please.'

Sir Hugo strode across to Witless with purpose, slapped him hard on the upper arm and Witless flinched. 'No worries about that, old boy. I'm just delighted to find someone so keen on the craft, that's all.' Then he turned to Tracey and shook his hand vigorously. 'I'm going to make you wait for the lab results I'm afraid, but you and I both know, don't we, just what killed this fairy boy, hmm?'

∞∞∞

Conway remained silent. She tossed her protective equipment with an angry flourish into the yellow disposal bag outside the morgue as Witless and Tracey exchanged wary glances. She did not wait for the men to catch up before striding towards the exit. As they emerged from the building, Conway was seen pacing by the car.

'She looks upset, sir,' said Tracey.

'Hmmm…' said Witless.

'Didn't you mind Sir Hugo getting your name wrong, sir?'

'Of course I bloody minded. I just chose not to make a thing of it. Anyway, he could have a genuine hearing problem, and if he hasn't, and it was intended to make me look foolish, he didn't succeed did he Tracey?'

'No sir, he could never do that sir.'

They'd reached the car, and still she did not acknowledge their presence.

'Conway!' said Witless. She tipped her head slightly towards him.

'Sir?'

'Do you remember where we left the dog?'

'Yes sir, over by the fire exit.'

'Then would you be so kind as to collect him? Perhaps you could walk him over to that patch of grass we saw in case he needs to go.'

Conway hesitated for a few seconds as if she was about to protest, then marched in the general direction.

'Oh, Conway?' Witless shouted after her, fumbling in his mackintosh pocket. She turned.

'You may need one of these poop bags....'

∞∞∞

Witless drummed his fingers on the dash and stared distractedly through the windscreen.

'You know, Tracey, maybe you just need to make friends with her. After all, she is the newcomer here.'

Tracey looked skeptical. 'I ***have tried*** sir, you've no idea. She hates me.'

'I don't think she does, but she is ambitious, and you're seen as the competition.'

'How can I be competition? She's a D.S. for God's sake.'

'You're a fella. That's reason enough for any woman hoping for a career in the force. Maybe it's up to you to offer an olive branch. Ask her out ….. She might bite your hand off.' He grinned.

'Yeah, that's what I'm scared of.'

Witless straightened up in the driver's seat. 'Whoa, here she comes, face like thunder. Look lively!'

The rear door opened and Conway stuck her head inside. 'Can one of you gentlemen assist me with this dog please?'

Tracey opened his passenger door and stepped out of the car. On seeing his pal, Rambo's back end shook with high velocity and he snorted like an asthmatic pig. Once settled in the car, with Tracey next to his new buddy, Witless buckled his belt and adjusted his mirror. 'I think we need to get back here tonight, speak to the night shift while everything's still fresh and no-one's been clever enough to think up any plausible alibis.'

'But sir, that'll be a double shift,' said Tracey. '… and I'm visiting Dad tonight. He's just had his operation.'

'I don't mind coming, sir. I've got nothing on tonight,' said Conway. Tracey smirked from the back seat.

Witless stroked his chin with one hand and sighed. 'Right. Well I'll tell you what's gonna happen. We meet back here for eight o'clock. That gives you plenty enough time with your dad, Tracey, and maybe a couple of hours kip. If we're done by ten, and I don't see why we shouldn't be, we'll all have a snifter in that pub down the road,' he jabbed a thumb in the direction. 'What's it called?'

'The Fishgutter's Arms, sir,' said Conway.

Witless grinned and turned the ignition key. The Morris purred into life. 'You see, Tracey? She can't be all that bad if she knows vital information like that.'

∞∞∞

Staff nurse Brenda Cole poured semi-skimmed into two tea mugs and gave each a quick stir with a plastic fork, while D.C.I. Witless studied the print outs in front of him. The office was tiny, with a notice board skewered with Thank You cards commanding attention.

'So, those other doors at the rear of the ward.... anyone could come and go through there and you'd definitely be aware of it?'

Brenda placed the mugs on the desk, opened a drawer and pulled out a tin of Peak Freans Xtra special biscuits.

'I only leave the ward once or twice in a shift to use the ladies' facilities, Inspector. I'm never gone longer than three, maybe four minutes at a time, and if I know someone's coming in, I'll ask them to hold the fort.'

'And no member of the public has access to those doors?'

'Absolutely not. Even though they're not pin code protected, the other doors leading to them are.' She sat down opposite Witless and removed the lid from the biscuits.

'On that night, can you recall asking anyone to ***mind the fort*** while you spent a penny?'

Brenda selected a jammy dodger and attempted to drown it in her tea.

'Well, no, I just nipped out quickly both times.' Popping the whole biscuit into her mouth, she lifted both hands to her head and removed a number of hair pins from her nurse's cap as she chewed, tossing them down on the desk. Witless was transfixed. Then she pulled off her cap and a mass of blonde hair tumbled to her shoulders. 'Just excuse me a minute while I take care of this.' Her fingers were straight in, scratching away like a dog's back legs just released from police cuffs. 'Oh, you have no idea how good that feels,' she said with eyes closed. 'If I didn't do this at least once in every shift, I'd go insane.' Then as if it never happened, she put everything back together as Witless tried to refocus.

'And you always do that …' he waved a forefinger at her head, '… routine in here, every shift?'

'Sometimes here, sometimes in the ladies' loo. Why?'

'Well, that just took you all of four minutes from start to finish, so if you did it in the ladies' two nights ago, then you'd be off the ward for eight minutes in all.' He cocked his head, peering at her from beneath bushy brows. Brenda's cheeks flushed and her hands fussed with some papers on the desk. 'Alright, that's a possibility…yes.'

Then someone knocked softly at the rear doors, before a maintenance worker poked his head around one of them.

'That's you all fixed, Brenda love. See you next time,' he said. Then he was gone.

Witless continued to stare at the staff nurse from beneath tortured brows.

'What's been fixed, exactly, Nurse Cole?'

Her pink cheeks reddened.

'One of the fire doors wouldn't close properly….I reported it more than a week ago, but you know how long it takes for some jobsworth upstairs to fill out a billet doux for these feckin' things they seem to classify as non-priority.' Brenda sighed heavily through flared nostrils and shook her head. 'Ten years ago, we'd have just rung the local handyman and paid him out of petty cash for a job completed the same day. But those times are long gone…'

'So you're saying this ward has been freely accessible from the outside for several days or more? To any psychopath who fancied a killing spree?'

Brenda could not meet Witless's stare. Instead, she picked up the biscuit tin.

'There's only one jammy dodger left, Inspector. Would you like it?'

CHAPTER 5 : THE GIG : ST MARTIN-IN-THE-FIELDS CHURCH HALL

Sylvie's failed attempts to mount the bar stool were starting to rankle. Four feet nine inches had been the summit of a lifetime's growth, but at sixty eight years of age she appeared to be shrinking. On the third attempt, and only with the aid of the reverend's interlocking fingered stirrups, she landed squarely on the soft vinyl seat with a triumphant sigh.

'That's fabby, Norris. I can just about see my flamin' forehead in this ancient ruin of a mirror of yours. Could you not find one with a bigger crack?'

Reverend Norris straightened his spectacles, brushed the dust from his palms and wiped the remainder on his black frock. 'Miss Broadstairs,' he gasped, 'this community hall was built around that very mirror. It's Victorian, I'll have you know.'

'That's as maybe, but just like Victoria, it's buggered and you know it.' Sylvie flapped an arm towards her handbag lying on a saggy, threadbare sofa at the far side of the room. 'Pass me my make-up bag will you Norris? And if you give me that cushion too, I might be able to see the rest of my face in this Godforsaken monstrosity.'

Norris handed over the bag and cushion. 'I have to go and check on Daisy, see if she needs help in the kitchen. Bobby will be in shortly, he's doing that mingling thing he does. Or is it eavesdropping?'

'I wouldn't know, Norris. But that boy's a terrible nosy parker.' Sylvie slotted the cushion between her buttocks and the seat. 'Oh, look at that. I can see me nose now!'

'Just so long as there's no impropriety….you know, we've had this discussion before.' The reverend threw her a scolding look.

'And I remember it well. No impropriety whatsoever, you can be assured of that. Right Norris, let's get on, we'll see you out there and thanks for the hitch-up.'

Powdering her face, she looked around the room. This place held some memories. At twelve years old, Sylvie worked her first job as cloaks attendant for the Saturday night dancers. The same mahogany coat rails stood next to the old sofa – the sofa she still searched for lost coins, buttons, or the odd chocolate raisin. Clarabelle still found it comfortable, curled up as she was now, her short nose twitching in dream mode, whimpering at intervals.

Sylvie dragged a hair brush through pure white, wayward curls and applied lipstick, doubtful it would impress anymore. And even if it did, why was she bothering to repeat the same old lines, gig after gig, to a gullible crowd she'd virtually robbed just to listen to the same old pile of garbage? Still, the calf-length tiger print dress she's bought off the peg from Oxfam that afternoon looked the business, and the matching headband with orange and black feathers gave her that mystical look she'd been after for months. Pity about the pink trainers, but she wasn't ready to give those up any time soon.

An intrusive whisper disturbed her thoughts. 'Sylvie, sweetums…'

'Christ on a bike!' She whipped around, smearing 'pinkish pout' by Revlon all the way down one cheek. 'What the hell, Bobby? I could be naked in here.'

'Well that's hardly likely to interest *me*, is it? If you happened to be George Michael however, I'd be sorely tempted.' Bobby closed the door behind him and scanned her from top to toe. 'Is that what you're wearing? Be careful you don't get shot by a game hunter.'

Sylvie huffed. 'Less of the sarcasm if you don't mind and tell me what you've got,' she said, turning back to the mirror to repair the damage. Bobby shooed Clarabelle from the sofa and sat down. She growled.

Bobby unbuttoned his jacket and crossed his legs. 'Well, I don't have a lot … but there's a woman in row three who told another woman in row four that she'd lost her husband.'

'And has she reported it to the police?' answered Sylvie, spitting on a handkerchief. 'Honestly Bobby, could you ***be more vague?***'

'I did say it wasn't much …. ***And*** … Sylvie, sweetums…. I may as well tell you this now, but there's a possibility I've stuck my dainty foot in it with Mrs. Tooley.' Bobby's chin disappeared inside his cravat and he dropped his gaze. 'But I think we can turn it to our advantage…'

'What have you done now?' she said, rubbing harder at the lipstick stain.

'I just asked her where ***Mister*** Tooley was tonight, and can you guess what she said?'

'She said he's stuck down a well and to send Lassie.'

'Don't be daft. She said he's gone. I thought she meant to Blackpool, 'cause she was talkin' about holidays a few weeks ago.'

'But she meant ***he's dead***.'

'Well, I didn't know did I? So I said why didn't she go with him?'

Sylvie plunged a mascara brush back in its tube. 'Oh, Bobby…'

'But we can use it …. Can't we?'

She turned to face him. 'It's too obvious. And I don't know a sodding thing about Sidney Tooley.'

'You know his name, that's gotta be a starter for ten. ***And*** she was carrying a set of false teeth. Widows like to carry keepsakes around like that, don't they?'

'Or maybe she was lending them to Daisy to crimp one of her pies.'

Bobby flicked a dismissive hand and grimaced. 'That's just too revolting…'

'Bobby, it's ***a no***, okay? Anything else?'

'Yes!' Bobby's voice rose an octave. 'Someone famous is in the congregation!'

'Audience, Bobby, it's an audience. We're not delivering a sermon.' She rolled her eyes, shook her head in despair. 'Okay, who's the celeb in the audience?'

'Only the greatest singing star in the country.'

'Vera Lynn? Oh my. We ***are*** honoured.'

Bobby pressed his lips together and crossed his arms with a dramatic sigh. 'Only Carolyn flaming Carr, that's who…'

The whites of Sylvie's eyes flashed for a second, she crawled down from the bar stool and staggered towards the sofa. Plonking her backside in a cloud of dust, her head lolled backwards.

Bobby shuffled along to give her more space. 'What the hell's wrong with you?'

'Carolyn Carr had an affair with my husband. Then I left him …. forty years ago.' She drew in a deep breath, tossing Bobby a sideways glare. 'And she's not the greatest singing star …. she's a warbling witch.'

'Well … okay, but she's hardly gonna remember you four decades later, is she?'

Sylvie sat bolt upright. 'Of course she will. We had a cat fight in the street. What the hell's she doing here?'

'I think you're worrying about nothing.'

They sat for moment, the silence only interrupted by more of Sylvie's slow, deep breaths.

'This is ridiculous. You're right, I'm a professional. It'll be fine. If she tries anything, I'll pull her bloody wig off this time. Which reminds me, do my head feathers look straight?'

Bobby leveled his gaze. 'As a die…'

'Good. And now it's my turn to point out … just a teensy-weensy defect.'

He rolled his eyes. 'What now? This is a new jacket by the way. Check out the elbow patches,' he said, rotating an arm.

'Very impressive I'm sure … but …' she flicked away some of his shoulder dust with a heavy hand. 'You really need to get some Head and Shoulders, Bobby. Dandruff is not a great look when you're in the public eye.'

Bobby flinched. 'What ***would*** I do without you, sweetums?'

'You'd have died in a ditch long ago, most probs Bobs. There, you look just fabby.' She glanced at the wall clock. 'So there's ten minutes left to blast off. Where's my ear piece?' Bobby produced it from his jacket pocket, turning towards Clarabelle, who stood, staring at him expectantly.

'What is it Clarabelle? Want to go walkies? Want a treat? How about a tickle?'

'Get real,' said Sylvie, 'She wants you to get out of her bloody seat….'

∞∞∞

As church halls go, St Martin's was larger than most with space for sixty five humans, but seats for only thirty three, and most of those were sick with wood worm. In better days, the velvet-draped windows carried themselves with elegance. But six decades on, their sweeping folds carried only dust, discarded sweet wrappers and an abandoned hornets' nest that Daisy Harbottle would not go near with her feather duster.

With two minutes to Sylvie's intro, Reverend Norris raised the hem of his frock to mount the stage steps, flashing white socks and Jesus sandals to the crowd. Someone whooped from the back row, and the reverend appreciated with a swish of the skirt, a nod and a smile.

'Good evening ladies, gents, and the stray cat who sauntered in from the cold, now sitting on the front row, a warm St Martin's welcome to you all!'

Necks strained to see the cat in question – a ginger tom with one eye, lounging on a hassock, licking its mucky paws.

'As your compère this evening, I want to make you all feel at home, even though I wish some of you actually were.' He grinned. 'I don't actually mean that ….you're very much welcome here tonight, except for maybe Miss Mountshaft, who remembered to bring my tax return, yet forgot my gingerbreads.' Norris threw his accountant a mock look of disapproval, which would normally receive a smile, but this evening she seemed rather morose, and he puzzled.

Sylvie took a peak through the curtains. Daisy Harbottle was seated at the piano, digits poised for the big intro. Bobby was slouched in the second back row, his paisley cravat knotted loosely at the neck, disguising a microphone.

'Miss Mountshaft's been crying,' he whispered.

High pitched feedback screeched through her earpiece, and Sylvie grimaced as she answered.

'Well I'll need more than that Bobby. I'm not bloody psychic.'

'Tell me something I don't know. She hasn't spoken to anyone, just sat there with a soggy hanky. Should I put an arm round her, ask her what's up?'

'Nooo, Bobby, too late for that. I'm goin' on now. Not happy about tonight at all .... picking up other voices from somewhere .... Maybe someone's playing with a CB radio. Oh, and look at that .... the local hack's in from the Gazette.'

Bobby scanned the audience. 'Where?'

'Two rows in front of you – far end.'

'Oh, Max Wade. Is he working, you think?'

'That lot are always working. He's not here for me .... He's got his eye on the warbling witch.'

Reverend Norris continued, 'However .... there will be refreshments at half time in the reception area, so without further ado, let's give a very warm welcome to the star of the evening .... that formidable psychic we all know and love.... Crystal Gazer!' Daisy's fingers danced across the piano keys and the not-so-spooky intro of Michael Jackson's Thriller filled the hall. Sylvie burst onto the stage, arms wide, as Norris took his place next to Miss Mountshaft.

'Thank you Reverend Norris, and thank you all for being here tonight. I can see we have one or two new faces in the audience, so don't be shy, we're all friends here looking for answers. And I'll do my very best to find those for you tonight.'

She hesitated a moment, spotting Carolyn Carr in the second row, still with that massive beehive perched on her stupid head, and the vinegar face beneath having aged even more. Yes, time had been exceptionally unkind to the starlet, and Sylvie's heart leapt with vicious delight. In the seat behind, District Nurse Eva Shawcross bobbed up and down like a dipper bird, straining to see beyond the vast mound. Impatience wearing thin, she prodded the offender in the shoulder blade. Carolyn fired a look of venom in her direction, mouthing something unreadable.

'So, I'll dive straight in folks, because the spirits seem like they're in a hurry.' Sylvie continued. 'I've got a bit of a strange one here, and this voice has been nagging me for the last few minutes....so bear with me a second.'

That second ran into five. Bobby shuffled in his seat and whispered into his cravat. 'Sylvie, sweetums! What the hell are you playing at? Are you okay?' She did not answer, but stared vacantly at the back of the hall. Suddenly, she thrust out her stomach, placed a hand in the small of her back and waddled across the stage. 'Oh...can't bear this bloody pain!' Her voice was child-like. 'Call the middle wife!' The audience gaped.

Sylvie paused the waddling and faced the audience. 'I need to tell you about my Charlie ..... how he got here.' Her eyes widened, the picture of innocence. '***My lover*** ... ' she covered a giggle with her hand, 'that's a ***naughty*** word ..... he planted a seed in my tummy and it grew ever so big...I fed it through an umbrella cord for nine bloody months.'

Miss Mountshaft's attention had been grabbed, and she stiffened. Reverend Norris switched puzzled looks from Sylvie to Miss Mountshaft and back again.

Sylvie groaned once more and duck waddled back across the stage.

'Jeeesus help me!' she cried. A moment of calm followed. 'Our Rosalind …. she called the middle wife …. But it had to be in secret.' Sylvie held a forefinger up to her lips and shook her head. 'No bloody telling!' Satisfied that she held the trust of the listeners, she continued. 'That middle wife … well, she delivers babies …. But not like the mail man….oh, bloody no …. Not that easy!' Sylvie lowered herself awkwardly to a horizontal position on the stage and spread her legs. 'So she comes and I'm lyin' on old towels on the floor like a dog, and then pop! The water bag I was keepin' in there in case Charlie got thirsty…. blew up all over the floor …. Then the middle wife, she starts tellin' me to push, then breathe, push, then breathe. And suddenly there he was, my beautiful Charlie …. I was so happy to see him … even though he was covered in puke. My arms went up for a cuddle, but the middle wife dangled him by the ankles and gave him a good spanking for climbing up there in the first place.' Giggles and a few gasps erupted from the audience, but Sylvie hadn't finished.

'I heard him cry,' she said softly, and sniffled. 'I wanted to fuss him, you know, tell him it was okay like. But then I came over all funny. The middle wife handed Charlie to our Rosalind. ***"She's a bleeder!"*** she shouted. I thought she was sayin' I'd done well, but when I looked, all my blood was on the floor. The whole bloody lot. They'd forgotten to put the stopper back in after the play centre came out.' She paused to wipe tears with the heel of her hand. 'And then it all went dark …. I couldn't hear my Charlie or anything anymore. I think I must have died.'

Sylvie lay for another moment. Some audience members whispered among themselves, while others stared, spellbound. Then slowly, she sat up and looked around in a daze. 'I…I'm so sorry folks …. That's never happened to me before.'

Bobby made his way to the front of the stage.

'Sweetums, are you not feeling well? Shall I call half time?'

'Maybe in a minute, Bobs.' Steadily, or rather unsteadily, she rose onto her feet and faced the audience.

'Well, folks …. that didn't do my old knees any good, I can tell you …. But now I'm wondering ….. if anyone in the room is called Rosalind, or knows a Rosalind maybe?'

There was a whimper from the back row, and Miss Mountshaft raised a hesitant hand. 'I'm Rosalind,' she said.

'I wonder …. Can we speak after the show? I just think there's a lot more to say about this.'

∞∞∞

Daisy Harbottle topped up the tea urn with water and switched it to 'heat.' True to form, it hissed back like an angry cat. A sharp tapping of fingernails on the serving counter behind made her swivel on swollen, tired feet, and she winced. Carolyn Carr's large, pointy head leaned across the counter. She beckoned to Daisy with a boney forefinger and attempted to whisper. 'I'd like to purchase two bottles of your special brew …. Just tell me where you can do the handover and I'll be there.' She tapped the same forefinger on the side of her nose several times and winked.

Daisy looked around. The reception area was beginning to fill up, and a queue was already forming at the hatch. 'Madam, we don't have a license to sell alcohol. But I can do you a tea, an instant coffee or a sparkling water…..'

Carolyn reached out and grabbed hold of Daisy's tabard at the shoulder, pulling her closer. 'You know what I'm talking about!'

Daisy flinched to avoid flying spittle. The queue was getting longer.

'Are you serving, love, or is there gonna be a punch up?' someone said. Carolyn released her grip. 'I'll see you in fifteen, outside. Don't come empty handed.' She moved away.

Daisy put on a smile. 'Sorry sir, what can I get you?'

∞∞∞

Max Wade, Gazette reporter lingered by the doorway, stroking his Pentax P30. His editor had flat out refused to reimburse the full cost, but the sacrifice was small compared to the status symbol and chic magnet now hanging around his neck. He watched, licking his moustached lips as Carolyn Carr was offered a seat and a coffee by her younger female companion. Then he raised the camera and took a shot.

Sylvie came into reception with Bobby on her arm. He plonked her into a comfy armchair, flapping like a mother hen while Reverend Norris disappeared behind the serving hatch with Miss Mountshaft.

'I don't think you should do the second half, sweetums,' said Bobby. 'If that was an act, I fear for your sanity, and if it was real, I fear for mine.'

'Don't be such a drama queen, Bobby. It wasn't even a full first half …. These folks might want their money back and your rent's way overdue. Anyway, this has never happened before so I have to run with it. It must be important, and I don't think Rosalind Mountshaft is the only intended recipient of that message.'

Bobby sat next to her. 'Really? Then who else?'

She gave him a look of disbelief. 'Well, ***me*** of course. You great wassock.'

Norris arrived, hovering with a tray. 'A Horlicks for Bobby and a Bovril for Miss Broadstairs.'

'Norris, can we dispense with the formalities? We've known each other for decades. Just call me Sylvie, please?'

He placed the drinks on the table and spoke to her feet, 'I will … try, certainly.'

'That's progress. Let's drink to that…'

Norris almost smiled, produced a business card and passed it across the table. 'Miss Mountshaft had to leave, and she asked me to give you this.'

'Oh ….. that's disappointing.'

'It seems her mother passed away this morning …. and she came here hoping to connect …. But something entirely different happened. Anyway, she had to dash. Maybe you can speak to her tomorrow.'

Bobby muttered from behind his Horlicks. 'Watch out…here comes another adoring fan at ten o'clock. And look, that stray cat with the boss eye's following her over.'

A Siouxie Sioux look-alike with multiple piercings and finger tattoos approached from the left, chewing on a chocolate digestive. Several heads turned.

'Hello … Hope I'm not intruding,' she said, swallowing hurriedly, 'but I think we may be related.'

'Oh, I get that a lot,' said Sylvie. 'People want to adopt me all the time. I'm pocket-sized you see, they want to take me home and sit me on the mantelpiece.'

'No, really. I'm your Millicent's grandaughter. I'm Ruby Porter.'

Sylvie gaped. 'Well now you've told me, how did I not see the resemblance? Pull up a chair and tell me all.'

As Ruby sat down, the ginger cat leaped onto her lap.

'Is he yours?' said Sylvie.

'No, he was on the bus, and he followed me here. Someone said he belongs to the Shoreline club. If he does, his name's Nelson.'

'Well ***if he does***, he's a long way from home,' said Norris. 'I'll get him some milk….' As Norris got up, Ruby dragged her seat closer.

'How's your mother?' said Sylvie.

Ruby flushed behind the piercings. 'Oh, I don't see her anymore ... we kind of lost touch. I had problems she couldn't deal with.... Not that I blame her at all...Look, Sylvie.... Crystal? I'm not sure what to call you.'

'Sylvie's fine.'

'Well, Sylvie, I'm here for a special reason.'

Sylvie scanned the room for earwiggers.

'Is this something you'd like to discuss elsewhere?' She stood up and indicated with a head twitch where she intended going. Ruby and the cat followed her outside with Bobby trailing at a cautious distance.

Out in the car park, Sylvie shivered. 'Holy shite .... It's brass monkeys out here ....'

'That's the seaside for you.' Ruby took off her cardigan, and slipped it across Sylvie's shoulders. 'This may not be your style ... but it's warm.'

The giant safety pins and tacked-on pocket made her smile. 'Thank you ... now give me the gossip.'

'I ... had a boyfriend .... David. He was your Ernie's youngest son.'

Sylvie paced up and down to keep warm, rolling her eyes. 'That doesn't surprise me .... One of many I'm afraid.'

Ruby gave a sardonic laugh. 'Yes, anyway, we were two lost souls trying to feel better, you know? We went on a bender one weekend … and not just booze … it was stupid …. First time for me, but not for him. So I don't know how it happened. It should have been the other way round, but it was David who died.'

'What was it? What did you take?'

'Cocaine. I snorted, he injected. Maybe that was the difference.'

'Not that I know much about drugs, but was the stuff okay? I mean, did he have a regular dealer?'

'I don't think he did. He'd just about given it all up, but then he had a setback. You see he was trying to get in touch with family, having lost his mother. Then it didn't work out and he was so depressed. But that's all it takes to relapse.'

'I'm so sorry. When was this?'

'Six weeks ago. I haven't touched any substance since, I promise you.'

'Hey, I'm not fit to judge. I once scoffed a whole tray of fresh cream horns. No bakery would employ me after that.' Sylvie shook her head. 'Life takes us many places, and sometimes we make wrong choices.'

'I was hoping you might make contact with David tonight …. Or teach me how to do it …I can pay you, I have a job now and everything.'

'Oh, Ruby, it's not something anyone can learn. Sometimes the spirits just choose, you know? They pick us out when the time suits them. We don't really have a say in it.'

Ruby looked down as the cat slalomed between her legs.

'Where do you live, Ruby?'

'We have …. ***I*** have a flat on the riverside. It's right on the end with a glorious view.'

Sylvie heard voices across the car park. She turned to see Carolyn Carr's beehive nodding aggressively beneath a lamp post. Then she spotted Daisy, still in her tabard, handing over a carrier bag in exchange for what looked like money.

Bobby popped his head around the exit door. 'You've got seven minutes, Sylvie. Best get a wiggle on.'

'Okay Bobby, you go ahead …. I'm right behind you.' He went back inside.

She opened her handbag, scrabbled around inside. 'I don't suppose you've something I can write my phone number on?'

Ruby stuck out her arm. 'Write it on there. You're in a rush.' Sylvie produced a biro and scribbled her number on Ruby's pallid skin, careful to avoid the dragon tattoo, then she tossed the pen back inside her bag and snapped it shut. 'I have to go, but call me…' She headed for the door and turned before disappearing inside. 'Don't you forget mind.'

'I promise.'

Back in the cloakroom, Clarabelle lifted her sleepy head off the sofa as the door creaked open and Sylvie entered the room.

'Oh poppet, I've spent no time with you at all tonight, have I?' She bent to eye level with the dog, stroking her head. 'And now I have to bugger off and leave you all over again …' Clarabelle puffed a warm blast of air through her nostrils and plopped her chin back down on the sofa. The door creaked again, and in sauntered a ginger cat. He stopped at the sofa and stared up at Clara. She raised her head in mild interest and sniffed the air. The cat leaped up beside her and lay down. 'Oh Clara, look … You made a friend.' The door creaked a third time, and Bobby poked his head inside. 'Sweetums…You're on.' Sylvie sighed, stood up and followed Bobby out.

Waiting in the wings once again, she hoped the second half would be no more than mediocre. Tiredness was creeping in, and she felt very old. And there were the voices again, *'I want, we want, let us in…'* coming through the earpiece. She tried to ignore them as Reverend Norris introduced her back onto the stage, but it was pointless. Taking in a deep breath, she painted on her best smile and walked out to greet the audience.

'Well folks, what a first half that was, huh? Let's hope we can match it.' Sylvie stared at the floor for a moment. 'I'm getting an older man with a gruff voice.' She tilted her head to one side and twisted her face. 'The voice is kind of familiar. He's shaking a fist at someone….it's not me folks, don't worry, but he's sure as hell mad about something ….' She drifted off again. Seconds passed, and Bobby whispered into his cravat. 'Sylvie… Wake up. You're doing it again.' But Sylvie wasn't listening. Not to Bobby, at least. Suddenly she straightened, clenching both fists and marched to the front of the stage, furious as hell.

'MURDERER!' she screamed. Her eyes snapped shut and her head began to roll on its axis. 'My flesh … my blood.' Then instantly calmer, she clasped hands behind her back and ambled around the stage, whistling The Sailor's Hornpipe just as someone clattered to the floor in the back row and slid beneath the seat in front. People bustled around, dragging chairs clear. Bobby was one of the first, crouching by the victim's side.

'It's that punk rocker,' someone said. But it was also Ruby Porter, and she was convulsing as she lay on the floor.

'Can everyone stand back please? Give her some space?' Bobby rolled her on her side as she became still, and felt for a pulse. 'Come on Ruby, let's hear yer ticker. Prove you're no vampire.' After a minute, he asked the crowd, 'does anyone have a mirror?' One of the women produced one from nowhere and Bobby held it beneath Ruby's nostrils. Then Eva Shawcross shoved her way in from the back of the crowd.

'I'm a nurse .... Let me through.' She gave Bobby a sharp nudge with her elbow to shift him, tilted Ruby's head back, pinching her nose. Then she covered Ruby's mouth with her own, shrouding both with a mane of dark hair.

'That was completely unnecessary,' said Bobby, rubbing at his bruised ribs. 'She ***was*** breathing.' Two very long minutes passed, while Bobby paced up and down and Sylvie descended from the stage. She got there just as Eva raised her head to reveal Ruby's lifeless face.

'Well, she's not breathing anymore.... is she?'

Chapter 6 : An inspector calls

It was 10.15pm and The Fish Gutter's Arms was packed and noisy. A sweaty barman weaved around tables gathering dirty glasses between fingers, under arms, anywhere they'd fit. Rambo had sniffed out a dry patch of floor for sleeping and D.C.I. Witless had actually removed his coat and loosened his tie. In the humidity, his wayward comb over begged for discipline. He took a swig from his beer glass and thumbed through the notebook on the table.

'So, Conway, what did you get from the night cleaner, Joe Parker?'

Conway slipped reading glasses over her ears and perched her notebook on a crossed leg. 'Joseph Damon Parker, thirty six years old, married, two kids. An employee for five years at Harton Hospital, no previous. Currently trying to give up smoking, so we can safely assume the nicotine patch found at the scene belongs to him. Claims not to know Ernie

Winters personally, only of his reputation as a bad drag act and womanizer.'

'So he was cleaning on the ICU ward at what time?'

'He says it was around 19.30 hours to 20.00 hours, give or take.'

'Estimated time of death is 23.00, so depending how long the toxin …. still not confirmed, would take to kill Winters ……' Witless glared at Tracey, more focused on scratching the sole of his foot which he'd freed from the shoe for a better experience. 'Tracey! You're meant to be taking part here, or at least making a better show of it.'

Tracey straightened up, returning his hands to the table. 'Sir, I was listening, truly I was.'

'What is it with your sodding feet anyway? Can't you leave them alone?'

'They're exceptionally dry, sir. Makes them itch something rotten, and they get so cold…'

Witless gave that disapproving glare from beneath the eyebrows. 'If you can put that to one side for the moment …. We're still waiting to hear the name of the toxin you and Sir Hugo were so secretive about this morning.'

Tracey slotted the offending foot into its shoe and straightened the hem of his trousers. 'Oh, I don't know if that's shareable sir. And we may not have been thinking along the same lines. I mean we could both have completely different ideas about it.'

'As I recall, animals and euthanasia were discussed.'

'Yes sir, that's true.'

'So I'm presuming you know the substance used to euthanize a calf?'

'I do sir.'

'Then might I trouble you for the name of that substance? I'm willing to exchange this information for a bag of pork scratchings?' Witless tossed his unopened scratchings across the table.

'And another pint?'

'Don't push your luck.'

'Of course not, sir. And thanks very much. It's Pentobarbital. Commonly known as Nembutal.'

'Wonderful.' Witless made a note in his little book. 'And how long would you estimate Pento ...?'

'...barbital, sir.'

'How long would it take to kill a human being?'

Tracey shook his head and stared at the floor. 'Depends on the dose, sir. And remember I've only witnessed it in animals. But a hefty dose used to euthanize a calf would kill it within a minute.'

'Right, and what about Monica Woodhouse?'

'I imagine about the same amount of time, sir.'

'Don't get clever with me, Tracey.'

'Course not sir. Monica's thirty two; divorce pending; three kids under ten. Didn't arrive on shift until 20.15 hours on account of sick child. The nearest she got to the ICU that night was a neb through the windows on passing.'

'You had all that in your head, Tracey?'

'Yes, well I know her already, sir.'

Conway lifted her eyes from the notebook, her attention grabbed. 'And just how well do you know Monica Woodhouse, D.C. Tracey?' she said.

'We went to the same school. I took her to Saturday club at the Odeon once.'

Witless threw down his pencil and blew air threw his bottom lip. 'And you didn't think to mention this before?'

Tracey looked confused. 'I haven't spoken to her for the last twenty years sir.'

'You could still be accused of bias. That might have just pissed on the chips. I'll have to think. In the meantime, keep your gob shut and your body away from hers.'

'Wouldn't dream of it, sir.'

'IS THERE A D.C.I. WITLESS IN THE HOUSE?' the pub landlord yelled from behind the bar, waving a telephone handset in the air.

Witless raised himself from the vinyl seating, dragged a trouser fold from his anus and headed towards the bar.

'Evening all ….Witless here.'

'Witless, get your arse over to St. Martin's church hall. There's been another suspicious death.'

∞∞∞

Rambo leapt from the car unaided, clutching Tracey's pork scratchings between saggy jowls.

'Have you ***seen*** this one?' said Tracey. 'I was looking forward to those.'

Seymour Witless stepped out from the driver's seat, straightened his tie and thrust an arm into his overcoat. 'What can I say? He always clears up when anyone leaves the table. I'm sure he'll let you have one if you ask nicely.'

Tracey turned up his collar, rolling his eyes as Conway strode off ahead of them.

'She's not giving an inch, sir. I may as well give up.'

'No-one on my team gives up, Tracey. That's the law,' said Witless, striding after Conway.

'What do I do with Rambo, sir? It being a crime scene and all,' said Tracey, in hot pursuit.

'Bring him in. He might sniff out the wrong 'un.'

A uniformed officer greeted them at the church hall doors with shoe coverings and gloves. Witless huffed and snatched them from the officer's hands. 'Second time today with all this bloody malarkey, and it's my sodding bedtime!'

Conway glanced around while she waited, already kitted out and impatient to be making a move. 'I don't think the dog should be in here sir,' she said.

'Oh ***don't*** you now?' said Witless. 'Well perhaps you should wait by the door with him Conway.' He snatched Rambo's lead from Tracey's grip and handed it to her. She hesitated. 'Can't D.C. Tracey do it sir? ***I am after all*** his senior, and I need to be closer to this case.'

'Are we going to waste time arguing, Conway?' He pressed the lead into her hand, closed her fingers around it and turned. 'Come on Tracey,' he beckoned, 'you're with me. Let's see what we've got here.'

First responding officer Sergeant Eccles fell into step with them as they entered the hall. 'Evening, sir. Sorry you've been dragged out at this hour.... It's a young girl, name of Ruby Porter according to the local psychic.'

Witless mocked surprise. 'Amazing powers! Will she know who I am? I need reminding.'

'The coroner's been called .... Should have been here by now...'

'Yes, well, I shouldn't hold your breath Sergeant......Good God!'

Ruby Porter lay on her back at the end of the hall with heavy make-up smeared across pale cheeks, jeans slashed at the hips, knees and thighs.

'It appears she's been attacked by wolves,' said Witless.' What do you think, Tracey?'

Tracey considered for a few seconds before leaning in. 'I believe it's a fashion trend, sir,' he said softly.

Witless returned the quiet exchange, 'This may surprise you, Tracey .... but I don't live under a rock. Where are the Scene of Crime Officers? Sergeant Eccles?'

'As I understand it sir, the female recently lost a partner to drugs. That's why we didn't call in the SOCO's. Could be self-inflicted.'

'Could be, Sergeant. But we can't just assume, can we?'

'No, sir,' said Eccles, nervously fingering his cap.

Over by the piano, Daisy and the reverend exchanged hurried whispers, oblivious of the D.C.I.'s interest. Witless returned his attention to the crowd.

'So, what happened exactly?'

Bobby stepped forward, raising a hesitant hand.

'Excuse me, sir, Bobby Mason …. Crystal Gazer's aide … '

'Just plain English will do, if you don't mind …' said Witless.

Bobby folded, then unfolded his arms and began gesticulating. 'I was…um …. in the second back row when I heard a crash.' Bobby's hand moved up to his hair, then to one ear for a good scratch before he continued. 'Well, I looked across and spotted a vacant seat where Ruby had been sitting, so I guessed it was her straightaway. Felt for a pulse, but wasn't sure there was one, or it was very faint. Then I borrowed a mirror and ....'

'Then I took charge, Inspector. I'm the district nurse.' Eva Shawcross interrupted. 'There was no sign of life, so I tried mouth to mouth for several minutes. But sadly, she did not recover.... And it's true what the other sergeant was saying .... She was a drug user who'd recently lost a partner.'

'And you know this .... how?'

'She's a patient at our G.P. practice, Bedside Manors.'

'Right, well we'll still need to take statements from those involved and a full list of names D.C. Tracey? Can you see to that please? And where is this Crystal Gazer?' Witless scanned the room.

As if by magic, Sylvie appeared at the hall's entrance. Beneath one arm, Clarabelle cuddled in close, a pack of pork scratchings held between her teeth.

'That would be me, Inspector,' said Sylvie. 'You've a face like a chewed toffee as usual.... and if you don't close that mouth of yours someone will be along to park a dirty great bus inside it.'

Witless closed his eyes and gently shook his head. 'I cannot believe this…'

'I knew it had to be you when I spotted that sex crazy dog of yours on the door,' she continued, advancing towards him. 'I only just prevented my Clarabelle having one of her panic attacks. You still haven't had him fixed, have you?'

Massaging his temples, Witless assumed a calmer voice. 'It's on my list, Miss Broadstairs.'

Sylvie scoffed. 'Maybe I believe you … And in case you're interested, some drunk in a dinner suit just tripped over your dog and is threatening to sue.'

'What drunk?'

At that point, a disheveled, bald man in a frilly shirt and coat tails stumbled into the hall and attempted to collect himself. 'Reginald Sm … Smythe, M.B.C.…H ... Bleurgh …. Hic!' Close behind him was Sir Hugo Stubbs, dressed in similar garb, though less ruffled.

'Ah, Shitless! So good to see you again …. and Tracey, what a pleasure!'

Witless stood frozen while Sir Hugo grabbed Reginald by the arm, just as he was about to topple again. 'So sorry about my friend Reggie the coroner …. A few too many sherbets at his own leaving do, so I thought it best to drive him,' he said, guiding

Reggie towards a seat. 'Can I just park him .... aargh ... here, old man? And then I'll take a quick shufty at the cadaver.'

Once seated, Reggie's eyes closed and his chin bounced around his chest like a snooker ball in a jump shot. Looking rather pleased with himself, Sir Hugo brushed imaginary dust from his lapels. 'Now, let the dog see the rabbit.'

'Well, Sir Hugo, this young lady collapsed during the performance for no obvious reason,' Witless explained.

'Any fitting or vomiting before she expired?'

'Yes, there was some fitting.' Bobby added. 'But not vomiting.'

'There seems also to be some speculation of a drugs overdose,' Witless added.

With gloved hands, Sir Hugo examined Ruby's arms and carefully pulled up the legs of her jeans.

'Except ***there was no drugs overdose***....' Sylvie interjected.

Witless glared at Sylvie, while Sir Hugo's face lit up.

'You know this for a fact, madam? You know this woman?'

'She's a relative of mine, and I strongly believe this was not self-inflicted.'

'No track marks, certainly. But there is a number on her arm written in biro. Could be a clue,' said Sir Hugo.

'I wrote that number on her arm.'

'Then I'll need to speak to you as a matter of urgency,' said Witless. 'Sir Hugo, would you agree with Miss Broadstairs that this would appear to be a suspicious death?'

'I never make assumptions, not at this early stage. Could be anything from poisoning to an aneurism. Fitting without vomiting suggests any toxic substance is unlikely to have been taken by mouth. I'd need to get her on the table, to be certain, so it's best not to speculate at this stage.'

Witless paced up and down, stroking his chin.

'Do you need me to sort this out for you Inspector?' said Sylvie. 'You remember how useful you said I was on that last ***murder*** case?'

Witless sighed. 'Can we not go into that ***again***?'

'Excuse me, chappie-in-charge?' Carolyn Carr's beehive threatened collapse as she tottered forward from the back of the crowd waving a white leather-gloved hand. 'How long must we stay here?

It really is so inconvenient …. I have a driver waiting outside with nibbles.'

'Nibbles?'

'Err … oh, um …. What do you people call it? Takeaway! Yes, that's it.'

'And you are?'

The starlet guffawed. 'You mean …. You're being serious? You don't know who I am?'

'I wouldn't be asking otherwise, would I?'

She held out another gloved hand. 'Carolyn Carr ….. singer, entertainer, writer and ….' She leaned towards Witless's ear and lowered her voice, '...private dancer.'

'Look at that geriatric hussy, Clarabelle. All chicken fillets and no knickers,' whispered Sylvie.

Witless's eyeballs ping ponged from side to side as the local celebrity stepped back with a smile crammed full of pricey veneers stained with lipstick. He dropped his gaze to the floor and cleared his throat again.

'Erm … yes, well, Ms. Carr, I'm afraid you can't leave until we've taken everyone's details. And this can go as quickly as you all choose.' Miss Carr's bottom lip turned itself inside out and bounced off her chin. 'Oh poo!' she said.

'Righto, Shitless!' said Sir Hugo. Time to call in the cavalry, what?' Witless took another hard slap to the arm, swayed with the impact, but managed to stay rooted.

'Okay, Tracey, let's get the SOCO's out here.'

'Yes sir,' said Tracey, making for the exit. Passing Sir Hugo, he paused, leaning in to whisper, 'Sir Hugo, your friend Reggie appears to be on fire.'

Sir Hugo looked across, and sure enough tendrils of smoke curled skywards from the sleeping man's shirt pocket.

'Good God!' said Sir Hugo. 'I knew he couldn't have finished that bloody cigar.'

∞∞∞

Sylvie lay with her throbbing feet resting on the cloakroom's lumpy couch. By her side, Clarabelle extended her tongue from time to time, wrapping it around Sylvie's pink toes in a long, comforting lick. The cat had been displaced to the floor rug, where he lay snoring like a drain, a back leg kicking out, Kung Fu style. Sylvie's eyes were closed, until a rapid tapping at the door made her start.

'Holy shite!' came out of her mouth just as Reverend Norris peered around the door. His droopy jowls and frantic brows gave the impression he was permanently in turmoil, when in fact he was known to have extended periods of calm, particularly during Daisy's classical piano recitals.

'So sorry to disturb you, Miss Broadstairs, but the inspector wondered if he could use this room for interviews?'

D.C.I. Witless appeared behind him. 'An hour at most, Miss Broadstairs. We're all eager to get to our beds after tonight…'

Another voice from behind ***him*** needed no face to confirm its identity. 'I can't wait to get into bed, Inspector…'

Sylvie stood up and shrugged. 'Who am I to object? I take it you don't mind if I retreat to the bathroom? I can have a soak in there and you won't be disturbed.'

'That will do just fine,' Witless agreed. The reverend scowled discreetly, and Sylvie gave him a sly wink.

'You can come in, Carolyn …. I promise not to bite you this time,' said Sylvie.

Carolyn swept around the men and surveyed the room, with mouth downturned.

'You expect me to be interviewed in here? It smells like a farmyard, the couch is filthy and ….'

She looked down and raised a foot. 'I'm sticking to the Goddam floor!'

'And you still smell of that tacky perfume – what's it called? Ah yes, Chanel number 2.'

Carolyn scowled. 'Number two?'

'Exactly.' Sylvie smirked, picked up her shoes and padded bare foot towards a door in the far corner.

'Give me a knock when you're done,' she said. 'And watch yourself with that one, Inspector. She'll have you on toast for breakfast.'

Closing the door behind her, Sylvie took two steps across the tiny room to the corner sink, and turned on the tap. Then two steps back again, she pressed an ear to the door.

CHAPTER 7 : THE RUNAWAYS

Her interview completed, Daisy Harbottle emerged from the vestry with a sullen face. Heading back to the hall, she chewed on a forefinger, then thrust a hand inside her pinafore pocket and pulled out a roll of fivers. With a smug smile, she tucked them back inside and strode on, only to collide with Reverend Norris leaping out from the Gents.

'Oh, Norris!' Her hand leapt to her throat, 'Don't ***do*** that to me.'

'Daisy…' He looked furtively around and grabbed her by the elbow, steering her into the broom cupboard. Closing the door softly behind them, the reverend pulled out a wallet from his cassock. 'How much have you collected tonight?'

She drew back her chin and gave him the once over. 'And why might that be any business of yours?'

'Because for one thing, you're conducting illegal trade on my premises, and for another, the place is crawling with police…'

Daisy folded her arms across her chest and looked away. 'Still don't see how the amount is any of your concern…. And these are not your premises, they're the Good Lord's'

He held out a palm. 'Give it to me. If I can tell that's no handkerchief in your pocket, then one of these officers will see it too.' The hand was still outstretched, and the fingers now doing a ***come hither*** movement. With reluctance, Daisy surrendered the cash.

'There's fifty quid there Norris, so don't you go diddling me.'

∞∞∞

D.C. Richard Tracey, having emerged from the study, headed down the hall to claim his next interview victim when he heard voices from the broom cupboard. He listened for a moment, then quickly backed into the cloakroom as Norris and Daisy re-emerged, going their separate ways. Tracey peered through the crack in the door, oblivious of his intrusion upon his D.C.I.'s interview with Carolyn Carr.

'Erm… can we help you, D.C. Tracey? You appear to be lost,' said Witless.

Tracey whipped around. 'Sir!' he said, eyes wide. 'I'm so sorry .... You're right, lost my way....'

'Well, do come in. Take the weight off those poor sickly feet of yours. Miss Carr is just leaving.'

Carolyn stood up from the couch with hesitance. 'Right, well ....you know where to find me, Inspector.' She dusted off her buttocks, fingered the beehive and made for the exit. 'And don't forget about my invitation .... Any time.' Tracey opened the door obligingly, and with a flirty finger wave, she was gone.

Tracey closed the door.

'Sir, I think Reverend Norris and Daisy the cleaner are up to something.'

Witless smirked. 'Why? Did you catch them in the broom cupboard?'

Tracey became animated. 'Yes! .... Well, I don't mean ***in that way***, but ...' With a quick scan of the room, he dragged a dog-eared footstool closer to the couch which he attempted to sit on. It was no more than six inches high, and Tracey's gangly legs concertinaed up to his hairline.

'There were definitely raised whispers behind closed doors, and when they came out neither one looked happy.'

Witless pondered. 'We've all had those disappointments, Tracey. I'm sure the reverend will get over it.'

Just then, the bathroom door opened and Sylvie emerged from her long soak.

'Did the pair of you forget about me by any chance?' Her eyes flitted across the room. 'Is that a new yoga pose, Detective? And where's Clarabelle? Where's my bloody dog?'

∞∞∞

Sylvie strode with purpose down the corridor, followed closely behind by Seymour Witless.

'Miss Broadstairs,' he said, struggling to catch up. 'I can't permit you to leave the building yet …. not until you've been interviewed. Where are you even going?'

She stopped abruptly and faced him. 'Maybe I'm going for pizza …. ***or*** …. to commit murder.' She turned, continuing en route towards the hall. 'I'll decide whichever in the car…. This is all ***your*** fault. If you want an interview, you'll have to come along …. because I have no time to waste when my Clara could be in mortal peril.'

The foyer was empty apart from two uniformed officers guarding the doors.

'Oh, bloody hell ….' Said Witless, scanning the doorway. 'Where's ***my*** bloody dog?'

∞∞∞

D.C. Richard Tracey continued his search for the missing Chihuahua inside the building. He knocked briefly, then opened the vestry door. D.S. Conway was perched on the edge of a wicker chair having seen better days. She tugged at the hem of her skirt as he entered, attempting to conceal a rip in her tights. Opposite, sat Eva Shawcross, district nurse.

'What's going on, D.S. Conway? Where's Rambo?' he said.

'He's tied to the railings outside, Detective.'

'Are you sure about that?'

Eva Shawcross smirked. 'Is Rambo a suspect, them? My, the press will be all over this one.'

'D.S. Conway, can I have a word, please?' said Tracey.

With lips pursed, Conway stood up and followed Tracey into the corridor.

'Did Witless tell you to conduct interviews?' he continued.

Conway removed her spectacles and prodded them against his chest. 'I'm using,' (prod) 'my initiative,' (prod) 'and, D.C. Tracey …. ***maybe it's not your place to ask.'***

Tracey retreated one step. 'Right …. well, if you spot a Chihuahua anywhere, perhaps you can alert an officer …. and detain the animal if possible.'

'I'll consider it my priority. Now, if you don't mind, I really need to get on.' She stepped back inside the vestry and closed the door on him.

∞∞∞

Out in the car park, Witless and Sylvie split up. 'Check behind those sheds over there.' Sylvie shouted, wagging a pointed finger into the abyss. 'I'll do a circuit of the cars.' Witless shrugged with upturned palms but then sped off in the direction.

A pair of wooden sheds cast gigantic shadows across the tarmac. As he approached the first, an owl's hooting suddenly startled him. 'Shit!' he said, snatching a torch from an inside pocket. Under the play of torch light through a grimy window, a vagrant snoozed beneath a pile of woven garden sacks, his face half-covered with a crumpled fedora, an upturned wine bottle by his side. Witless found the door ajar, crept inside and nudged the man's foot with his own.

'Rise and shine, Hoggy. It's the witching hour …'

Hoggy's hand flew to his eyes for shade. 'Turn that ruddy thing off, Seymour, for hell's sake.'

Witless diverted the torch beam onto his surroundings. A rusted perambulator circa 1950's containing a pile of old books topped with a near-fossilized remnant of a half-eaten sandwich; Hoggy's push bike, propped against one wall, recovered by the police diving team five years prior, now glowing luminescent.

'What's with the luminous orange, Hoggy?'

Hoggy ruffled his tatty mane of ginger curls. 'Did that body yous was lookin' for ever turn up, Seymour?'

Sylvie's face poked around the open doorway, complete with smirk. 'No, it didn't, because ***there was*** no body, was there, Inspector? And by the way, does nicking a tramp take priority over finding my dog?'

'I is no tramp, missus. Seymour and me …. we's old friends.'

'Hoggy's right, Miss Broadstairs. There's no harm in him.'

'How long have you been kipping here anyway, Hoggy?'

Hoggy sat up, perched his elbows on his knees and rubbed his eyes. 'Couple of weeks .... maybe longer.' He looked up. 'It's all legit .... Norris lets me stay, in exchange for odd jobs. Fixed a toilet leak yesterday.'

'That's very commendable. Ask Norris for the loan of his razor. I swear that beard of yours has grown an extra six inches since last time I saw you.' The brows on Witless crinkled as he sniffed the air. 'Have you been smoking weed?'

Hoggy looked wounded. '***Tha knows*** I only smokes cigarillos... Can hardly afford ***even those*** these days anyways.'

'Hmm ... we may need to talk to you, so don't go anywhere, right?'

Witless made for the door, and Sylvie backed out.

'I'll get the car. We can have a cruise around,' he said, striding towards his vehicle.

'Not so fast, ***Seymour***,' she said, following after, 'I've just seen that Gazette hack slobbering all over Carolyn Carr's young protegé in the car park.'

Seymour partially turned but didn't slow down. 'Define slobbering?'

'Like your dog's doing right now to my Clarabelle behind that white Chevrolet over yonder.' She nodded across to the far side of the car park.

'You found them?'

'I have indeed, ***Seymour,***' she mocked. He was defeated.

They'd reached the Chevrolet, where an empty pork scratchings wrapper blew out from under the chassis. At the rear, Clarabelle, Rambo and Nelson the cat crunched greedily on its contents.

'This may be all too much for D.C. Tracey when I tell him,' said Witless.

∞∞∞

It was freezing inside the Morris Minor, and the furry dice hanging from the rear-view mirror swung from side to side as Witless parked his backside in the driver's seat.

'Are you getting in or just playing doorman for the next tornado?' Rambo and Clarabelle were already settled on the back seat having a smooch fest with tongues, while Nelson sat on the tarmac outside.

'I can't leave the cat out there. Look at his dejected little face,' said Sylvie.

Witless blew air heavily through his nostrils. 'Alright. But he's gone the minute you are.'

Nelson didn't need much persuading. He was in like a rocket, and Rambo grumped as he forced a space between the dogs. Satisfied, Sylvie climbed into the passenger seat and shut the door, swaddling herself in Ruby's oversized cardigan. Something in the pocket jingled.

'So, what is it you want to tell me?'

'Excuse me, Miss Broadstairs .... but ***you're*** meant to be doing the telling, not me.'

'Okay Seymour, I can tell you're a fan of the rigmarole, so what do you want to know?'

Witless took out his notebook and fished for a pen in the dash. 'After conducting my interview with Carolyn Carr ....'

'You mean the warbling witch?'

Witless sighed. 'If that's what you prefer to call her, yes. Anyway, following that interview, I find you two have a connection to a recent murder. What do you say to that?'

'Well of course we have a connection. We were both in the same room when Ruby died. ***That's why we're being interviewed, is it not?'***

'I'm not talking about Ruby Porter's murder, I'm talking about Ernie Winters. You both have a connection to ***him, do you not?'***

Sylvie turned white. 'Ernie's been murdered? You're having me on. Crazy person that you are…'

'Two nights ago,' Witless spoke slowly, '….Ernest Winters, we believe, was pushed down the fire escape at The Shoreline, then someone finished him off in Harton General's Intensive Care Unit last night. The press haven't been notified as yet ….'

'Shite almighty!' she said. 'And I thought she was telling fibs.'

'Telling fibs?'

'I was listening at the door. I heard her say she was in the audience to connect with her dead lover. I thought she was full of the brown stuff…'

'You were listening at the door? So you weren't having a soak after all?' Seymour's brows formed wavy lines.

'Jesus, I know I'm small but ***even I*** couldn't fit inside ***that*** sink.' Sylvie puzzled for a moment. 'So how ***was*** Ernie finished off, as you so crudely put it?'

Seymour considered through the windscreen. 'I'm meant to be ***asking you*** if you have any ideas about that.'

'Well, I'm guessing the easiest way, if he was already hooked up to drips, oxygen, whatever, would be to interfere with the flow of any of those things.'

'Precisely …. So where were you the night before last between 20.30 hours and 23.00?'

'Watching TV, at home.'

'Can anyone vouch for that?'

'No ….. Yes! Bobby came over around 9 o'clock, after a row with the boyfriend. I made him a cuppa and a hot cross bun with Red Leicester …. He's not keen on Blue Stilton.' She fumbled with the clasp on her handbag. 'Would you like one, Seymour?'

Witless began salivating. He wrestled with his hunger but it threw him to the ground and sat on his chest. 'You carry these around with you?'

Sylvie was already peeling back the cling film. Rambo raised his enormous head and forced a jowl flapping sneeze as the essence of mouldy cheese wafted through the car. 'I've eaten nothing all day …' Seymour whimpered. Slowly, she prised open his hand and placed the bun inside it. The hand sped to his mouth and he chewed greedily with a gratifying sigh.

'Well, Seymour, looks like I've found your weak spot ….' She sniggered, then frowned as she spotted Judy Conway approaching the vehicle. The D.S. rapped on the driver's side window.

Witless spun around, still chewing, and offered an eye roll to Sylvie as he turned the winder anticlockwise.

'What is it, Conway?'

Conway's eyes missed nothing. 'Sir, it's after midnight. There are only four left to interview. Perhaps we can do those tomorrow?'

'Yes, that's fine, Conway. And next time, perhaps you should ask your senior before you decide to abandon his dog in a fit of resentment.' Conway pursed her lips, swiveled around and stomped away.

∞∞∞

Chapter 8 : Finding where to start

Despite the late bedtime, Sylvie was up with the larks and drinking Bovril with a four-minute boiled egg on the side. Clarabelle had hers scrambled, while her other eggs remained, hopefully, unfertilized. The rain clattered down like machine gun fire on the perspex roof as a wad of cotton wool sprang from Sylvie's ear, landing on her plate. She picked it up and sighed. 'Oh Clarabelle, I'm too old to be living in a caravan, even if it does have a state-of-the-art flushing toilet.' The dog looked up and waved her tail in the air. 'I don't suppose you want to go out in the rain anymore than me, do you? Even though we might bump into Nelson?' Clarabelle's tail wagged faster. 'Oh you do?' Sylvie picked up her plate and carried it to the sink. 'Come on then, let's find your raincoat.'

The windscreen wipers struggled to cope on the drive back to St Martin's, but she'd covered it so many times it probably could have been done blindfold anyway. Parking up, she tightened the chin strap under her fisherman's hat, locked the steering wheel and stepped out onto the gravel. Clarabelle jumped out after her and they ran for the hall's entrance doors.

'Why, good morning,' greeted Reverend Norris as Sylvie dripped and Clarabelle shook herself, showering the entrance hall with gay abandon.

'Is it really, Norris?' said Sylvie, sliding the hat to the back of her head and scanning the room. Hoggy was snipping the stems of the Devil's Trumpets he'd picked that morning for Daisy's flower displays, while she filled the vases from a large pitcher.

'Um… you do know they're poisonous?' said Sylvie. Hoggy waved silicon gloved hands across the room in her direction. 'I do knows, missus. I gets these from the bin after the rozzers went home last night. Still plenty of life left in 'em. That's tax payers' money, tha knows.'

'So it is, Hoggy, so it is.' Sylvie grasped Norris's elbow, ushering him nearer the door. 'So, Norris, I'm calling on Miss Mountshaft today about …. you know … what happened here the other night. Is there anything you can tell me about her family?'

Norris considered, with spectacled eyes wandering around the room. He kept his voice low. 'She's a very private person Miss Broadstairs, but I know she had a sister that died .... oh, long time ago now, because I found the entry in the parish records by accident. Now, what was her name again?' Stretching a thumb and forefinger across his brow, he stared at the floor. Then, pointing skywards with jowls flapping, he suddenly said, 'Dorothy. Yes, that's it .... Dorothy!'

'Fantastic, Norris .... At least I have a name now. And oh, just a word of warning about those Devil's Trumpets ....'

'Oh, you mean the flowers? So pretty, aren't they?'

'They are, but deadly if ingested. A friend's husband ended up in hospital after cutting them from his garden. He was ill for weeks.'

The entrance door suddenly burst open and Judy Conway presented with a perfect scowl, shaking a golfer's umbrella into the hallway with the wield of a sword. As the raindrops hit her, Clarabelle gave a tiny yelp.

'And where might these poisonous blooms be, Reverend?' said Conway, following the direction of Norris's eyeballs with her own. Daisy Harbottle paused her arrangement and frowned.

'As long as you know how to handle them, miss, they're fine. It's not illegal to bring them indoors, so far as I'm aware.'

'No, but since we suspect that someone was killed here yesterday by ingesting a toxin, and given the fact that you have full access to the kitchen and the serving counter, I think it would be better if you came down to the station with me now.'

'You're arresting me? You can't arrest ***me***, I have a sick husband at home with no-one else to care for him.'

'I'm not arresting you .... yet. Just asking you to accompany me to the station for further questioning. Get your coat.'

Norris retrieved Daisy's mackintosh from the coat stand. 'Don't worry about Arthur, Daisy. You'll be home in no time, and if you aren't, I can always ask the district nurse to call and give him his insulin.'

'Tha's done nuthin' wrong, Daisy Harbottle,' said Hoggy, tossing down his scissors. 'Just tha remember that!'

Still in shock, Daisy allowed Norris to help her on with her coat, whereupon Conway seized her by the arm and marched her outside.

'Well,' said Sylvie, 'if anyone deserves a kick up the arse with a builder's boot it's ***that one.***'

Norris spoke to the ceiling. 'Oh Lord, keep an arm around her shoulders and a hand over her mouth.'

∞∞∞

Snapdragon Lane snaked downhill towards the cliff tops like an invitation to suicide. This white-knuckled pensioner whimpered softly, hunched over the wheel of her Mini Metro with one foot quivering over the brake pedal as she concentrated on the degree of force required for her ultimate survival. Cottages trimmed the road in a haphazard plan of mixed sizes and shapes like a lineup of adolescent students in senior school. Sylvie bent her head to read the door numbers.

'Some of these only have names, Clara …. Henry's Hideaway …. Cozy Nook ….. Old Bat's Belfry ….. oh, this is the one, number nine, The Nut House…. That's a warning … possibly. No sign of Bobby yet … fashionably late again.'

Lace curtains began to twitch all around as she pulled in and Rosalind Mountshaft appeared in the open doorway dressed in twinset and pearls. Sylvie clambered out of the car and held the door for Clarabelle. The rain had stopped and the pavement steamed beneath the sun's rays.

'Good morning …. Miss Mountshaft?' she greeted with a hopeful smile.

'Thank you for coming, Miss Broadstairs. Do come in.' She stood aside as Sylvie scooped up the dog and entered.

'I should warn you, Miss Broadstairs, I do have a bird.'

'Oh, how nice. Not a giant eagle I hope?'

'No,' she laughed uneasily. 'But he does like to take part when I have company.'

'Well, all opinions are welcome, of course.'

The living room was small but cosy, with a real coal fire burning in the grate. In one corner stood a very tall, metal cage, furnished with a string ladder, a mirror with bells attached and a fully stocked feeding device.

'Oh, do sit down, Miss Broadstairs.' She prepared to pour tea into fine china cups then seated herself. 'And meet Cyril,' she continued with a smile. Sylvie thought perhaps she was going blind. Miss Mountshaft's eyes definitely pointed towards the cage, but there ***was no bird,*** as far as Sylvie could see. She glanced around the room. Still nothing.

'Erm… what kind is he, Rosalind? I can call you Rosalind, can't I?'

'Of course you can,' she chuckled. 'We don't stand on ceremony here, do we Cyril?' She addressed the cage directly. 'He's a Dusky Lory. The love of my life, aren't you Cyril, dear? ….Yes, I thought you might say that.' She chuckled again.

'Erm, yes, he's charming.' Sylvie tried hard to refocus on the job in hand. 'So…. I wondered, Rosalind, about last night during the performance …. Sorry to have to call it that, because it really wasn't a performance at all. I felt … I was embodied by a sweet, innocent child taking me through a traumatic event …. and I know you were moved by that, and …'

'She was my baby sister,' Rosalind interrupted, dragging a tissue from a box of Kleenex. 'She was the sweetest person in the whole wide world.' Dabbing at her eyes, then her nose, her face suddenly darkened. 'And that man took it all away from her.'

'Which man …. was that, Rosalind?'

'Ernest … flaming Winters. That's who!'

Sylvie's eyeballs almost sprang from their moorings. 'Really? That's the man who …. was murdered just a couple of nights ago?'

Rosalind's nose-wiping hand fell to her lap. 'Indeed. And may he rot in hell, God forgive me.'

'Do you feel up to telling me what happened?'

Rosalind composed herself within seconds. 'Dottie was barely seventeen when we found out she'd been seeing him. That's mother and me, I mean. She was never quite right in the head, you know. Not like you and me ….'

Sylvie's doubting eyebrow arched itself to the max. 'And she got pregnant? I mean, ***he got her pregnant,*** of course.'

The whites of Rosalind's eyes flashed. 'She didn't know what was happening to her body. Mother never told her about the birds and the bees. Nor me, for that matter. Daddy went to see Winters. He took a hammer.'

'Christ on a bike! …. I mean …. sorry, Rosalind. And is …. Daddy ***still around?'*** she said, nervously scanning the room for manly things.

'No, he's long gone. They said mother killed him, but he tripped on a vine and fell into the pond. Skull cracked open like a walnut on the way down and pffft! So tragic.' She shook her head in despair, then sipped her tea.

Sylvie took another deep breath. 'Can I ask …. What happened to the child?'

'Oh, the baby? Daddy took it to Ernest, said he had to raise him. And he did …. Or he tried, for a while. We weren't allowed to visit. But I heard he got married soon after and they raised Charlie for a few years, but I've no idea what happened after that.'

Sylvie's heart began to somersault inside her chest. 'And you're ***absolutely sure*** the child's name was … ***Charlie?'***

'Oh yes, they picked the name together. When it was explained to Dottie she was having a baby she couldn't have been happier, even though he still refused to marry her. Such a naïve little soul, God bless her. And when I saw you re-enact the birth on stage, it was so real … and hard to bear.' Rosalind pierced Sylvie's eyes with her own. 'How could you have known…. that was exactly how it happened?'

'That is quite beyond me too, Rosalind.' Sylvie's mind raced. She needed to think. 'Well, thank you for sharing your story. We really should be going.' Sylvie got up and went to pick up Clarabelle from the floor. But the dog's eyes were fixed on the bird cage, or more specifically, the hanging mirror inside, as it swayed and jingled back and forth.

'Cyril does love kissing his reflection, Miss Broadstairs,' she chuckled again, and it seemed she'd come the full circle of emotions. Sylvie scooped up the dog once again and headed for the door.

'It was lovely to meet you, Rosalind …. ***And you,*** Cyril,' she said, tossing a brief nod and a smile to the bird cage.

'Well, next time, perhaps you can meet mother,' Rosalind smiled. 'She just insisted on resting this afternoon.'

Sylvie was almost out of the door when she turned. 'But I thought your mother had just passed …. Oh, heavens …. ***passed her driving test?'***

'Oh, goodness, no. Wherever did you get that idea? The only thing mother's ever driven is us lot round the bend!'

Back on the street, Bobby waited by Sylvie's car.

'Where the hell have you been, Bobby? ***I needed support***.' Bobby returned a wave from Miss Mountshaft with a toothy grin.

'I can't explain out here … she's still watching.'

Sylvie unlocked the car. 'Get inside then.'

Once behind the driving seat, she took a few calming breaths. 'Jesus, Bobby. Wait 'til I tell you what just happened in there ….'

Chapter 9 : The Backstabber

Rambo leapt from the passenger seat of the Morris, waddled across to the police gates and cocked his leg. A ground floor window flew open and Chief Inspector Jim Craddock's head popped out. 'Witless!' he yelled across the yard. Seymour Witless grabbed a briefcase from the back seat and looked up.

'Sir?'

'Get yer arse in here, pronto!' The window snapped shut. Witless strode towards the entrance where Tracey was waiting. 'Do ***you*** know what's going on, Tracey? Because as usual, I'm clueless.'

Rambo's lead trailed behind him as he followed his master inside and Tracey snatched it up. 'Only bits … but you need to know that Conway's brought Daisy Harbottle in for questioning.'

Witless kept walking. 'And who told her to do that?'

'No-one, so far as I know …. But she was in there with Craddock early on this morning and he's been fired up ever since.'

Witless glanced at his watch. 'We've got that briefing in five minutes. I can give him two at the most. Catch up with you then, Tracey.'

'Yes, sir.'

Witless reached Craddock's office, knocked and entered. Craddock stood by the window in full golfing gear, clicking the knob on the end of his biro. He threw Witless a narrow-eyed stare.

'I've been hearing things this morning, Witless,' he said, pausing for effect. Click.

Witless closed the door behind him. 'That's not good, sir. Have you seen a doctor?'

'…Things that make me rather unhappy….' Pause. Click, click.

'Sir, my team are waiting for me. Can we do this later?'

'Always something more important, isn't there, Witless?' Click click.

'Well, two people ***have*** been murdered sir, and I think finding the killers to be pretty important.'

Craddock sat down, clicked the biro twice more and threw it onto the desk.

'Have you heard of sex discrimination, Witless? Hmm? Do you know how many times the force has been accused of discrimination in its lifetime? Hmm? Are you aware that you are one of the perpetrators of such a crime?' He did the narrow eyes again.

'Erm… Yes, no and no, I don't believe I am, sir.' Witless still held onto the door knob. Then the telephone buzzed. Craddock picked up the handset and killed the call.

'Apparently, in the last week, you have allowed your D.C. to remain on the Winters' case ***despite knowing*** him to be an acquaintance of one of the suspects. You've also spent social time ***involving food*** inside your vehicle with another ***female*** suspect, and humiliated a ***female*** officer on several occasions with degrading remarks and by giving her dog duties. What do you have to say to that? Hmm?'

Witless checked his watch again. 'Can we finish this later, sir? We have the lab results back, and things are beginning to move forward with both cases. I really must get back out there.'

Craddock began clicking his tongue against the roof of his mouth. Click, click. Witless sighed heavily, threw open the door and marched out, leaving it swinging behind him.

He thundered along the corridor to the incident room, burst through the door and slammed his briefcase onto the front desk. Rambo's head sprang from the floor beneath and he snorted.

Conway sat in her usual front of centre position with a smirk spreading across her face and Tracey rubbed a sockless foot against the back of his calf.

'Right! Results are in, you'll all be pleased to know,' said Witless. 'Seems like we've waited long enough, so…' He opened the briefcase and pulled out some papers, adjusting his arm length for focus. 'Starting with Ernie Winters ….' He directed his gaze at Tracey. 'The toxicology report revealed, as we thought … Pentobarbital in the blood samples – I won't get into the volume per litre, but it was sufficient to shut down his respiratory system within minutes. The discarded syringe, also had traces of the chemical but no fingerprints. Other prints taken from the scene can be accounted for as belonging to staff members. It's now understood that an exit door was accessible from outside for a period including the evening of Winters' murder. Now, this is interesting …. Winters' gaff was burgled the same night he was pushed down the fire escape. The entrance door was jemmied and the place overturned as if someone was searching for something.'

'Any idea what, sir?' said Tracey.

'As yet … ***that would be no***. The flat was barely furnished – typical bachelor's residence, apart from the drag act costumes. And oddly enough, an extensive collection of clocks.'

'Rather unusual for a womanizer …' said Conway.

Witless flicked his eyes briefly towards her, grimaced, then continued.

'Also, at the scene of the accident at the Shoreline, the contents of Winters' handbag were strewn across his body when the ambulance picked him up.'

'You think his handbag was searched too, sir?' asked Tracey.

'It certainly looks that way…'

'Or it could have just burst open during the fall,' Conway interjected once again.

'It's possible …. But an inside pocket had been unzipped and emptied also.'

A smirk played across Conway's face and she swung a leg across the other. 'Well, as everyone knows, men don't always close their zippers, do they sir?'

An awkward silence filled the room. Witless cleared his throat, fingered his comb over and turned to the next page.

'So, on to Ruby Porter. Toxicology revealed an abnormally low level of glycogen in the liver, and low glucose in the blood samples, despite the fact her stomach contents contained half-digested chocolate biscuits. It's extremely difficult to test insulin levels in blood due to its fast rate of degradation over time, but because of the other findings, we can conclude that insulin was involved. No alcohol was present and no other drugs.'

'Was she diabetic, sir?' said Chinless from the back of the room, tapping a rolled up newspaper against his leg.

'Nice to hear from you, Chinless… no, she was not diabetic. Nor was she a drug user. At least there's no evidence of that …. But, Sir Hugo found a needle mark to the side of the neck. The needle pierced the common carotid artery, which could have been the insulin route directly into the blood stream, speeding up its action. The injection site was quite bloody…in a place difficult to reach if she'd done it herself, and even if she had managed it, she would have had to be left-handed, which she wasn't.'

'Would the attacker be someone with a medical background, sir?' Asked D.C. Tracey.

Witless paused for a moment. He took out a handkerchief and dabbed at the beads of sweat on his forehead. Loosening his tie, he sat behind the desk and tossed down the paper print outs.

Conway scrutinized every movement.

'Are you feeling alright, sir? Should I get someone to help you?'

Still, he did not glance in her direction.

'I'm perfectly fine, thank you. Just a little warm.' He focused once again on the pages in front of him.

'To answer your question, Tracey, not necessarily a medical background. The neck is an uncovered area; it can be accessed from behind with a sideways projection. The attacker could have taken a lucky shot in a short space of available time, not knowing much about carotid arteries at all. So, it could have been administered during the interval of the performance. Death seems to have been caused by organ failure, on first observations, primarily the heart in this case due to lack of glucose supply. We need to establish .... And I know these questions were asked before, but they need to be asked again of all those witnesses present that night .... We need to know exactly who Ruby was seen with, who she spoke to, even who she looked at. Or anyone who was taking an interest in her particularly. You all have details of those you need to speak to. So that's about it for now, and I'll catch up with some of you at St Martin's, and the rest of you back here.' Chatter broke out among the team as they left the room, but Conway didn't move from her seat. Witless stood up, collected his papers and slotted them inside his case with a disgruntled expression. Finally, he looked up.

'Aren't you moving, Conway?'

She continued to smile. 'I might … ***when I decide.'***

'I thought you had a suspect waiting to be interviewed?'

'Daisy Harbottle can wait a few more minutes, I'm sure.'

He snapped the briefcase closed and rested both hands on top. 'Do you have some sort of problem with me, Conway?'

'I think you know that already ….***sir.'***

Witless shuffled from one foot to the other. 'Look, Conway …. I don't know why you've seen fit to pounce on Daisy Harbottle all of a sudden. Her statement …. which you took yourself incidentally…. clearly said that she was a carer for her sick husband. How long has she been waiting in that interview room? Has she even been given a hot drink?'

'I don't think that's any of your concern anymore, ***Witless***.'

His eyebrows crumpled, half blinkering his eyes. 'If you have something to say, Conway, just say it.'

'Daisy Harbottle's sick husband is diabetic. She's very used to administering insulin …four, sometimes five times a day.'

'The statement didn't mention that.'

'Did it ***not,*** sir? I must have found that out afterwards.'

'But you didn't know the toxicology results when you brought her in. I just read them out to you.'

'Looks like luck was on my side then, or call it a ***woman's intuition***.'

The door opened and Chief Inspector Craddock's Pringle clad torso appeared from behind it.

'A word, Witless … now!'

Chapter 10 : The Investigation Deepens

The aroma of all things meaty taunted Sylvie's taste buds until they could take no more. She sucked back a wayward dribble of saliva.

'Can I help you?' asked the counter assistant.

'Two large savoury dips with ***everything on,*** please.'

'You want stuffing?'

'Oh, frequently….' she said. The assistant stared blankly.

'Um, … yes please. ***Everything.***'

'Crackling?'

'Absolutely.'

'How about mustard?'

'Shite almighty.'

'Beg pardon?'

'Please …. Yes.' She forced a smile.

A second counter assistant gawped through the shop window. 'Have you seen that, Marcie?'

'What?' said Marcie.

'That cheeky beggar parked up on our forecourt right in front of the sign.'

'Oh, yeah. What a nerve. The sausage delivery guy won't be happy. Heh heh.'

'Well, they'll just have to shift. Can you tell them after you've served the little old lady?'

'Who the hell are you calling old?'

'Sorry, what did you say?'

'Just saying, this place …. worth its weight in gold.'

'If only they paid us in gold…. heh heh.' Marcie bagged the order and lobbed it onto the counter. 'That'll be £1.80.'

Sylvie scratched around inside her purse. 'There's a couple of gold coins for ya. Heh heh.'

'You want change?'

'That's usually the custom. Heh heh.'

'You takin' the piss?'

'Me? I'm just ***a little old lady****...'* Sylvie grabbed her order and made for the door. 'Heh heh!' was her parting shot.

Out on the forecourt, she tugged on the driver's door and threw the sandwiches into Bobby's lap, tossing her buttocks onto the seat.

'Ow, ow, ow! said Bobby. 'Willy's on fire!'

She sparked up the engine. 'Serves you right for telling me to park here.'

Marcie appeared in the shop doorway, gawping like a halibut. The Metro squealed with premature acceleration and was gone.

∞∞∞

From the outside, the Shoreline club could have been mistaken for a massive beach hut on legs. Thrown up before the end of the tax year to spend the last of the council's yearly budget, its foundations creaked, electrics fizzed and the plumbing had its own percussion section. An aged poster splashed across the front wall read, 'SUNDAY – PIE 'N' PEAS with A SLOW STRIPTEASE.' Sylvie screwed up her sandwich wrapper, opened the dash and tossed it inside to join the others. 'Well, that was a tasty stop gap 'til tea time,' she said. 'How's yours goin' down Bobby?'

Bobby had almost finished, but he held a double strip of pork crackling between finger and thumb. 'Erm … what do I do with this?' he said with disgust. Clarabelle whined from the back seat and Sylvie's eyes expanded in horror.

'What the hell's wrong with you? That's the best bit!' She snatched it from his grasp and wedged it between her lips. 'Now …. I know this place. Did a few gigs here actually and Prudence is an old ***acquaintance*** of mine,' she said, in between crunches. 'But she could also be a suspect, so just be careful what escapes from that gob of yours.'

Bobby wiped the grease from his fingers with a paper napkin. 'Everyone's a suspect according to you…. By the way, did you pay for those sandwiches?'

'Ex … cuse me!'

'Well, you did leg it out of there with a fire-breathing she-devil in pursuit.'

'She was being …. ***annoying.***'

A side door opened and a youngish woman exited the building with three small children. She bundled them into a Ford Escort before driving off.

'That woman's familiar,' said Bobby.

Sylvie opened the driver's side door just a smidge. 'Well, if it comes to you in the next ten minutes, do share it, won't you? Otherwise the curiosity might kill me. Come on, we're runnin' late.'

A waft of mould hung in the air as Sylvie led the way to the concert stage. Below a spotlight, Prudence performed rippling hip bumps for Marlon Brando as she draped a feather boa around her neck singing, ♪ ***Hey, big spender ....*** ♪

'Shame it's just a poster, eh, Prudence?' Sylvie grinned from the centre aisle as Prudence swiveled around.

'She's big,' whispered Bobby from behind Sylvie's shoulder.

'Behave, Bobby,' Sylvie fired back.

'Well, gast my flabber! Could that possibly be? It's never Sylvie flaming Broadstairs?' She said, stepping down from the stage.

'The very same!' said Sylvie.

'Just an acquaintance, is she?' said Bobby. She answered with an elbow poke.

'Tis me, Prudence .... Maybe a little older than the original, but much, much wiser.'

Prudence spread her arms, wading in for a hug, and Sylvie panicked as her kidneys & liver flew south. There was no other way out. She feigned a coughing fit.

'Oh, my poor darling, would you like a drop of the hard stuff?' Prudence fussed. 'Ernie has bottles hidden everywhere.'

'No, Pru, really I'm fine. Just have to be careful these days, you know. Oh, by the way, I'm being rude …' She turned to Bobby. 'This is my trusty assistant and fiancé, Bobby Mason.' It was Bobby's turn to cough. And to receive a second elbow to the ribs.

Prudence retreated a step. 'Oh? Well …. that's wonderful news.'

'Maybe you should tell your face that.' Sylvie laughed uneasily, linking her arm with Bobby's and rubbing his shoulder with affection. 'He's a lovely wee fella.'

'I'm pleased for you. It's about time you settled down …. you monkey, you!' At this point, a fleshy hand reached out to pinch Sylvie's cheek, but she dodged it just in time.

'So, have you come about Ernie? Let's sit, and I'll make you a coffee ...we have a machine and everything these days.'

'That would be great, Pru. We'll have two double frothy ones in a bucket with two straws.'

Pru was already at the little bar, pressing buttons as the pair sat down.

'What the hell are you up to now, sweetums?' whispered Bobby. ***'I couldn't look more gay if I tried!'***

'Just play along, won't you? We can break up tomorrow if you're that uncomfortable ….' She checked the hearing distance was a safe one, then continued. ***'Prudence proposed to me once.*** Hard to believe, I know. And as you've just witnessed …. she can be a bit full on …. so, if you want to keep your job …'

'There we go … Frothy coffees all round,' said Prudence returning with a tray. 'And some milk for the little one.' Clarabelle stood on hind legs as the dish was being lowered.

'Thanks Pru, you're a star. We were just wondering …. how it all happened, that night. We know there was some sort of raid, and Ernie ended up at the bottom of the fire escape?' She cradled the mug and took a sip.

'That's right. I was in the corridor … we were all in a flap. Ernie got through the back door, then I heard an almighty clatter. Nelson freaked out …. Dashed out after him.'

'So, Nelson couldn't have tripped him up?'

'Absolutely not .... He was still inside when we heard the fall.'

'Did you go outside to investigate?'

'Of course I did. I mean the man gave me the cringes, but I couldn't have ignored that noise. I called the ambulance.'

'And did you see anything out there? Any***one***?'

'It took me a while to get from the top to the bottom of that spiral staircase ... those things are never wide enough, are they? And, to be honest, I did think there was someone .... There were shadows, and I was nervous, so I delayed .... Just a few seconds. My heart was going like the clappers .... I mean, if there was a murderer, I didn't want to be the next victim, did I?'

'So, how many ***seconds*** are we talking, give or take?'

Pru shook her head. 'Not sure ... maybe twenty? Thirty at the most. I know that sounds bad.'

'Doesn't matter how it sounds, as long as it's the truth,' Bobby interjected, reminding Sylvie she needed to stroke his arm again.

'I'm straight as a die, me, Sylvie knows.'

'That's not how she's coming across exactly,' whispered Bobby, from behind a nose wipe.

'So how did he look .... when you got down there?' Sylvie went on. 'Did you notice anything out of the ordinary?'

'Well it was ***all*** out of the ordinary.... His bag was three feet away, and open, with the contents scattered all around which I thought was unusual .... because he guarded that bag with his life. It was always either slung over a shoulder during performances, or tucked tightly under his arm at other times. I asked him if he had the crown jewels in there, and he just said, ***"As good as, Prudence. As good as."*** But I'll never know what he meant now.'

'That's good information, Pru. Just one more thing ... there was a young lady leaving with three youngsters just as we arrived, had she been visiting you?'

'Oh, that's our Monica ... my niece. She works at the hospital, and those three darlings call me Nanna now that my sister's passed on. I just love being a nanna.' She gushed.

'Has she ever been to one of Sylvie's gigs?' Bobby asked. 'Because I could swear I've seen her before.'

Prudence pressed a forefinger to the side of her cheek, then wagged it a few times in the air. 'You know, I believe she did talk about going somewhere like that, soon after her mother died, but I don't think she was too happy with the performance,' she laughed. 'So, it couldn't possibly have been one of yours, right?'

'Absolutely not, Pru,' Sylvie humoured. 'I'm a professional.'

'I tell you what, though …. It's rather convenient Ernie's out of the way ***now,*** nudge nudge.'

At this point, Bobby and Sylvie were united in puzzlement.

'How do you mean?' asked Bobby.

'Well, isn't it obvious? You're free to marry now, aren't you?' She chuckled.

'Oh, that's ***right*** …. Ernie and me …. we never bothered getting divorced,' Sylvie recalled.

Prudence leaned forward, lowering her voice. ***'I say, you didn't murder him yourself, did you?'***

Chapter 11 : The Rejects Hang Out

Seymour Witless emerged from Craddock's office a crumpled man. On autopilot, his feet trailed the familiar path to the Evidence Room, where he leaned on the counter, buzzing for attention. D.C. Tracey came to the window. 'What can I do for you, sir?'

Witless straightened up, staring in disbelief.

'What the hell are you doing here, Tracey? You're meant to be out there, ***catching murderers.***'

'Sudden change of plan, sir. Craddock's orders. My involvement in the Winters' case was a conflict of interest.'

'And what about the Ruby Porter case? You're fine to continue on that one, surely?'

'D.S. Conway wanted me off both, sir. There could be a connection between the two. Funny thing was, I suggested that connection to her first thing this morning before she saw Craddock.'

Witless sighed. 'So she's taking over both cases?'

'Yes sir.'

'And how do you feel about that?'

'I think you can probably guess, sir. I'm gutted.'

Witless thought for a moment, stroking his chin. 'When you're done here, could you manage a pint in The Fish Gutters?'

'Maybe more than one, sir. Can I ask, sir …. your reason for stopping by here?'

'Believe it or not, Tracey, I was gonna ask if you had a cardboard box to clear out my desk. Then I planned to write my resignation letter.'

'But you're not going to do that now?'

'Let's say … I need to consider that decision a bit more before doing something I may regret. I've been asked, no, ***pressed*** …. to take some leave.' He sighed, tapping his fingers on the counter. 'And speaking of regrets …. I know sometimes I come across as a complete twat with a heart of stone, but I've been meaning to ask, Tracey …. how's your dad after the knee surgery?'

Tracey beamed. 'Well, he's fallen head over heels with the district nurse, so that's a good sign I reckon. Unless he marries her of course, then my inheritance goes up in smoke. And guess who the nurse is?'

'Not Eva Shawcross, by any chance?'

'That's the one.'

'Well, bugger me…'

'Maybe you should stop saying that sir.'

'Whatever do you mean, Tracey?'

'Well, sir, it's one of those things we have to be more careful about these days. Someone might take you up on it.'

Witless straightened up in surprise. 'Well, I never thought of it like that. It's a changing world, that's for sure.'

'I'll be in the bar around 3 p.m. sir. At least here we have regular hours.'

'Make the most of it, Tracey. Oh, and by the way … has Conway booted Rambo out too?'

'Thankfully not yet, sir. He's under my desk.'

'You won't forget to bring him with you, I hope.'

'No chance, sir. We're best buds now.'

Witless managed a weak smile. 'See you later …'

∞∞∞

Daisy Harbottle's damp raincoat stuck to her legs as she shifted in the hard wooden chair. An energy-saving bulb dangled above her head, failing its basic purpose for the sake of thrift. Every few seconds she glanced at the clock, nibbled her bottom lip and checked that the uniformed officer by the door hadn't dozed off, standing up. She couldn't remember what time they had brought her in there, but it seemed like hours ago, and the silence was torture. When the door eventually opened, she jumped like a toad in a tank full of piranhas.

Judy Conway's kitten heels clacked across the room as she approached the table, fingering the radiator on the way.

'Why isn't this switched on?' She addressed the constable.

'Erm … not sure ma'am, but quite a few are switched off this morning. Most likely down to budgets, like everything else.'

She threw him a disdainful look and dragged a chair from under the table with a nerve-jangling scraping noise. The officer following some distance behind her was Chinless, looking fearful with more than a touch of hesitance. Conway checked the seat – possibly for drawing pins before she sat, and the table top for wet puddles before setting down her files and notebook. She flipped a switch on the recording machine beside her and spoke into it. 'Interview with Daisy Mildred Harbottle, September 4th, 1986, ten seventeen hours, with D.S. Judy Conway and D.C. Gordon Chince.'

'Scuse me .... Ma'am,' Daisy interjected.

'***I haven't asked you anything yet,*** Daisy Harbottle. Just wait for your chance to speak.'

Chinless's eyes rounded in terror, flipping from left to right and back again. His lips firmly pressed together.

'Daisy Harbottle, what is the precise nature of your work at St Martin's?'

'Well, I just do what needs .... Cleaning, some cooking, serving, that sort of stuff.'

'You're experienced, are you not, in administering insulin on a daily basis to your husband?'

'Up to a point .... I mean, I'm no expert, but the NHS aren't interested so much in the technique so long as it saves them a daily home visit. They never turn up on time anyways. My Arthur was still sitting waiting for his full English at half ten before they showed up in the beginning. I mean, he needs feeding, ***he's a bloody big man.'***

'Yes, well, poor sad Arthur. And how much insulin do you keep in the fridge at any one time? How many syringes do you have?'

We get a month's worth of insulin, no more. And the syringes .... Have you seen those bloody things? Glass - ***and sodding metal*** –unscrew into a million bits, boil 'em up in a saucepan. Now here's a tip, to save gas ...' Daisy leaned in, as she often did with women of the parish. ***'You can boil an egg in the same pan!*** A nurse told me that.' She sat back in the chair, folding her arms across her chest. 'And I'd appreciate it ... if you didn't call my Arthur a poor sod.'

Conway frowned. 'I can assure you, ***I did not*** call your husband a poor sod, Daisy Harbottle. I said ***poor sad*** Arthur .... The recording will prove it .... Just in case you were thinking of issuing a formal complaint.'

'The recording ***won't*** prove it .... I'll bet you a tenner.'

'Of course it will .... And D.C. Chince will confirm it too.'

At the sound of his name, Chinless straightened up, feigning interest but remained silent.

Daisy leaned forward in her chair, unfolded her arms and nodded at the recorder. 'I tried to tell you .... But you wouldn't bloody listen, would you? The machine won't confirm anything, because you flipped the bloody ***pause button***. The ***record button*** is the one with the red dot ....' She pointed. 'That one there! You see?' She sat back in the chair again, refolded her arms and rolled her eyes at the constable. He responded with the briefest wink.

Chapter 12 : The Warbling Witch

In less than two hours, heavy rain had transformed the caravan park into a swamp. The Metro's tyres splattered, sucked and squished as they rolled into the bay next to Sylvie's metal home. She jerked on the handbrake and exhaled.

'I don't know why you want to come back with me, Bobby. Don't you think it's better to face him head on, instead of running away all the time?'

'I'm ... I'm not running away, exactly. Just need a bit more time to prepare myself.'

'Prepare yourself for what? You don't know he's going to end it, do you? He might just be waiting for you to make the first move. You'll never know unless you try.'

Just then, a mewing sound came from the back seat. Sylvie and Bobby turned in unison.

'Nelson? Where in the name of buggery did ***you*** come from? Bobby, did you know he was in here?'

'No, ***not a clue***. He must have sneaked in when we came out of the Shoreline. He's a master for cadging lifts, I'll give him that.'

'And you, Clarabelle... What a sneaky one, keeping quiet. What do we do with Nelson now?'

'Show him your photo albums, that'll put him to sleep nicely.'

'You're not too old for a clip round the ear, Bobby Mason...I suppose he could come inside .... for a bit.' She opened the driver's side door, a foot hovering over the mud while she decided the driest spot to land it. Nelson was no such ditherer. He was out, frolicking in the puddles like a newborn lamb discovering its legs. Sylvie picked her way over the mud, fumbled for a door key and leapt onto a dry doorstep. Bobby stuck to her back all the way, with Clara tucked under his arm.

'On the count of three, Bobby, as fast as you can, okay?'

'I take it Nelson stays outside now?'

'Too bloody right he does.'

The door closed just as Nelson cottoned on, and he began to wail like Mariah Carey in a stranglehold.

Barely had they removed coats, when there was a tapping at the door.

Bobby's wide eyeballs met with Sylvie's. 'Nelson's freaking me out now…'

Sylvie drew back the net curtain. 'Yer daft noggin. It's Hoggy, Seymour's pal …. He's got a trailer on the back of his pedal bike.'

'Do we hide, or should I get the peashooters out?'

'I think …. I may let him in…' She cracked open the door. Rainwater dripped from the rim of Hoggy's fedora onto his beard.

'Aye aye, missus ….. don't know if tha remembers me, but Norris sent me over with stuff for hiding.'

'What …. stuff, Hoggy?'

'It's Daisy's brew. That copper woman might be back again …. And she's no Seymour, tha knows. She'll have Daisy hanged good 'n' proper if she finds it.'

'And how much …. of ***Daisy's brew*** is there?'

'Only half a dozen, missus. Just a tiny corner will do, if tha has one.'

'Okay, bring them in, Hoggy.'

But the door was open too long, and Nelson took his chance.

'Shite on a stick! Grab him, Bobby!'

'But .... this is ***my best pulling shirt*** ....' Bobby pleaded.

Before anyone had a thought, Hoggy was in like Flynn with the perfect rugby dive, staining his already stained shirt with more .... stains. But Nelson slipped through the trap with razor sharp trickery. He took a bounding leap at the wall, clinging on for dear life to a picture frame of Sylvie's daddy above the fireplace. Clarabelle squealed and dove behind the sofa.

'I nearly had him there, missus ....' Hoggy peeled himself off the floor. 'The bugger won't get away a second time ...' He took off his hat, tossing it down on the sofa, then spat on his palms and rubbed them together.

But when he picked up a chair, swinging it above his head, Sylvie held up a hand in front of his face with a firm, ***'No!'*** and he instantly froze. Then she grabbed a towel from the sink, swaddled the traumatized cat with it, unpicking his claws from the plasterboard one by one.

'Perfek!' said Hoggy. 'Bottles is in t' corner. I'll be off now, missus.' And with that, he retrieved his hat and was gone.

Sylvie shook her head despairingly at Bobby as she held Nelson tight. 'So I take it sticking him under the shower is not on the pulling shirt's list of duties either?'

Bobby gave his best puppy dog eyes as the door was rapped on again.

'What the hell? It's like Piccadilly flamin' Circus round here ….' Sylvie cracked open the door for a second time. Carolyn Carr's beehive nodded unsteadily, as the face said, 'I'd like to purchase a bottle of the special stuff …..' and the gloved hand waved a tenner in the air.

'Have you … ***did you follow Hoggy here?'***

Carolyn flipped a finger towards the Daimler with its engine ticking over behind her. 'Hudson followed him, actually …. On my instructions, of course.'

Sylvie's brow furrowed, but she snatched the note from the witch's hand and opened the door wide for her to enter.

'What are you planning to do with that thing, trussed up like a turkey?' Carolyn said, eyeballing Nelson's face peeking out from the towel. 'I'd recommend gas regulo six for ninety minutes. But be sure to skin it first….'

'He needs a bath. Don't suppose you have any ideas how to go about it?' Sylvie closed the door behind her.

'As a matter of fact …. ***I have*** washed a cat before …' She clocked the bottles stacked in the corner. 'I presume you have a toilet with a lid?'

Sylvie threw her a look of suspicion. 'State of the art toilet … complete with lid.'

'Cats tend to hate water …. So, you have to be crafty.'

'Well, you'd know all about that ….'

Carolyn scowled. 'Indeed.'

'And this cat? It's not a normal cat. Happens to love water …. Laced with a good measure of mud … as you can see.'

'I'd still do it the same way…' she walked across to where the newly-delivered bottles enticed.

'Which is?'

'If you'll have a drink with me …. I'll tell you.'

'Bobby, get the corkscrew and three glasses …'

Bobby grimaced. 'Is that a good idea? I mean …. We don't even know what it is. Those bottles have no labels.'

A whoop of laughter escaped from the warbling witch's mouth, and Clarabelle recoiled behind the sofa. 'Such a sweet boy… where did you rescue him from?'

'He's a fully qualified barista, lion tamer and bodyguard all rolled into one. I head-hunted him from a prestigious law firm.'

'Yes, of course you did. Okay, Mister Qualified, can you fetch me a cork screw and three glasses?' She tilted her head, peering at Bobby through heavy fake lashes. 'Pretty please?'

With reluctance, Bobby obeyed while Carolyn took a seat, sweeping one varicose-veined leg across the other.

'The simplest solution …. is to add plenty of shampoo to the toilet.' She began to gesticulate. 'Grab the cat by the scruff of the neck and ***plunge*** him in there; slam down the lid before he has a chance to escape. You may need to sit on it, to be extra secure. The cat performs its own agitation program, coating its fur with soap. The next stage …' At this point, Bobby appeared with three wine-filled glasses. She took one from him, and downed half in one gulp.

'You do know,' said Bobby to Sylvie, 'this is cannabis wine …and these are ***large*** glasses?'

Sylvie gave him a wink. 'It's okay, Bobby. So, Carolyn, what is ***the next stage?'***

'The next stage is …. Hit me again, Mister Qualified.' Bobby handed her a second glass. 'You flush the toilet several times for a good rinse … then … hic … open all the doors for a clear escape route … hic … lift the lid and stand clear. That cat will self-dry as it speeds over the hilltops …never to be seen again.' She cackled like a swamp witch and picked up the final glass.

Sylvie took a seat herself, cradling Nelson in the crook of her arm. He started to dose.

'So, Carolyn … ***why did you*** come to my gig at St Martin's the other night? I mean, I realize you wanted to contact Ernie, but you hadn't been properly together for years, so why was it so important to you now?'

Carolyn took another half glass in one mouthful. 'We were still seeing one another … hic … right up until two weeks before he died. Then he just ***buggered orf***… along with something very valuable of mine he was supposed to be minding for me….hic. I wanted to know what he'd done with it.' Bobby and Sylvie exchanged puzzled looks.

'What did he take, Carolyn?'

Her lips parted, showing perfect veneers, now with a tinge of green. 'Wouldn't ***you*** like to know?' She shuffled back on the sofa, eyeing Sylvie up and down. 'I'll tell you what ***I'd*** like to know…. You must have wondered too …. What did Ernest ever see in a tiny sparrow ***like you?'***

Sylvie dropped her gaze to the sleeping cat, swaddled like a newborn in her arms. 'I was a convenience to care for his son. I think you knew that already. But Carolyn, ***we were both wronged by the same man***. If you tell me what he stole from you, maybe I can help you find it.'

The witch took another slurp and swallowed.

'Come to think of it …. hadn't seen it for years. Maybe he sold it …. hic …bastard!' Carolyn began to drift off, staring into space.

'She's too far gone, sweetums. You'll get nothing out of her now,' said Bobby.

'Carolyn!' urged Sylvie. ***'What did he take?'***

Her eyelids flickered. 'A thousand ….. bloody carats of flawless diamond …. A sight for sore eyes… the Maharaja of Bapod … Baro … Oh bugger the … hic … bloody place …but the year was … thirty-nine.' Carolyn's head flopped back against the sofa and she began to snore like a jackhammer. Sylvie went to the door, opened it wide and beckoned to the driver outside. He climbed out of the car and came towards her.

'You might want to take Miss Carr home, Hudson. She's away with the fairies.'

'For God's sake, not again ....' he said, stepping over the threshold. 'Come on madam, looks like you've outstayed another welcome.'

Like a scene from The Bodyguard, he tossed her across his shoulder and carried her to the door.

'Hang on ....' said Bobby, retrieving Carolyn's hairpiece from a sofa cushion. 'She'll be needing this.' With Hudson's hands full, Bobby shoved the beehive inside the chauffeur's pocket, giving it a pat as they left. Sylvie held the door open a little longer to watch Carolyn being dropped onto the back seat of the car and the door being slammed on her knees. The squeal could barely be heard.

She sighed and closed the door. 'Someone's gonna have a few bruises on them knobbly bits tomorrow, Bobs. And tonight, you can sleep on the sofa with Nelson. Me and Clara are having the bed.'

'But what about my shirt?'

'I'll lend you something fitting to wear, don't fret. Now, where's that nightgown with the daisies?'

'You needn't bother. I won't be a toy for your amusement.' Bobby tensed his jaw, with nostrils flared. 'I'll be going back home tonight....***after*** I've taken you out for a drink. You did good today, and that calls for a reward.'

'We did good, Bobs, but all these tiny scraps of information need connecting up. I may need my notebook. And Bobby, as much as I hate the witch, she was right about one thing you know.'

'What's that?'

'You ***are*** a sweet boy….'

Chapter 13 : Hoggy & the Great North Run

Daisy stepped off the number 19 bus just in time to see hubby Arthur being loaded onto a white minibus with mud splashed windows. Two care workers had him by the arms, propelling his top half towards the entrance faster than he could shuffle his feet, supervised by Eva Shawcross. Daisy dashed into the road with cars honking and swear words peppering the air.

'Oi! You lot! .... Where the hell do you think you're going with my flaming husband?'

Eva whipped around. 'Oh, so they've let you out?'

'Let me out? I was never ***in*** for your information! Just tell me what's going on.'

The district nurse lowered the mobility step on the bus, and went to lift Arthur's foot onto it. 'The paperwork's all been signed. Arthur can no longer be cared for at home, so he's off to Senior Moments care home until he can be found a permanent place.'

Daisy caught her breath. 'I haven't been gone five sodding minutes and you leap on him like a pack of vultures. Just take him back inside …. This is ridiculous …. I'm bloody well here now, aren't I?' She grabbed at Eva's sleeve, and the nurse shook her off.

Arthur was now being strapped in with a tartan blanket over his knees, looking rather perplexed. He glanced up. 'Daisy? What's happening? Where's this hellish place you're sending me to?'

'I'm not sending you anywhere, Arthur. I'd never do that.'

Eva slid the door shut on the conversation with a resounding thud as it locked into place.

'You may be here now, Mrs. Harbottle, but for how long? And is he safe in your care?' She tossed Daisy a disapproving glare, slapped the heel of her hand against the driver's side window twice and the engine fired up. 'Give Arthur a wave, Mrs. Harbottle …. He needs to feel reassured.' But Eva was the only one up to waving, as the bus moved off and disappeared around the next corner.

Daisy let herself into the house, leaning against the back of the door until it clicked shut. She walked steadily through to the kitchen, where the smell of burnt toast lingered and the butter knife stuck out of the open tub on the drainer, with black dust sprinkled all around. She sighed and padded across to the front window. Another bus pulled up across the road and as it moved off, Hoggy appeared from behind it, sucking on a cigarillo stub like a newborn. With a brief tug on the brim of his hat, he was on his way over. She straightened up, hands flying up to her damp hair. Before he could knock, Daisy swung open the door.

'Hoggy? Where's your bike? What are you doing here?'

Hoggy took the ciggy from his mouth and smiled in his lopsided way. 'Norris asked to borrow it. Said he wanted to follow the Great North Run. But I thinks he wants the Gazette to take his picture. The mad vicar in a black frock ridin' a luminous bicycle.'

Daisy's lip began to tremble, and Hoggy threw down the ciggy, stepped over the threshold and wrapped his arms around her. 'Oh Daisy, tha's home now. What's the bother?'

'They took my Arthur away, Hoggy,' she sniffed. 'He didn't know what was happening. I think he thought I'd planned it all.'

Hoggy frowned. 'They done ***what?*** Well that's gotta be a bloody mistake …. They'll hasta bring him back, won't they?'

'Maybe, I don't know …' her face was way too close to his. She could feel his heart beating against his chest, and this closeness was something she'd not felt in so many years. She met his gaze, and before she knew what was happening, they were sucked into a lip lock. He grasped her hand and led her upstairs.

The marital bed was unmade, and Arthur's discarded pyjamas lay on the floor in the perfect shape of a murdered corpse. Surprising herself, Daisy took the lead and untied the string holding up Hoggy's trousers. 'I think I may regret this…later,' she said.

'Whatever happens later …. can keep,' he said.

As they were getting stuck into the whole experience, so to speak, there was a sharp knock at the front door.

Daisy bolted upright, grabbing at the sheet, desperately trying to cover her naked breasts. 'Oh Jesus Christmas! …. You need to go … that could be anyone.'

Hoggy threw back the covers and edged his naked body towards the window. 'Tis only Seymour. He's not gonna tell no-one.'

'What? That copper? Are you mad?' Daisy was up, snatching Hoggy's clothes from where she'd tossed them ten minutes earlier in a fit of madness.

Tucking them under his arm, she shoved him down the stairs towards the back door.

'I'm sorry, Hoggy …but I can't risk the neighbours seeing, not with everything else they'll be gossiping about already.' She opened the back door, pushed him out and closed it behind him. He gazed helplessly at her through the glass panel, and she blew him a hasty kiss. Before he knew what to do, he heard the sound of cheering from the crowds lining the Coast Road egging the runners on, all dressed in the maddest costumes. Some were barely clad in anything but budgie smugglers, carrying banners advertising worthy causes they were running for. So Hoggy took his chance, raced across the field and merged with the runners, still in his socks clutching his clothes beneath one arm. The rain was a light mizzle, but still it persisted.

Daisy answered the door in her dressing gown.

'Mrs. Harbottle, is Hoggy here?' asked Seymour.

'Does it look like it, Inspector?' Daisy tightened her gown around her neck. 'I was just having a lie down … a lot of distressing things have been happening.'

'Yes, I heard you were taken in for questioning by D.S. Conway. I take it no further action was necessary?'

'That's not what she said. She told me not to leave town … that they'd want to speak to me again … and then, when I gets home … I find that bloody Eva Shawcross carting my Arthur off to a sodding care home.' She shook her head in despair. 'He was so upset, Inspector. You have to do something … it's just not right.'

Seymour scratched the back of his head and grimaced. 'I've been taken off the case, Daisy. It's out of my hands now. But I'd never have treated your family that way.'

'Can you help me? Please, Inspector?'

'I don't know … if it's possible. Where do you think Hoggy can be? I know he was here.' Seymour nudged the discarded cigarillo on the garden path with his toe.

She sighed. 'He joined in the bloody race …. Daft sod. You'll find him no bother …. He's running in his birthday suit…'

Seymour cruised the Morris through the adjoining roads, but traffic barriers stopped him getting close enough to the runners. In a fit of temper, he got out of the car and shifted a couple of blockades from his path, but as he drove through, a rather beefy Marshall, clad in a hi viz vest, flew out with flailing arms and yelled, 'STOP! Or you'll be arrested!'

Seymour braked, wound down his window and showed his warrant card. 'I'm a police officer …. I need to get close to the runners. Can I use the grass verge?'

Exceeding Seymour's expectations, the Marshall saluted, army style, shifted a few more barriers with his little pinky and guided him through. As he steered the Morris over the grass verge, Seymour smiled with the smugness he'd always detested in a villain, but right now was the best feeling in the world. He was within feet of the runners, searching for a mane of matted ginger curls atop a naked torso. It only took a few minutes to spot him. With both sets of cheeks incredibly flushed, Hoggy's expression was desperate.

'HOGGY!' Seymour yelled from the car window. But there was so much noise. Cheer leaders chanted by the roadside, tanked-up pub crawlers had ventured out for the homeward stretch despite the rain - swearing, singing, mooning and throwing up.

'HOGGY!' he yelled again. Then he remembered the megaphone he'd used for his last hostage situation. He groped around under the passenger seat, attempting to steer with the other hand. Then he felt it. 'Bingo!' he said, for want of a better word, dragging it clear. Praying the batteries still had life, he switched it on and held it to his mouth.

'HOGGY!' This time the whole population of South Shields winced with ear pain, but Hoggy's attention was finally grabbed.

'GET IN HERE, YOU FLAMING NUTTER!'

Hoggy's knees sprung higher and his willy bobbed up and down as he steered himself sideways around the runners, narrowly avoiding a pile-up.

His sweaty buttocks squeaked as he landed on the passenger seat, turning Seymour's smugness to disgust in a nanosecond. He u-turned back the way he'd come, onto calmer side streets and pulled into the side of a road free of onlookers. Tugging on the hand brake, Seymour swept his eyes over the naked Hoggy.

'This is a completely new side to you, Hoggy, I've not seen before. Do you always run marathons in the nude?'

Hoggy gave Seymour a sideways glance. 'Half marathon … ***not*** a marathon.'

'Right … half marathon. Well, do you?'

'Oh yeah, I likes to feel the breezes on my skin. It's the business.'

'And why carry your clothes under your arm….' he circled a forefinger in the direction, 'like that?'

'Just in case I gets cold, or I needs to jump on a bus to get home. ***Tha knows how it is***.'

'Right, and just one more thing…'

'You're goin' all Columbo on me now, in't ya?'

'You're not a murder suspect, Hoggy, no, I was just curious. Do you always run ***half*** marathons naked, ***and wearing a condom?'***

Hoggy still kept his face forward, though his eyeballs danced from side to side. 'Only when it's raining,' he said.

CHAPTER 14 : THE UNOFFICIAL MURDER TEAM

The sun had finally broken through the dark clouds and The Fish Gutter's Arms was bursting at the seams. Tables and chairs set up on the pavement outside were crammed with stragglers draped in foil capes from The Great North Run, their proud families, canine pets, Uncle Tom Cobley and all.

Collecting his pint from the bar, D.C. Richard Tracey picked his way through the animated taletellers with Rambo in tow until he reached the lounge doors. But beyond them, the buzz of excited chatter was deafening. He tried the snug, scanned the room and found a vacant table in a secluded corner. Grabbing it quickly, he lifted one of the legs and looped Rambo's leash around it. Then he took out his notebook. He was halfway through his pint and two pages of notes when Seymour Witless peered around the door. Tracey acknowledged with a wave of his pen and Witless approached, closely tailed by Hoggy, now fully clothed. Tracey threw Hoggy a narrow-eyed stare and stood up.

'Sir, it's good to see you. Can I get you a drink?'

'That's all right, Tracey.' Witless plunged a hand inside his trouser pocket and pulled out a crumpled note. 'Hoggy can get them, can't you?'

'Hoggy took the note, his face beaming. 'Sure as hell I can, Seymour. Can I gets some nuts?'

'I think we've had enough of your nuts today, Hoggy, don't you?'

Hoggy's face looked like Rambo's when he'd been denied a Hob Nob.

'Oh, go on then,' Seymour relented. 'You deserve something for the entertainment I suppose.' And off he went.

'You can sit down now, Tracey. You're not on duty and I'm not your boss anymore.'

Tracey sat. 'Are you sure you can trust him with your money sir? Who the hell is he, anyway?'

Seymour pulled up a couple of chairs. 'I've known Hoggy for years, went to school with him. We just chose different paths, that's all. He's a bit eccentric, naïve at times, but solid when it comes to friendship.' He looked at Rambo curled up on the floor, twitched his nose and frowned. 'Who gave him the beer shampoo?'

'Scuse me, sir?'

Witless flapped a hand at the dog. 'Look at him. He's covered in beer stains!'

'Oh, he is a bit yellow. More likely lager, sir. ***We did*** have to fight our way through two bars of sloppy drinkers.'

Hoggy returned with more beers and his nuts in a packet this time. As he sat down, drinkers at the next table nudged one another, drained their glasses and left. Hoggy watched from behind dipped eyelids.

'Pay no attention, Hoggy. How many times have I told you?' Witless slapped Hoggy's leg. ***'We don't give snobs the time of day!'*** They both said in unison.

'Now, Tracey, how are they treating you behind the serving counter?' Witless slurped the froth from the top of his glass.

'It's a bit dull, if I'm honest, sir.'

'Dull enough that you have to make notes about it in the pub?'

Tracey gave a tiny laugh. 'Oh, this?' He closed his notebook. 'Just a force of habit I suppose. You never know when something might be of use later.'

'Such as?'

'Oh, it's nothing sir. But I was documenting the evidence from the Ernie Winters' case this morning, and I'm finding it difficult to just do that without thinking about the wider investigation. If you get what I mean.'

'Sadly, I do, Tracey. I'm not ready to give up on it either. Especially since I was taken off the case for sex discrimination, a crime of which I'm innocent. Then of course there's the consumption of a hot cross bun. Could be a hangable offence if Craddock has his way.' He supped some more from his glass. 'Just makes me all the more determined.'

'We needs to get Daisy off the hook,' Hoggy chipped in. 'This thing's turned her world upside down. Arthur needs rescuing from that nasty care home, and I has a plan.'

'I don't think we'll be using any of your crazy plans, Hoggy…. and by the way, it's easy to see where ***your*** priorities lie,' said Seymour. 'But it's the killer we need to find first, then Daisy can have her world restored to its upright position, yes? Anyway, if Arthur comes back, there'll be no more nookie for you, will there?'

Hoggy looked wounded. 'I doesn't know what tha means, Seymour. Methinks tha makes up stories in that head of yours again.'

∞∞∞

Sylvie pulled into the side of the road outside the Fishgutter's Arms. All that was left of the Great North runners outside were half a dozen discarded silver capes wrapped around table legs or else chasing one another in the breeze.

'Do you think Clarabelle will be okay on her own, Bobby? I feel terrible leaving her behind.'

Bobby loosened his seat belt. 'I'm sure she will. You do spoil her, sweetums …. what with the TV on and everything. I hope she can change the channel because Crufts is on at nine o'clock.'

Sylvie unbuckled her belt too. 'I want her subdued, Bobby, not excited by all those handsome dogs' bodies. She's due on heat and I'm taking no chances.'

'Not even with Nelson? You ***are*** cruel, chucking him back outside.'

Sylvie's eyes rolled. 'I dare say he's used to it …. Someone else can give him a kipper. He's had all of mine.' She opened the driver's door just as a massive shire horse was beginning to overtake. 'Jeezuuuz …. I nearly shat meself! Sorry love!' she yelled to the rider. The rider turned her head and acknowledged with a hand wave.

'You know who that is?' said Bobby.

'I think I do, Bobby. Is it the district nurse from the gig?'

'***It is*** .... Eva Shawcross. Well, who'd have guessed? I'd never have taken her for the horsey type.'

'People are never quite what they seem, Bobby. Come on then, might as well put our heads together over a cocky tail.'

Bobby smoothed out his hair and fingered his eyebrows. 'I'm always up for a few of those, as you know.'

A combined waft of stale smoke, toasted sandwiches and strong urine hit the visitors' nostrils as Bobby pushed open the pub's side entrance door. Two men were having a heated argument outside the Gents' toilet.

'***Just where*** do you get the nerve from? To ask me this, after everything that's happened?'

'Aw come on Seymour, you're not gonna see me sleepin' on the streets? Your own flesh and blood?'

'Listen here, Twatface, I have no conscience as far as you're concerned. Not anymore! We are done!' With that, Witless spun around, stomping straight onto Sylvie's tiny foot.

'Aargh .... Seymour! Watch the effing bunions...Christ on a bike, look at the size of those monster feet.'

Witless stopped in his tracks. 'Miss Broadstairs ... Ever your charming self, as always. I'm sorry ... miles away.'

'So I see.' She raised the injured foot and traced a circle with it in the air. 'Well, seems I won't be suing you this time.'

'By the way...' came Twatface's retreating voice, ***'she wants her dog back.'***

Witless gawped as Twatface disappeared through the exit. ***'She can want all she bloody well likes. And it's not her bloody dog!'*** he muttered to himself.

Sylvie glanced furtively around. 'Having a spot of bother, Seymour? I'm an expert on family matters if you need an ear to cry on.'

Witless looked flushed. His tie was loose, his comb over had wandered and his eyes were fixed in the narrow position.'

'I'm fine as I am, thanks,' he said. Sylvie leaned in closer.

'As a matter of fact I'm glad I ran into you, or you ran into me ... whatever ...Anyway, Bobby and me ... we've been doing a bit of digging, on a different matter .... and funnily enough there are too many coincidences with one or maybe both of those cases you're investigating that I think we ought to be sharing.'

'Oh Yes? Well, maybe you should contact D.S. Conway about that ... she's the one heading up those two cases now. I'm on leave.' With that, Witless headed back to the snug.

She turned to Bobby. 'There's no way I'm sharing our precious intel with Judy highfalutin Conway. C'mon Bobby .... We're not taking no for an answer.'

Inside the snug, Seymour was being served at the bar.

'If you'd like to know what the intruder was searching for at Ernie's place,' said Sylvie from behind him, 'we're more than willing to exchange that information for a Screaming Orgasm and a Slippery Nipple.'

Seymour reddened even more. 'I beg your pardon?' he said, resisting the urge to turn around.

'A Screaming Orgasm and a Slippery Nipple. Look, It's on the board.' She indicated with a hand flap.

'Alright … Just keep your flaming voice down … ***please*** …. I still have tatters of a reputation to uphold.'

'Whatever you say, Seymour. We'll just grab a seat.'

Hoggy held out his bag of nuts. 'Would you like a couple, missus? I didn't pick them off the floor, honest.'

'No, Hoggy, you enjoy them. I'm sure that's a real treat for you. Well, good evening by the way and D.C. Tracey I believe?'

'That's correct, Miss,' said Tracey, bending his back with a scrape of his chair.

'Don't get up … please. This is Bobby, who I think you've met before. He's chair monitor for tonight …' Bobby dragged two chairs across from the abandoned table and pushed one under Sylvie's bottom as Witless returned with the drinks.

One by one he lifted the drinks from the tray. 'One of ***those*** …. for Miss Broadstairs, and one of ***these*** …. for Mr. Mason. I have got them the right way round, have I?'

'Well, Seymour, you may have thought I was past the screaming orgasm stage, but in fact you'd be quite wrong,' she said, swapping her drink with

Bobby's. 'Now I do expect you to take notes, because if you've had more than two pints, you'll kick yourself in the morning when you can't remember we were ever here.' She took a sip from her cocktail glass.

Seymour humphed as he sat down and pulled a notebook from his jacket pocket.

'Whatever you have to say … you can speak freely in front of Hoggy here.' He waved his pencil in the air, stuck out his tongue and moistened the end of the lead. Then he made a note of the date and time.

'Right …' said Sylvie. 'On the night Ruby Porter was killed and the night of my performance on stage, I had two visitations from separate spirits.'

Seymour slapped his pencil down on the table.

'Oh, come on, Miss Broadstairs! We know that's a load of nonsense …. I thought you had some ***real information*** to pass on…'

'But I do, Seymour! If you would just hear me out?'

Seymour grimaced and retrieved the pencil. 'Alright, I'm listening.'

'The first was the spirit of a young girl …. She was one of Ernie's lovers. Dottie was her name … actually she had the mental age of someone much younger … anyway she died giving birth to Ernie's child, Charlie.'

Seymour was now starting to write, and even Tracey opened his notebook again and picked up his pen.

'Now this is where ***I come into the picture,'*** Sylvie continued. Seymour gave her a puzzled, but tell-me-more look.

'I met Charlie and Ernie on a park bench taking a sandwich break. It was egg and raw onion … funny the things that stick in your head, or even in your teeth for that matter. Anyway, cut a long story short, we were married and I raised that boy until he was eight years old. Ernie had countless affairs, kindly shared a venereal disease with me which was the final straw and I told him I was leaving and taking Charlie. But he wouldn't let me take the boy, and I knew I had no legal right … and we were still in the middle of a world war, so I had to leave him behind…. I can't tell you how difficult that was.' She paused for a moment.

'The woman I left him over, was Carolyn Carr. She was an upcoming singer at the time, and has done remarkably well since, as you know…. '

'Did he give her the clap too?' Hoggy asked.

'Who knows?' Sylvie said. 'Maybe ***she*** did the giving. Anyway, so then we fast forward a few years … more than a few, actually, and Ernie is murdered. Carolyn comes to my gig hoping to ask her dead lover what he did with a certain treasure she entrusted in his care.' Sylvie paused for a moment, shooting Seymour a meaningful look.

'What treasure was this, Miss Broadstairs?'

Sylvie hesitated.

'If you'd rather whisper in my ear, that's fine.'

Sylvie cupped a hand over her mouth, leaned in and whispered. Seymour's eyes almost sprang from their sockets.

'I see,' he said. 'And do we know where this item is now?'

Sylvie shrugged. 'Not a clue. Unless the murderer has it.'

'So Ernie didn't reveal where it was …. when he ***visited you*** that evening?' he mocked. 'Perhaps he whispered it to you and you decided to keep it to yourself?'

'Not at all. I didn't know anything about the …. ***item*** until Carolyn Carr told me today.'

'Hmm …. And why would she mention it to you? You're sworn enemies, aren't you?'

'There are ways and means, Seymour.'

'So …. what is the connection with Ruby Porter, then?' asked Tracey.

'Well, the connection is …***family*** … and that includes me, apparently. And also Ruby's boyfriend who died from a drugs overdose only weeks before that night … his name was David, and he was another of Ernie's illegitimate children. That all may be a coincidence … but Bobby and me … we would like to do some more digging …. Maybe search family records, that kind of thing. Also worth mentioning … is Prudence from The Shoreline, whose niece is an employee at Harton General, and Rosalind Mountshaft who was Dottie's sister.'

'Hang on there a minute,' said Seymour. 'Do we know the name of this niece who works at the hospital?'

'I believe she said the name Monica? But not the surname, sorry.'

Seymour scratched his head. 'Now that could be useful. Do carry on ….'

'Well, it turns out both these women disliked Ernie, to put it mildly. Prudence has a preference for gaiety, but that didn't stop Ernest trying it on, at any opportunity, and of course she didn't like the way he treated me.'

'Gaiety? What do you mean by ***gaiety***, Miss Broadstairs?'

'Well, you know, the art of being GAY.'

Bobby sniggered, and Sylvie gave him a shove.

'And what about this Mountshaft woman? What could she have to do with anything? She wasn't even at your gig.'

'Oh, but she ***was*** there, Seymour, and she left during the interval.'

'Well did anyone else leave during the interval?'

'I don't think so, Inspector,' said Bobby. 'My job is to keep eyes on the punters at all times, and as far as I can remember during the second half, the only empty seat was Miss Mountshaft's.'

'We'd better hope you didn't nod off at any time then,' said Seymour, adding more to his notes.

'Oh, and it's worth mentioning ….' said Sylvie, 'Bobby and I had meetings with both these ladies, and while they may have their own eccentricities, I did not see the word 'murderer' written across either of their foreheads. But there's always a possibility I could be wrong of course. Slim though it is.'

'So … that's another of you psychic abilities, Miss Broadstairs?' said Tracey. 'You can see labels on people's heads?'

Seymour checked Tracey's expression for sarcasm.

'Are you blathered, Tracey?'

'No … not at all sir. But there are more things than you and I know. Why, my dad saw my mam just before his operation, and she's been gone fifteen years.'

'Oh my God, that's amazing,' said Bobby. 'Did she tell him how much she loved him, and not to worry?'

'Not really. She scolded him for sending her off with no knickers on.'

Hoggy tipped back his head, lifted the bag of nutty crumbs to his open mouth and tapped it against his bottom lip. As he chewed and then swallowed, all eyes were upon him.

'What I wants to know is …. who belonged to that leg you found abandoned on the A19 last year? I reads the papers tha knows, and I hasn't seen anythin' about that. Happen it was all hushed up … for some reason or another.'

Seymour winced. 'I told you, Hoggy, there's nothing to know…'

'So's *it was* hushed up, then?'

A smug smile crept across Sylvie's face. 'Hoggy's a right to know, Seymour. Even if it is painful for you.'

'Oh, if it's gonna be painful,' said Hoggy, shaking his head, 'I doesn't want to be upsettin' no-one.'

'It's more … how can I put it? An embarrassment. Yes, that's a better word.' Sylvie continued to smile.

'Well, go on …. Don't be stoppin' there!'

Seymour gave a relenting sigh. 'The body belonging to the leg we found …. still walks around, minus the real leg of course …. which fell from the back of a van on its hospital route collecting clinical waste bound for the incinerator. Miss Broadstairs, believe it or not, identified the leg in question from a tattoo on the outer calf.'

'Bloody amazing!' said Hoggy, gazing at Sylvie in awe. 'What a woman!'

'And now, Hoggy,' said Seymour, 'shall we tell these good people why you changed your name to Hoggy? Another embarrassing tale, perhaps?'

Hoggy's eyes flipped to the exit. 'I doesn't really think that's of any interest, Seymour.'

'Hoggy was one of the hostages in a bank raid back in '68. When he gave his statement to police and they asked him his name, well, he had to confess.'

'Confess to what?' said Bobby.

'That his name was Robin. Robin Banks.'

'That embarrassment were only temporary ….. for me,' said Hoggy, draining his glass. 'But yours, Seymour …. ' He sucked in air through pursed lips and shook his head. 'I reckon yours is likely to stay around a lot longer. It being a full-scale murder enquiry at the time.'

Seymour cleared his throat and shifted in his seat. 'I think, Miss Broadstairs, your plan to search family records sounds like a good one. If you can trace all of Ernie Winters' offspring, that would be extremely useful.'

'Sir …. There's something I'd like to speak to you about,' said Tracey.

'Oh, and here's another one with a name and a half.' Hoggy interrupted.

'What are you on about now, Hoggy?' said Seymour.

'Your young fella here, Dick Tracey. Now there's a name worth hangin' onto.'

'It beats me how anyone gets Dick from Richard,' said Bobby.

A lop-sided smirk spread across Hoggy's face. 'Maybe tha just has to ask him nicely.'

Bobby and Sylvie exchanged a secret smirk, Tracey stared deeply into his pint and Seymour's eyes rolled.

'Well, spit it out Tracey ....What's this thing you'd like to speak to me about? Unless it's of a personal nature?'

Tracey fired a glance at Hoggy, busily scratching his armpit inside his shirt, then examining his fingernails with deep concentration.

'Hoggy?' said Witless, feeling for another note inside his trousers, 'would you mind getting another round in please? But wash your hands first, if you don't mind.'

'Oh, not for me, Hoggy, I'm driving, said Sylvie.'

'No bother, I'll get tha some nuts.' Then off he went again, snatching the note en route.

Witless leaned in. 'What is it, Tracey?'

Tracey hitched his chair closer. 'You know I told you I was documenting those items from the Winters case today?'

'Yes ... what about them?'

'It's just … I don't think they were examined properly.'

'You mean they missed something? Like what?'

'That handbag … the fake designer one? I could feel something in the lining.'

'Well that happens a lot, Tracey. My wife was always losing lipsticks, nail files, all manner of things in the linings ***of her*** handbags.'

'But this feels like a key, sir.'

'Well, those too … but did you tell anyone?'

'No, sir. ***I'm telling you***.'

'I see. And I suppose you're wondering how you can tear that bag apart without anyone official knowing about it?'

Tracey took a drink, sweeping his eyes around the room. 'I never said that sir.'

'But you were thinking it?'

'For hell's sake, you two,' Sylvie interrupted. 'Stop dancing around the houses and think of a plan. How securely is evidence stored? Who's allowed to access it? Is it possible to remove an item temporarily, replace it the following day without anyone finding out? And by the way, I'm a dab hand at invisible repairs.'

'Invisible repairs?'

'I think she means at sewing, sir,' said Tracey. 'My mam could do those too.'

'Fascinating,' said Seymour.

'I think it could be done, but it would need perfect timing…Give me a few days on the job to see how the land lies.'

'Actually,' said Sylvie, 'I have a set of keys too somewhere. Ruby gave me her cardigan when we were talking outside in St Martin's car park. There were keys in the pocket.'

'They must be her flat keys,' said Seymour. 'Damn! I can't remember the flaming address.'

'I don't know the number, but she told me it was on the corner overlooking the river. I can find it.'

'I don't want you doing anything risky off your own back. We don't know what we're looking for yet.'

'We'll consult you when we've worked out a plan, won't we, Bobs?'

'Erm, yeah, absolutely.'

'So, Seymour, you never told us why Hoggy calls himself Hoggy?' asked Sylvie.

'Oh, that's a nickname we gave him at school when he was milk monitor. He'd hog half the milk for himself before he brought the crate to class. We all suffered from brittle bones because of Hoggy.' He drained his glass and gave Sylvie a wink. 'No, that's a fib. He actually saves hedgehogs from dying, don't you Hoggy?'

'What's that, Seymour?' asked Hoggy, setting down the tray of drinks from the bar.

'I'm just telling Miss Broadstairs about all the hedgehogs you've saved.'

'Oh, I loves 'em, missus. If you finds a poorly one, just you brings it to me. I can make splints for broken legs, potions for sickness, you name it.'

'No, he didn't do any bank robbin' despite his name, but he did rob the bloody milk, the flippin' toe rag.'

CHAPTER 15 : CLARABELLE GOES MISSING

With daylight rapidly fading, Sylvie headed for home having dropped Bobby off at his place. She felt rather pleased with herself, eyeballing the beer mat with Seymour's scribbled phone number laying on the dash. Maybe he was beginning to take her seriously after all.

But turning into the caravan park, her mood suddenly changed. The sound of a TV grew louder the closer to home, and when she spotted the caravan door swinging on its hinges, all became clear. Performing back flips inside her chest, the old ticker needed a few of those calming breaths she practiced just before a gig. She pulled in alongside the van, tugged hard on the handbrake and sat for a moment with eyes closed, inhaling slowly on the count of six. But she didn't get that far. A balled-up fist thumped on the driver's side window and her bowels threatened immediate evacuation. Clenching her buttocks, she opened an eye to a cross-looking neighbour breathing steam on the window.

'What the divil you doin' sleepin' in the bloody car with yer flamin' TV blastin' away?'

Sylvie wound down the window. 'Mrs. Hanratty, sorry about that, I've just got here.'

'Who's having the party then? I've missed the start of Midsummer Murders now.'

'I've no idea. Don't suppose you saw anyone arrive or leave at all?'

'My curtains are clamped shut by 8 p.m. If you want someone to guard the place, get yerself a bigger dog!' With a flounce, Mrs. Hanratty spun around in her pom-pom slippers and marched back to her caravan.

'Oh, bollocks.' Sylvie said to herself with a sudden thought. ***'Please be okay, Clarabelle.'*** She opened the dash and pulled out the heavy flashlight she'd bought from the pound shop the previous winter. ***'In the absence of a baseball bat, you'll have to do.'***

Leaving the driver's door open, she edged towards the caravan and gasped as she peered through the window Every cupboard, drawer and hidey hole had been ransacked. ***'Bastards!'*** Anger sent her inside without another thought. She side-stepped around piles of beige underwear, precious photographs, toilet rolls and tinned dog food. The fridge door was open and the freezer compartment emptied onto the floor. Two fish fingers swam in a puddle of melted ice. In the bathroom, she picked up her blood pressure medication from the floor, popped an extra pill and swallowed with a grimace. Then she sniffed the air with creased up brows. It must be said her nose had some involvement too. ***'What is that smell?'*** she said out loud. But there was no Clarabelle to listen. She went back to the living room and lifted the telephone handset. It was still working. ***'Phone number, phone number,'*** she muttered, retracing her steps to the car and then back again.

'Seymour!' she said as the line connected. 'I've been burgled. Can you come over?'

∞∞∞

Seymour Witless drew up in a taxi as Sylvie searched the Begonias for Clarabelle.

'It might help if you ***switch the flashlight on,*** Miss Broadstairs,' he said, paying off the driver.

'Oh, Seymour, am I pleased to see ***you***.' she said, fiddling with the switch. 'Flaming pound shop rubbish ....'

'Now what's gone on here? Anything missing?' He approached the van, pulling on latex gloves.

'Just Clarabelle, I think. But everything's such a mess, and the door's a bit bent.'

'Well, that's one of the drawbacks of living in a tin box. The first response team should do a makeshift repair. But you'll need a replacement door. I'll sort something out for you, don't worry.' Seymour stepped over the threshold with caution and surveyed the damage. 'Looks like they've been pretty thorough. Is anything broken? Do you have insurance?'

'An old age pension doesn't stretch that far, sadly, not when you have to run a gas guzzler as well. A good tidy should sort it.'

'Well don't touch anything, not yet. You'll have to call this into the proper people. That'll trigger a visit from my nemesis D.S. Conway no doubt, and I don't want her to know I was here first. She'll flip her lid.' He pulled another card from his jacket and wrote a number on the back. 'Ring this number; tell them what's happened and your connection to the Winters and Porter cases.'

'What if they ask who I was with tonight? Do I keep you out of it?'

Seymour winced as he pondered. 'Eurgh …. Well, if they ask, it's not a crime to bump into someone in a pub …'

'Which is ***exactly*** what happened…'

'Indeed. And then to have an innocent drink with them …. '

'As compensation.'

'Compensation?'

'For the foot injury.'

'Erm, yes. But maybe shorten the time of that drink, just a little?'

'And we discussed …. what? The Great North Run?'

'The same as everyone else was discussing …. And what a jolly time we had doing that … for five or ten minutes?'

'No more than that …. Oh, and by the way, I was meaning to ask you – who was that man you were arguing with in the pub?'

Seymour pretended to look vacant.

'You know the one …. who goes by the name of Twatface?'

'Ah, yes, well, Twatface used to be my brother.'

'I see. So, he did something unforgivable to deserve this estrangement?'

'He ran off with my wife, Miss Broadstairs.'

'Well, you know what they say … when a man steals your wife, there's no better revenge than to let him keep her.'

'Except now, she's chucked him out of their little love nest – the place I'm still paying for incidentally, and he suddenly wants to reconcile with me. Well, I'm having none of it. The pair of them can rot.'

'That sounds very final, Seymour. But maybe you're just that tiny bit curious to know the ins and outs of what happened …. And what about the dog she wants back? I take it she means Rambo?'

Seymour sighed heavily and flopped onto Sylvie's couch. 'We had an agreement over the dog. Rambo was a time-share, if you get my meaning. This was before Twatface came on the scene. We'd already been separated a while by then, and it was all very amicable. We split the house money when it was sold and bought separate places. I offered to pay the mortgages because she couldn't afford hers, and Rambo would stay with me when I wasn't working. Once Twatface got his foot in the door, however, she had no time for the dog and I've had him full time now for months. With the help of dog sitters, of course. So if she does want him back, there'll be a court battle because I'm not having him passed from pillar to post all over again.'

'Quite right. And where is he now?'

'Tracey's sitting with him at mine. We were having a chin wag when your call came through. Speaking of which,' he looked at his watch, 'you should call that number now and I'll get out of your way.' He stood up.

'Before you go, Seymour, will you go into my bathroom and tell me what you can smell?'

Seymour offered a narrow-eyed stare. 'Miss Broadstairs, I can appreciate you may have had a dreadful shock, and perhaps an urgent visit to the bathroom was necessary, but you don't need a detective's nose to confirm that, surely?'

'I'm not having you on. There's seriously an odd smell in my bathroom. Come hither.' She pulled him by the sleeve towards the tiny room at the rear of the van and pushed him inside. 'Now, what are you getting, Inspector?'

Seymour crinkled his nose. 'It's very faint. I'm not sure. Tortoises, maybe?'

'Tortoises? Where the hell do you get that from?'

'It smells like my pet tortoise used to smell. ***You did ask.***'

'Hmm,' said Sylvie. 'I've always had a strong sense of smell, I'm just not sure about this one. It'll come to me sometime when I'm least expecting it.' She grabbed his sleeve once again. 'Right, time to be on your way, Seymour.' She dragged him to the open door and hustled him through it. 'I'll get on the phone as soon as you're gone.'

Seymour hit the ground and steadied himself before making one more point.

'It might be a good idea, Miss Broadstairs, before the cavalry arrives .... to get rid of those suspicious looking .... ***items*** .... behind the sofa.'

'Items, Inspector? Oh, you mean .... my new herbal shampoo? Good point, I'm on it.'

∞∞∞

As the door closed behind him, Seymour peeled off the latex gloves and shoved them back inside his pocket. The same pocket with the hole that had lost him several coins over the last few weeks and a lottery ticket he would never be able to check for winning numbers. Ever. As he walked, he recalled Miss Broadstairs' claim to invisible mending skills. He must remember to slip the malfunctioning pocket into the conversation at the next team meeting. Perhaps she'd accept another of those embarrassing cocktails by way of payment. It felt strangely satisfying to have his own secret murder investigation team. And even stranger that a geriatric fake psychic was his second-in-command so to speak.

A walk home in the autumn night air was always good for thinking. Reaching the site exit and about to turn left onto the main street, he spotted two police vehicles approaching, their blue lights flashing from some distance away. With precise footwork, he spun through one eighty degrees and headed in the opposite direction.

∞∞∞

Chapter 16 : A visit for Mr. Tracey senior

Monday morning began typically for Eva Shawcross, district nurse. In the ten minutes she'd been on the road, she'd cursed the driver with all the time in the world to waste, abused the gear box controls and tried a dangerous lane swap amid furious honking horns.

Turning onto Chillbottle Road, a rare parking space beckoned outside old Mr. Tracey's two-up, two-down semi and she pounced on it in two blinks.

The door was ajar as usual, and Eva stepped onto a pile of mail.

'Mr. Tracey? Royston?' she called out, picking up the mail with a spare hand. 'It's Eva, the nurse. How are we feeling today?' She nudged open the living room door with an elbow. Royston Tracey was perched on the sofa's edge, his bandaged knee out on show, as was the rest of him from the waist down. Bloated ankles mapped with spider veins hung like clock pendulums from non-matching knees and an impressive wad of grey chest hair poked through the stringed holes of a droopy vest stained with blood.

'We are feeling as free as a bird. But who knows, there may be an early malignancy waiting for its chance to pounce. You should give me a thorough examination, just to be sure.'

'Oh, Royston,' she said, averting her eyes. 'Do you need some help getting dressed?'

Royston shook his head and smiled. 'Don't need it. Didn't feel like pants this morning. Oh dear, not shocked are you?'

'Not shocked, no. I thought perhaps ***you*** might be embarrassed.'

'Gave that up many moons ago.'

'Well, you were wearing pants the last time I was here. And I can see you had that silly nipple ring installed, when I advised you not to. Didn't you notice it was bleeding?' Eva placed her bag on the floor and took a seat.

'Yes, but I just thought …my favourite nurse might see to it for me.'

A rustling noise from outside the room diverted their attention.

'It's only me, Dad,' announced Richard Tracey as he padded through the hallway, a Tesco carrier in each hand. 'Oh, Dad…,' he said, setting foot inside the living room. 'You haven't started ***all that*** again, for heaven's sake …and where's the blood coming from?' He dropped the bags, snatching Royston's dressing gown from the back of a chair and draping it across his father's lap.

'I ***am*** allowed to dress how I like in my own sodding house.' He tossed the gown aside.

'But you're not dressed at all, are you? And while that may be fine when you're not expecting visitors …. what are you going to do in residential care? You'll kill all the old dears with your dangly bits out on show.'

'And not as many dangly bits as I used to have.'

'You lost a diseased testicle that would have killed you before now.'

'I lost my manhood. That's what happened.'

'And now you may be losing your marbles.'

The gown was back on, and being tucked under both of Royston's legs. 'Where on earth are you bleeding from?' Richard took a closer look.

'Your father's had his nipple pierced; ***against my advice I might add***. I'll clean it up and take a proper look.'

'Thanks, nurse. Why on earth would you get a nipple ring at your age, Dad? And how did you get to a piercing studio? What if they won't take you at Windy Nook now?'

'Oh, deary me. Why don't you ask someone who ***gives*** a toss? I'm not goin' into any piggin' old people's home, thanks very much. And the nipple piercer does house calls. Her name's Electra.'

'Oh, Electra! I knew her old man, Agamemnon.'

'What's he on about, nurse? I rue the day we sent him to that ruddy college.'

'Look, Royston,' said Eva, 'why don't I change your dressing, clean up that wound and then leave you two alone? I've got Mrs. Warboys in fifteen,' she said, checking her watch.

'Yes, of course,' said Richard, 'you must get on. And Dad, just behave yourself for Miss Shawcross while she puts you back together. I'll be in the kitchen hiding these groceries in places you'll never find them.'

Royston shook his head. 'He's not joking you know ….'

Eva donned surgical gloves, parted the chest hair and examined the piercing.

'I don't see any infection, lucky for you, but this Electra person should have shaved around the area first to make sure it was surgically clean. But anyway I've got some sterilized wipes here.' She took a pouch from her bag, opened it and dabbed at the wound. 'I want you to keep an eye on this, Royston. Healing takes longer when you get old, and if it starts to hurt or gets sticky, contact me at the surgery.'

She unraveled the old knee dressing in record speed. 'The clean one will have to last a few more days. I won't be back until the weekend, so try not to get it wet, won't you?'

'No time for a chat then? How's that young man of yours?'

'Oh, he's fine, but not that young anymore. Neither of us is.'

'Everyone's young to me, nurse. Is he back at work yet?'

'Next week, he should be.'

'That's good. You've enough on your plate as it is. How are the gee-gees?'

'Still being fed and watered. By the way, speaking of horses, you're the dark one, aren't you?'

'I'm a dark horse? What do you mean?'

'You didn't say your son was a policeman.'

'And can you tell that by the size of his feet? Because he's not wearing his uniform.'

Eva gave a tiny laugh. 'Of course, how else? There! All done.' She bagged the old dressing and took it to the bin in the kitchen.

'Sorry about my dad, nurse,' said Richard. 'He used to walk around half naked when I was a kid. Mam used to scold him all the time and I thought he'd left that nonsense behind him.'

'Don't worry about it. I've seen bare bodies before. But he is vulnerable on his own, and sitting naked with the door open is not a good idea.'

'You're right. I need to have a strong word.'

'Okay, well I'll be off. See you another time Mr. Tracey.'

'Yes of course, see you later.'

Hearing the front door close, Richard emerged from the kitchen.

'Have you had breakfast, Dad? I've got sausages. Fancy a fry-up?'

'That poor lass .... Her fella's not well you know, it's that post traumatic stress thing and she just lost her mother a few weeks ago.'

'Don't you be worrying about her, I'm sure she manages fine from what I hear.'

'What do ***you*** know? I reckon she deserves a leg up.'

'What kind of a leg up?'

'How much have I got in the Nat West our Richard?'

Richard sat down. 'What's got into you? You can't be giving your money away to anyone with a sob story.'

'I've nowt else to do with it, have I? I could make somebody happy before I climb the heavenly ladder. It's either that or get more nipple rings.'

'Dad, you're only seventy eight. You could live another ten years yet. And when you go into residential care, you'll need all the money you've got. What if you need a motorized wheelchair or one of those motability scooters? Think of the fun you'd have with one of those.'

'I'm not moving anywhere! They'll have to carry me out of here in a wooden box. Anyway, get those bloody sausages on, I'm starving.'

Richard got up. 'Right away, sir,' he said, heading back to the kitchen. 'Do you want toast or fried bread?'

'I want a flamin' stottie. And never mind hiding them because I saw the Greggs bag when you came in.'

'Nowt wrong with your eyes then.'

∞∞∞

Chapter 17 : A new way in

Sylvie had barely slept a wink all night. The makeshift repair on the caravan door was about as useful as a chocolate fireguard and Clarabelle was still missing, possibly kidnapped. Doors, drawers and tables stained black with fingerprint dust, cried out to be cleaned, but the motivation was lacking. As she lifted her tea mug, there was a tap at the door and it swung open with a grinding squeak as if by sorcery.

'That's some lockin' system you've got there, missus,' said Hoggy from the paving slab serving as a doorstep. By his feet sat an impressive box of tools and against one shoulder, a caravan door leaned unsteadily like a drunken sailor.

'Where did you get that?' Sylvie stepped outside for a closer look. 'It's the same make and model as mine.'

'Funny that, i'n't it missus? Seymour had me up with the larks and round the scrappies first thing.'

'But … you've ***never*** carried this …. Not on your own. Where's your bike?'

'Seymour dropped me arf at the entrance. Said he couldn't risk comin' in …. just in case, tha knows.'

'Right, well thank you, that was very thoughtful. Can I get you a hot drink?'

'No, missus, I is just fine. Hope tha don't mind me sayin' but tha's lookin' mighty rough this morning.'

'Yes, well, considering I'm fuelled up on two hours sleep, enough caffeine to kill a horse and a Jacob's cream cracker, I reckon I'm doing okay.'

Hoggy tipped his hat. 'Aye, well, best get started. Tha's had a nasty shock, so gets thaself indoors and stick them trotters up.'

'Okay, I'll do that Hoggy. And thanks…' As Sylvie turned to go back inside, a car turned into the site's entrance. She'd been expecting someone, just not this early.

Shapely legs, supported by impractical shoes emerged from the driver's side, while Chinless poked a reluctant face around the passenger door.

'D.S. Conway and D.C. Chince,' she announced as she stepped out, raising a warrant card. 'We'd like a few words regarding last night's incident.' Chinless did not move. 'Chince? Would you mind?' She offered him a head flick complete with glare and he clambered from the car.

'Who is ***this*** person?' Conway examined Hoggy's bum cleavage as he bent over his tool box.

'Oh, I's just the handyman, missus. Hoggy's the name.' He straightened up, wiped both palms on his trousers and presented a hand for shaking. 'Maybe tha sees me in church hall.'

'Ah, yes, I remember.' She returned the warrant card to her shoulder bag. 'I may need to speak to you too, at some point. Can't you do that job later?' She waved a dismissive hand at the toolbox. 'This interview with Miss Broadstairs will be confidential.'

Hoggy withdrew his handshake offer along with his hand. 'Nae bother, missus … I gots the Walkman here and a set o' plugs for the lugs. Only voice I'll be hearing is Hugh Cornwell's.'

'Who's that? Some other hippy?' she sniggered.

Hoggy sucked in air and shook his head. 'Oh, missus, that's fightin' talk that is. Cornwell belongs to the best punk rock band in the world.'

'Yes .... well, we must get on. Might we go inside?'

Sylvie stood aside from the doorway and gave Hoggy a wink. He nodded and switched on the music player.

Once inside, Conway strolled around the limited space, arms folded.

'Rather an odd place to live, a caravan, don't you think?'

'Clearly I don't, seeing as how I live in one. Though there ***were*** some odd things about it when I first moved in.'

Conway raised an eyebrow. 'Such as?'

'Well, there was the poltergeist for starters.'

'Really? I expect it felt threatened when a psychic moved in.'

'You'd think, wouldn't you? But no, it was a stubborn bugger. Took a whole week of walking around stark naked 'til it couldn't take any more.'

A grin spread across Chinless's face far too obviously.

'D.C. Chince… pay attention.'

Chinless straightened his face and thrust his shoulders back.

'Yes, ma'am.'

'How long have you lived here, Miss Broadstairs?'

'Seven years, four months and two days.'

'That's very precise.'

'It was the day Thatcher's government took over and designed a capitalist Britain.'

'A day that will go down in history for women's equality.'

'Just a pity it had to be ***that particular*** woman.'

'Oh, might have guessed. You're a socialist.'

'And proud of it.'

'Hmmm. Let's not get into politics, shall we?'

'Is your team looking for my dog, D.S. Conway? Because if not, I'd like to get on and do it myself.'

But Conway appeared not to have heard. Her attention was grabbed by the claw marks in the wall left by Nelson the previous day.

'Take this down, D.C. Chince.' Chinless whipped the notebook from a top pocket and poised his biro in readiness.

'Deep scratch marks and mud to fireside wall – query forensics' sampling.'

Sylvie smiled. 'Yes, best get onto that, D.C. Chince.' Then her smile faded as Conway picked up a dog-eared, black and white photograph from behind the mantel clock.

'What a cute kid. I have one around the same age.'

'Charlie was about three years old when that was taken. Lovely child, but awful picky with his food.'

'Mine's the same. Can't get my child to eat fish at any price. Can you suggest anything else …. equally as good for you …. that I could swap it with?'

'That's easy. Swap it with a cat. Cats will eat fish 'til the cows come home.'

Conway grimaced. 'You know, Miss Broadstairs, I thought we almost made a connection there. But you just can't help yourself, can you?'

'And I thought you might just smile, D.S. Conway.'

Conway replaced the photo and gave the mantel clock a gentle stroke. 'Are you fond of antiques, Miss Broadstairs, like Mister Winters?'

'Well, I wouldn't call him that, exactly…'

'Let me put this more clearly …. ***Did Mister Winters' clock collection inspire your love for old clocks?'***

'The clock collection in Mister Winters' flat belongs to both of us, D.S. Conway. We both contributed items to that collection. I still have some of the receipts, including the receipt for that one under your finger.'

'I see. Well, I imagine as his legal widow, you're likely to cop for the lot, so to speak. You might even find one that works … since this one appears to be only useful as an ornament. What value would the entire collection be worth? Any idea?'

'It's been such a long time since I've seen them. But, maybe two or three thousand?'

'Times that by three and you'd be closer to the mark.'

Sylvie's eyebrows leapt skywards. 'Well, that's quite a sum. And did the burglar not attempt to steal any?'

'Completely ignored them. Which you might expect if the intruder was about to inherit them anyway … and of course ***you*** have family connections ***to both*** recent murder victims.'

'So, what are you saying exactly? That I broke into Ernie's flat ***for what reason?'***

'To steal this clock, perhaps? As some sort of compensation for the hellish marriage he put you through?'

'We've been apart for nigh on four decades. So I suddenly thought, I know! It's about time I got my own back on that bastard and dug out the old balaclava for a spot of house breaking…'

'Where were you last evening, just for the record?'

'I was in The Fishgutter's Arms having a screaming orgasm.'

Conway's nostrils expanded in tune with her eyes. 'Miss Broadstairs, if you continue to be obstructive as well as disgusting, you will be arrested and detained at my pleasure.'

'I beg your pardon ***Your Imperial Majesty***, but I'm being neither obstructive nor disgusting. A Screaming Orgasm is a calorific cocktail containing vodka, coffee liqueur, amaretto, cream and milk. And I was with Bobby, before you ask …. and one or three others.'

'We'll check that out, of course. D.C. Chince … I hope you're still taking this down?'

Sparks were beginning to fly from Chinless's notebook. 'I've got the ingredients down, ma'am, but not the quantities. I wonder if this might double as a dessert?'

Conway turned her head away and rubbed at her temples.

'So, Miss Broadstairs, because of your family connections to these two individuals... you will remain a person of interest, and ...'

A burst of song from Hoggy interrupted the discourse as he began to attach the replacement door.

♫Can she escape that clitoris?

Tribulation of wimen

That's what I teach, teacher man. ♪

Conway sucked in rather more air than necessary. '***And*** it's not beyond the realms of possibility that this was staged to look like a burglary.'

'What idiot would break into my caravan just to stage a burglary?'

'An idiot like you, Miss Broadstairs, or your side-kick out there ... to make you look like a victim.'

♫Aw shit, I fixed the caravan!

Maybe I'll suck beer the whole summer

And that's no bummer ...♫

'Now you're being ridiculous. I'm hardly likely to make this mess, only to have to clean it up after. Not with my arthritic knees. And what have I done with the dog? Murdered her too? When you gonna start looking for her, incidentally?'

'The murder team doesn't hunt for missing dogs, Miss Broadstairs.'

'Not even murdered ones?'

'You've likely hidden it somewhere. Stuffed it under the caravan, possibly.'

'Not with these knees…I can assure you.'

Hoggy's battery-operated screwdriver whirred as he sang some more.

♪Bold and brown, inside a bun

Shoots me down with my machine gun… ♫

'Have you checked for missing items?'

'Yes, I told you. My dog's missing.'

'We don't seem to be getting anywhere here, D.C. Chince.'

Hoggy started to bang with a rubber mallet.

♬ I'm just bangin' around

Yeah just bangin' around ♪

'We'll get out of your way, Miss Broadstairs. If anything significant crops up from forensics, though I doubt that very much, we'll let you know.' Chinless thrust his notebook back into his pocket and followed Conway to the door.

Passing Hoggy, she leaned in. 'If I find out those lyrics aren't real lyrics, Mister … Hoggy… you'll be arrested for disorderly conduct or harassment. Perhaps even both.'

With earplugs still in situ, Hoggy couldn't hear a word.

'Yes, missus. Same back at ya with bells on.'

∞∞∞

Chapter 18 : Coffee Joe's

Seymour Witless stared into his coffee cup, trying to decipher the image in the froth. Sculpted by a talented barista, it began life as a heart, but somehow had morphed into the elephant man. Coffee Joe's captured the perfect balance between Fenwicks and The Greasy Spoon, with enough indulgence of the former and all the inclusiveness of the latter. He tore the top off a tube of sugar and poured it from a height.

'Inspector, fancy seeing you here.' He couldn't mistake the soft Irish lilt belonging to staff nurse Brenda Cole. He turned his head to confirm. She was dressed in civvies and her hair was down, sweeping across her shoulders just like in the Silvikrin adverts. He raised his bottom from the upholstered seating. 'Can I get you a coffee, Nurse Cole?'

'Sure that would be lovely but I've been in here way too long. Are you expecting company?'

'Not for ten minutes. Take the weight off your feet.' He really ought to stop saying that. Someone might take offence. 'What would you like?'

'She slid along the bench seat facing. 'I'm fine, really, but glad I ran into you. Please sit for a moment.'

'What is it?' He sat back down.

'I hope I didn't give you the wrong impression after our interview.'

Seymour puzzled. 'In what way?'

'I do so respect the responsibility of my job, Inspector. I should have jumped up and down a bit more to get that outer door fixed sooner than it was. The care of my patients is my main priority. I'd hate for you to think otherwise.'

You reported it soon enough. I don't see what more you could have done. I know the NHS is driven on a budget. It's bound to make your working conditions intolerable.'

She offered a shy smile. 'I wonder…have there been any developments on the Winters' case? Or maybe you can't tell me…'

'It's still very early days. And anyway, someone else has taken the lead on that one. I'm stepping back for a while.'

'Oh, I'm sorry to hear that. Should we expect more interviews with the new lead then?'

'Quite possibly, but I wouldn't worry about it too much.'

'It must be hard, letting a case go just like that. I could see how committed you were in solving it.'

'Still am, if I'm honest. Part of me sees it as a competition now. I'm still trying to piece it all together on the quiet. I did give you my phone number, didn't I? Just in case something else came to mind about that night?'

'You did, Inspector.' She patted her handbag and gave her shoulders another tantalizing sweep with the hair. 'Rest assured I won't hesitate to call.'

The shop bell sounded as D.C. Richard Tracey appeared at the entrance, holding the door wide for his father with armpit-supporting crutches. Both men wore grumpy faces, and Royston actually wore trousers too.

'Here's my company now, Nurse Cole. But it looks like the numbers have doubled.'

Brenda Cole stood. 'Ach, I'll be leaving you to it, Inspector. See you later .' He watched as she hip-swiveled her way to the door.

'Eyes front, sir,' said Richard Tracey, seating his father. 'We can't afford any distractions during business talks.'

'No, indeed,' said Witless. 'This is your dad, I take it?'

Royston offered a hand. 'That's me, ***much as he hates it***. Pleased to meet you.'

Witless offered his own, and they shook. 'Likewise. Are you the new recruit by any chance?'

'Can you believe …' said Richard, '…the old bugger followed me here in a taxi? And he's left Rambo alone in the house.'

'Oh, that could be a bad move,' said Witless, with a chin stroke. 'You may not have a sofa left when you get back.'

'No worries about that,' said Royston. 'I put him in the yard with a friend.'

'A friend? What friend?' Tracey's forehead corrugated.

'Some tiny dog poking its nose through the fence. Both of them all waggy-tailed to see each other, so I let it in.'

Witless squeezed his eyes together in pain. 'Was it a Chihuahua by any chance?'

'How did you know?'

'Forget it. You never saw that dog, and you certainly never let it into the yard, right?'

Royston shook his puzzled head. 'If that's what you say, then it's wiped from my memory.'

'Excellent. So, Tracey, have you had a chance to check out the item we discussed at the last meeting?' he took a slurp from his coffee cup, and licked the froth from his upper lip.

Tracey leaned in. 'Tomorrow, at 1 p.m. my office colleague takes his sergeant's exam. As long as the coast is clear, I can transfer the item to an A3 size brown envelope and conceal it inside my overcoat, which I shall wear for the purpose. However, the sooner I can transfer it to another location, the better.'

'How about if I call in for a chin wag around 1.20 perhaps? With a reciprocal overcoat enabler?'

'Bloody Norah,' said Royston. 'Did the pair of you join M.I. flippin' five when I wasn't looking?'

'Something like that, dad. Oh, look over there, sir. It's that hack from the Gazette.'

Witless's dark eyes swept across the coffee shop, landing upon Max Wade with his Tom Selleck moustache, deep in conversation with a pretty young girl swishing her pony-tailed head from side to side as she spoke.

'So it is, Tracey. And that's Carolyn Carr's companion from the gig at St Martin's. No guessing what'll be front page news by tomorrow.' He took another slurp of coffee. Then both watched Royston staring at a young man sitting at a table close by. The man's hair was dyed in multi-colours and gelled into spikes, ninety degrees from his scalp.

'What you staring for granddad?' he said, with amusement. 'Thinking about how much you missed out as a teenager, fighting all them wars and stuff?'

'Not really,' said Royston. 'I was just thinking … around twenty years back, I had sex with a peacock. So now I'm wondering if perhaps you could be my son.'

Witless sprayed coffee spontaneously from his nostrils, drenching the table. And Tracey was thankful he hadn't ordered the cheese toasties yet.

∞∞∞

Chapter 19 : It's all about the keys

Hoggy wiped the sweat from his forehead, tossed a screwdriver back into the toolbox and snapped it shut.

'That door's as good as new, missus,' he said, giving the paintwork a fond rub with his polishing rag.

'That's just fabby, Hoggy. Now how do you feel about me giving you a ride back to St. Martin's?' Sylvie emerged from the caravan in a strawberry mackintosh and pink trainers, tightening the strap of a yellow fisherman's hat beneath her flabby chin.

'Very good of you, missus. But hang on ….' He thrust a hand inside his trouser pocket, pulled out a set of keys and waved them in the air. 'Don't forget to lock up.'

'Good thinking,' she said, snatching the keys and turning them in the lock. 'I'll stand you a pint in The Fishgutter's next time. Oh, and by the way, do you want to take Daisy's special brew back with you? I had to hide it under the van in case madam plod found it.'

'Might be safer where 'tis for a bit …. 'til they find out who this ruddy killer is anyways. Imagine it's safe enough?' Hoggy peered under the van, his stare being met by a single green eyeball, glowing from out of the dark. 'Looks like you've a guard on duty under 'ere missus.'

'Not Clarabelle, I'm guessing?' Sylvie had one leg in, one leg out of the driver's side.

Nelson made a dash for the open door and leapt from the drivers' to the back seat in a nanosecond. 'Oh, it's you, is it? You didn't guard our Clara that well last night, did you, Nelson? Suppose you want a lift too?'

∞∞∞

For a Monday morning, Chillbottle Road was way more chilled than usual. Special offers splashed across desperate shop fronts distracted Sylvie's eyes from the road, and she wisely pulled around a corner and hunted for a parking bay.

'What's up, missus? I doesn't do shops.'

Sylvie tugged on the hand brake and unbuckled her belt. 'Don't be daft. I've just had the most brilliant idea, Hoggy, and you're not allowed to dismiss it, understand?'

Hoggy's eyes turned into scary saucers. 'I's not gettin' no hair cut!' he said, hands flying up to his tatty locks in protective mode.

She shook her head. 'Wouldn't dream of it. That bonce hasn't seen a pair of scissors since Noah learned to swim, and like him, I'm a wildlife preservationist in case you didn't know.' She looked down at his feet. 'But you can't go around in odd shoes …. 'specially not ones full of holes, not with winter looming.'

Hoggy dropped his hands into his lap, but the eyes remained suspicious. 'Not all ***that*** odd. One brown, one blue.'

'One brown slip-on with accidental peep-toe, one blue lace-up with … is that a blood-stain?'

Hoggy showed a bloody palm. 'Screwdriver slipped, missus.'

'What on earth are we gonna do with you?' She pulled a packet of wipes from the dash. 'Clean yourself up with those on the way.'

The shoe shop was almost devoid of customers, except for one elderly lady with a tiny head and huge bunions that wouldn't fit inside any type of shoe, judging by the number of try-ons scattered around her footstool. She puffed from the effort of it all.

'Just see to these folks, pet. I'll have another go with the Hush Puppies,' she told the assistant, who sprang up from her knees like she'd been saved from the gallows. Her hair was streaked with randomly placed lime-green plaits.

'What can I serve you with today?' She said to Sylvie, with a fixed grin like Gromit's Wallace.

'I thought maybe you could show me a refrigerator.'

'Oh, you want The Icehouse up the road. Shall I show you where to go?' The assistant began to walk to the door. Hoggy remained at the rear of Sylvie's left shoulder with a look of fear about him.

'Sorry, love. It's all fun and games until someone doesn't pick up on the sarcasm. No, we just need something weatherproof for my friend here.'

The assistant still looked like she'd been asked to board a spaceship. Sort of glassy-eyed with bared teeth.

'Hoggy …. Go pick something off the shelf before my feet take root and my brain cell dies of boredom,' Sylvie whispered. Hoggy jumped to it, and returned with a pair of green tasseled moccasins, wielding them under her nose.

'These look snazzy doesn't they, missus, and good for hidin' the grass stains.'

'Yes, Hoggy. Try them on .... assuming you've picked the right size?'

'I's not stupid, missus,' he said, kicking off the old shoes with a quick flash of yellow toe nail, and slipping on the new.

'How do they feel?'

'Like new shoes.'

The bunion lady watched with fascination.

'My son had toe nails just like your boy's there,' she said. 'Came back from football and they'd all come off inside his boots.'

'Ouch! That must have been uncomfortable.' Sylvie empathized.

'He had this condition called toelio; a bit like polio, but just affecting the toes.'

'That's interesting, because I have a condition affecting my knees. I'm just realizing it must be kneasles.' Sylvie kept smiling at bunion lady, against her better judgement. Hoggy was now walking up and down the red carpet, flexing his feet and admiring his new footwear in front of a long mirror. He performed a full squat, keeping a straight back with magnificent balance and squeezed out a tiny parp of wind.

'Still comfortable, Hoggy? Or would you like to try something else?'

'No, missus, I loves 'em. But price tag says £14.99 – that's a bit much.'

'You're forgetting, Monday is pensioners' discount day. These are half price …. aren't they …..' she squinted at the assistant's name badge, 'Karen?'

Karen looked suddenly startled, once again. 'Erm … to meet the terms and conditions for the pensioner's discount, the shoes must be for the pensioner. So your son wouldn't qualify, I'm afraid.'

'But Karen, the shoes ***are*** for me. Me and my boy share everything … including shoe size and toe conditions. He does all the testing and I do the wearing. It's only fair.'

Karen's cheeks reddened on her way to the till. 'That'll be seven pounds fifty then. Will madam be wearing the shoes, or would she like them boxed?'

Sylvie turned to Hoggy. ***'We'll*** be wearing, don't you think, Hoggy?'

Hoggy beamed in his own lopsided way. 'Oh yes, missus. They be smashers.'

'Fabby!' Sylvie paid the money, picked up Hoggy's old shoes from the floor and headed for the door. Bunion lady's jaw dropped, whether from admiration or joral thrush, it was difficult to know. But as a parting greeting, Sylvie turned and said, 'Oh, I forgot to say, my ex husband from a marriage that lasted barely 24 hours, had an embarrassing case of smallcox. But I did enjoy the wedding cake.'

Out on the street, Hoggy couldn't resist staring at his reflection in every shop window he passed. While he was thus occupied, Sylvie zipped across to a street waste bin and dropped his old shoes inside it.

'Missus!' shouted Hoggy. Sylvie thought she'd been rumbled, but Hoggy was pointing down the street. 'Looky! There's yer mate.' She followed his finger and found Bobby, struggling in their direction carrying a fully-loaded black bin liner.

'Bobby? What's happened? Have you been chucked out?'

'What? Noooo.... Just been to The Poshwash with a few smalls.'

'For who? The whole town?'

He gave a tiny laugh. 'Well, you know, gotta make extra money somehow .... So, Hoggy, nice shoes, pal. Where are you off?'

'We's off to St Martin's. I's been in a shop!'

'Yes, Bobby, would you like to come?' said Sylvie. 'We have stuff to talk about.'

'Is it juicy gossip? You have to tell me now before I burst.'

'Well, someone broke into the caravan last night while we were at the pub.'

Bobby dropped his laundry onto the path and went in for a hug. 'Oh, sweetums, that's awful. You really need to get that dodgy door fixed. Did they take much?'

'Nothing to take, Bobs. But they did make a mess, and Hoggy's fixed the door now, bless him.'

'So they must have been looking for the same thing they didn't find at Ernie's.'

'What may that be?' Hoggy asked.

'What everyone's looking for, Hoggy. Money.'

'Tell you what … if anyone broke into my shed for money, I'd be joinin' the search.'

'You're not alone, Hoggy. Well,that's a relief. So are we heading to St Martin's for a specific reason, or to pray for a miracle?'

She winked. 'Bit of both, I reckon. We can drop that stuff off on the way if you like.'

∞∞∞

Whatever state of dilapidation St Martin's church and its outbuildings had fallen into, its ancient yew tree continued to strike a pose of relentless guardianship over all it surveyed. It served as a landmark for travelers; a private place for sorrow; shelter from the rain and a home for the weirdest-looking creepy-crawlies you ever did see. As Sylvie cruised up the driveway in her sixty-ninth year, she remembered her first proper kiss beneath the yew's protective canopy of speckled shade. Joe Shufflebottom had been sneaking shy looks over the top of his hymn book for weeks at Sunday school, and Sylvie wondered if he would dare do anything else. It was after class on the first Sunday of June when he grabbed her by the hand and led her to expectation. Without saying a word, he planted a wet smacker on her optimistic lips and then he ran away. Disappointment persuaded her that the unfortunate event was nothing more than a lucky escape. And even if they ***had*** walked up the aisle, how could she or any unfortunate offspring ever live with a name like Shufflebottom?

Bobby brought her back to the present with a jolt. 'What the hell's that?' he said, staring at the yellow banner pinned across the events board outside the church hall doors. It read :

STAR ATTRACTION – FOR ONE NIGHT ONLY,
'MYSTIC MOHAWK' - RENOWNED

PSYCHIC TO THE STARS. WEDNESDAY, TICKETS £2

'What? ….well what a bloody nerve!' said Sylvie. 'How the hell did that happen? I've only been gone five sodding minutes,' she said, parking up at the first convenient spot. Releasing her belt with a dramatic snap and a fling, Sylvie cracked open the driver's door and stomped onto the tarmac. Nelson leapt out in front and took off for the sheds. 'Hoggy? Did you know anything about this?' Hoggy stepped out from the back seat, with head bowed.

'I just does what I is told, missus. Nuthin' more than that, honest.'

'I ***know*** you can read, Hoggy. Norris told me you'd read every one of those classics in your pram.'

Bobby caught up. 'That's impressive, Hoggy. So you were reading classics as an infant?'

A look of cringe swept across Sylvie's face. 'You great wassock. Hoggy keeps his book collection in a pram. I don't think it was actually ***his*** pram. ***Was it,*** Hoggy?'

Hoggy shook his matted locks. 'Nah, but finders is keepers. That's Romani law.'

'And it didn't occur to you to tell me about this ....' She checked the billboard again for the name, 'this ... Mystic Mohawk?'

'Thought maybe tha knows already .... I doesn't like upsettin' folks so I keeps schtum.'

'I'm not blaming you, Hoggy, not at all. Best just to ignore me when I go off on one like this.' She tugged on the church hall's door handles. 'I'm composed now, I promise.'

'Ah, Miss Broadstairs ....' Reverend Norris held up a copy of The Gazette from the table in the foyer as they entered the building. 'The murders have finally made it to the tabloids .... They even beat The Great North Runners to the front page.'

'Can I takes a squint at that paper, Norris?' Hoggy said. 'Is that a free seat there next to you?'

'Of course, Hoggy,' said Norris, pulling out a chair. 'I'm liking your new shoes, by the way. Now, how about a piece of Daisy's angel cake?'

'Ah, please, Norris, tha's very kind.'

Sylvie and Bobby leaned over his shoulder, scanning the front page.

'Just what I might have expected,' said Sylvie. 'A diabolical photo of Ernie in drag taken right off the promotion banner. And look at poor Ruby's picture. I wonder who gave them that?'

'Maybe Seymour knows,' said Bobby.

'Hmm. We need to have another conflab. Turn over the page, Hoggy. Let's see the runners.'

The photograph on the inside page was far more interesting.

'Oh, look! See that fella?' Bobby pointed to a figure third row from the front. 'That looks like you, Hoggy.'

'Where …. what?' said Hoggy with eyes on stalks.

'Oh, Hoggy, if that's not you it's got to be your twin,' said Sylvie.

'I has a twin? That's amazin'!'

'Aw, he doesn't have a number. Not even a vest. Shame, we won't be able to trace him.'

'Oh, there's a pity.' Hoggy exhaled.

'Is there more on the sports pages?'

'I bloody hopes not!'

'A bit. Nothing more than has already been revealed.' said Norris, flashing Hoggy a scolding look as he passed him a slice of cake. 'Would you like some Miss Broadstairs? Bobby?'

'Yes, okay, but, well the reason Bobby and I came was ….'

'To confront me about Mystic Mohawk, to ask me where my loyalties lie, etcetera, etcetera.'

'Something like that. Oh, and also Bobby and I would like to retrieve something I left here on Friday evening.'

'Of course. Feel free to look wherever you need. And incidentally, Mystic Mohawk offered to do a cut-price gig under the circumstances.'

'The circumstances being?'

'Preserving St Martin's reputation, Miss Broadstairs. Now the story's out, how long before your connection to both murder victims is revealed also? The bishop has insisted we dispense of your services until all this messy business is over.'

'I agree,' said Sylvie. 'One hundred percent.'

Surprise flashed across Bobby's face. 'Really? Now you're scaring me.'

'Really. Now, c'mon Bobbykins,' she grabbed Bobby's sleeve, half dragging him towards the main hall.

'I'll come willingly you know, sweetums. There's no need for force.'

Sylvie released her grip and gave him a hard slap on the back instead. 'Sorry, Bobby. See you in a minute, Norris.'

As the pair disappeared, Norris interrupted Hoggy's reading with a somewhat rehearsed statement, accompanied by a series of disapproving looks.

'Since I've got you on your own, Hoggy, there are one or two things I have to address.'

'Hoggy kept his eyes on the print. 'Oh yes, Norris? What be those then?'

'I understand that you've been drinking Daisy's brew to great excess and seeking her private company while her husband has been otherwise detained. Is this true?'

Hoggy looked up from the centre pages with a blank stare. 'So, ***tha did*** see me. Suppose I can't deny it then.'

'In that case, you also know that you have tempted Daisy to perform pleasures of the flesh outside of marriage, of which the church and The Bible disapproves?'

'Oh, Norris, I doesn't know about that exactly. In the book of Revelations for instance there's all kinds of shenanigans ....'

Norris held up a palm. 'Alright, I know you've read The Holy Bible and no doubt you've dissected it more than I have, but nevertheless, marriage is a holy thing and should be respected.'

'Okay, Norris. I gets the message. I shall apologise to Arthur when I sees him next.'

A look of alarm spread across Norris's face. 'Please, Hoggy, don't do that. Just …. finish your cake.'

Hoggy's attention returned to the newspaper. 'Norris, what's this thing **…. *arthritis***? How doest tha catch it?'

Norris's mood was unrelenting and he frowned. 'You catch it from drinking too much, drug abuse, and engaging in adulterous fornication, over and over again.'

Hoggy's eyebrows shot up to his hairline. 'Oh, I see,' he said.

'Why? Do you think you might have it?'

'No, Norris, not me, but it says here the Pope does.'

∞∞∞

Meanwhile, back in the cloakroom, all the usual places had been searched for Ruby's cardigan without success. But Bobby was delighted to find a sparkly waistcoat left behind by The Hot Hunks in 1979. He whipped off his jacket and thrust his arms into it.

'What do you think, sweetums?' he said, doing a twirl. 'Maybe I could wear it on stage as a warm up act.'

Having exhausted all cupboards and drawers, Sylvie was down on all fours, peering under the threadbare sofa. She raised her head.

'What sort of a warm up act? A striptease? In front of Miss Mountshaft and the reverend?'

Bobby's mouth turned down at the edges. 'Put like that …. maybe not. But how about a magic act? I could lock you in a coffin and run you through with a dozen swords,' he said, making stabbing gestures with his hand, '… or chop your head off in one of those guillotines with a double-sided blade.'

'If you want rid of me that badly, you only have to say. Keep it, Bobby, you look just fabby. And you never know when it may come in useful.' She struggled up from the floor onto her feet. 'Well, doesn't look like the cardigan's here. We may just have to go round to Ruby's and pick the lock.'

Bobby shook his head. 'No, not if it's anything like last time.'

'Hmmm. Maybe Norris has seen it. Let's ask.'

∞∞∞

Norris was busy opening his mail when the investigators returned. A box of tickets had just arrived from the printers. They were black with bold yellow lettering and framed with astral stars. Sylvie stood by his side, spreading her fingers on the table.

'Very snazzy they are, Norris,' she said. 'I only hope your ***Mystic Mohawk*** lives up to expectations.'

'I hope so too, Miss Broadstairs. Will you be coming on Wednesday?'

'Suppose we'll have to, won't we, Bobby? Check out the competition, see where we can improve. So how come my gigs never earned any flashy ticket printing?'

'Well, ***Mystic Mohawk*** has a greater following, apparently. Among the stars in particular.'

'And which stars might they be? I'm supposing he came with a recommendation?'

'Carolyn Carr, for one.' Norris proceeded to write names on envelopes from a list of attendees.

'Well, that figures. She'd just love it if I went out of business. So, who else?'

'I don't recall every one of the names she mentioned, but there were a few.' Norris paused for a moment. 'I don't relish pushing you out, Miss

Broadstairs. If it was up to me, of course I'd continue with your services …'

Sylvie patted him on the shoulder. 'I understand, Norris. You're stuck between a rock and a hard place. So, while you're feeling guilty, how about you give me two of those tickets at half price?'

Norris pressed his lips together and peered over the top of his spectacles. 'Take them for free. Never let it be said that Reverend Norris was an unkind man.'

Sylvie clasped his head and planted a smacker in the middle of his bald patch. 'Bless you Norris. You're a sweetheart.'

'Indeed.'

'So that list of ticket holders you have there … looks like all my regulars, plus a few more?'

'We're borrowing a few additional seats from St Mary's.'

'Fantastic. So that thing I came to look for …'

'Did you find it?'

'No. I was wondering if you or Daisy had seen it. A black cardigan with safety pins, a few holes and a patch pocket on the side.'

'Oh, that? Hoggy borrowed it for one of his hedgehogs. He and Daisy are nursing it in one of the garden sheds.'

'Hoggy again! That boy will be the death of me. C'mon, Bobby.'

∞∞∞

Daisy sat on Hoggy's makeshift bed while he stood by holding a hot water bottle. Cradled in her arms, a hedgehog, swaddled in Ruby's black cardigan was being fed through a dropper when Sylvie tapped three times on the shed door.

'Stand by your beds, you two.' She poked her head through the gap. Hoggy signaled with a forefinger placed over his lips. ***'Come in, missus, but keep it down if tha canst,'*** he whispered.

'I'll wait outside, sweetums,' said Bobby. 'There's barely room for three in there.'

Sylvie crept inside. 'Well, that's it, Hoggy. You'll just have to marry her now.'

Hoggy stared like a startled mouse. 'Missus? I is just bringin' gifts like those wise men did in the good book.'

'Keep your hair on, I'm only tuggin' on your leg. No, what I'm after, if you can manage to look carefully .... is a set of keys in the pocket of that cardy.'

'Oh, there's no keys in that there cardy. I knows that for sure.'

'Oh, bollocks and shite on a stick! Well, that's put the kibosh on it.' Sylvie pondered for a moment, turning to the door, then back again. 'And there's no doubt? You ***have*** checked?'

'I checked all right. Nuthin' in that pocket but fresh air.'

'Right, well, I'll leave you to it, then.'

'Stop teasin' Hoggy,' Daisy whispered.

'I'm bein' teased?'

'The reason I knows there's nowt in that cardy,' said Hoggy, groping around in his trouser pocket, 'is cuz I took these out of there not fifteen minutes ago.' He pulled out a key fob and waved it in the air.

Sylvie's eyes narrowed as she snatched the keys from him. 'You …. big bugger. I'll get you back for this.' Hoggy gave a crooked grin.

'I hopes you isn't thinkin' of doin' anythin' illegal missus.'

Then came a gentle tap on the door, and Bobby poked his head inside.

'Watch out! That lady copper's on her way over here, with a desperate look about her.'

D.S. Conway didn't knock, apart from the knock she gave Bobby as she cleared her path to the shed. D.C. Chince slunk up behind her like a nervous kitten.

She tugged at the shed door. 'What's going on here?' she said, her glance flitting from one face to the next.

'Shush, missus. We's just tending the sick. Does tha have a sickness that needs lookin' at?'

'Just a swollen ego,' Sylvie whispered.

'Mister Hoggy, I'm arresting you on suspicion of the murder of Ruby Porter. You do not have to say anything, but it may harm your defence if you do not mention when questioned, something you may rely on later in court. Anything you do say, may be given in evidence.'

'You ***whaaaat,*** missus?'

'Hang on,' said Sylvie. 'What the hell are you talking about? ***Where is*** your evidence?'

'Oh, I think you know very well, Miss Broadstairs. You're very likely his accomplice, just as ***he was yours,*** in your so-called burglary. And I should warn you not to go anywhere, as I will be speaking to you soon.' Conway flashed the whites of her eyes. ***'Very, very soon.*** We have a new witness, you may be disappointed to hear, who saw the pair of you this morning on Chillbottle Road disposing of an unmatched pair of bloodstained shoes.'

'But I put them in a proper bin,' said Sylvie. 'What did you want me to do with them? It was the bunion lady who blew the whistle, wasn't it?'

'D.C. Chince, remind me to bring an interpreter for gobbledygook to Miss Broadstairs' upcoming interview, won't you?'

'Yes, ma'am,' Chince answered on autopilot.

'The shoes are now being tested for blood type matching. If the blood on the shoes matches Ruby Porter's, Mister Hoggy will be charged. Take him, Chince.'

'But Hoggy didn't see me bin the shoes. If he had, he would have pleaded for their lives.'

'Too bleedin' right I would,' said Hoggy as he was ushered towards the door. 'Served me well did those shoes.'

'But that makes no sense,' Daisy puzzled. 'Ruby Porter wasn't stabbed. Where could the blood have come from, for Jesus Christmas sake?'

But Hoggy was already being hustled out of the shed.

∞∞∞

CHAPTER 20 : THE FLAT SEARCH

Sylvie's Mini Metro bumped its way over the uneven road leading down to the riverside development. Still in its early stages, the infrastructure was short of a few tweaks. But the river captured Sylvie's gaze like a balm for the soul; its surface sparkling beneath a timid sun, peeking now and then from behind a furiously-tinged cloud.

'I think my dinner's on the way up,' said Bobby.

Sylvie exhaled with irritation. 'Honestly, Bobby, where's your appreciation of beauty? I mean …. look at that view.'

'I can appreciate beauty … just not in the same places as you.'

'Between the glossy pages of Proud & Endowed, I'm guessing.'

'You so just made that name up.'

'Maybe I did, but it has a certain ring to it, don't you think?'

'Sweetums, do you know where you're going?'

'Not a clue, Bobby. But I'm sneaking in here, close to the exit ….. just in case we have to make a fast getaway.'

∞∞∞

Outside the block of flats, Sylvie dithered with the keys.

'I reckon it must be that one …' said Bobby, touching a square-headed key wearing a luminous yellow hat on the fob.'

'How in the name of buggery do you know that?'

'Because …. it glows in the dark, so it makes sense it's for the outside entrance.'

'Clever sod, that you are,' she said, trying it in the lock and pulling open the door.

'One of us has to be. Shall I lead the way? How many flights? Or are we using the lift?'

'No, not the lift. We might get stuck.'

'And you might get winded on the stairs.'

'Nonsense. We'll have to try each floor, and we're looking for a corner apartment with a sea view window.'

'Righto, sweetums. Shall I take your hand?'

'Bugger off, I'm not past it yet.' Sylvie gave him a push with the flat of her hand and followed him to the top of the first flight. She stopped to catch her breath. 'Bloody hell, Bobby.'

Bobby shook his head. 'I did offer help, did I not?'

'I dunno what you're on about, Bobby. I'm just overwhelmed by the décor. I could fancy living in one of these myself.'

'Right. Course you could. Are you ready to make a few more strides to the corner, or do you want a piggy back?'

Sylvie took off on her own. 'I'm just ignoring you now, Bobby. Come on you lightweight, catch up.'

Approaching the corner flat, an old man came out of his door dressed for winter in a trapper hat, fingerless gloves and a knotted woolly scarf.

'You's that couple, is you not? Always droppin' fish in the bins?' He glared, accusingly.

Sylvie shook her head. 'Not us, we're vegetarians. Aren't we, Peaches?' she said, tugging Bobby's sleeve.

'Oh yes …. very strict veggies.'

'Where's yer bin then?'

'Oh, we's bin to Margate ….on holiday,' Bobby continued.

'Naw, man! Where's yous wheelie bin?'

Sylvie nudged Bobby out of the conversation. 'We's really bin on holiday, and if some twat's nicked our wheelie bin, we'll hunt them down, never fear.'

The old man screwed up his eyes, turned his key in the door hurriedly, tested the handle, and shuffled away.

'Bloody hell, sweetums,' said Bobby. 'He might call the cops.'

'He wheelie won't, Bobby,' she said, standing on tip toe, peering through the corner flat's window. 'There's no-one in here. We may have got lucky.'

'Or they might be on the karsy.'

Sylvie grimaced and rang the doorbell. 'We'll soon find out.'

'What the hell you gonna say?'

'Haven't a clue, Bobs, but I'll find that out the same time as you.'

No-one answered, so Sylvie tried another key in the lock. It turned. 'How about that? Someone's watching over us.'

'So long as it's not the flaming Grim Reaper.'

Defying all gothic or punkish styles imagined by the house-breakers, the flat was painted in pastel shades, modern artworks displayed across the walls with more canvas paintings stacked up in the bedroom. The furniture was more M.F.I. than Fenwicks, with an out-of-place Victorian bed frame, beautifully iron-mongered.

'This is sad, Bobby. A young couple just starting life together.' Sylvie walked around, trying not to disturb anything. 'Wiped out within weeks of each other. I didn't even get the chance to know my own grand niece. If there's such a thing.'

Bobby found a letter rack posing as a sausage dog on the mantel shelf and leafed his way through it.

'No time for nostalgia, sweetums. That old fella might have set the warden on us.'

Sylvie composed herself. 'You're right, I'm getting maudlin in my old age. Anything in there, Bobs?'

'Here, take half.' He whipped out a handful of envelopes and handed them to her. 'These are bank statements, a couple of postcards, wage slips, how about you?'

Sylvie sat on a chair, opened a brown envelope and unfolded the letter inside. 'This is from Discover your Ancestry, and it's addressed to David Winters.'

'That's the dead junkie boyfriend, right?'

'And Ernie's son, according to Ruby.'

Bobby peered over her shoulder and read out loud.

'Dear Mr. Winters, thank you for your enquiry regarding your father, Ernest Winters' direct descendants. We are pleased to inform you that our investigation team has found matches with a number of individuals and we request that you contact our office for further information regarding these findings. Yours faithfully …'

'This is what Ruby was talking about. He must have been in contact with other siblings.' Sylvie leafed through the rest of her pile. 'Damn, I don't think there's anything more here. Looks like our next stop is the library. We need to see those tiny fishes.'

'You mean the microfiche records?'

'Those too. Oh, look at this …'

'What?'

'A stamped envelope with an unsent letter inside.'

'Addressed to who?'

'Ruby's mother. But there's no address.' Sylvie unfolded the letter inside and began to scan the pages. 'And by the way Bobby, it's 'to whom' not 'to who.'

'You're doing your owl impressions again. But I'll try and remember that. Is it worth a read?'

'Maybe for me it is,' she said, refolding the letter, shoving it back inside the envelope and into her pocket. 'We should get out of here. C'mon Bobby.'

∞∞∞

Clambering into the car outside, the getaways paused as a soft-topped Morris Minor pulled up alongside. Seymour wound down his window.

'Up to no good as usual, I see,' he said. 'Find anything?'

'Sort of,' said Sylvie. 'We need to look at those inventory records at the library next. Did you know Conway's arrested Hoggy?'

'Seymour's jaw hung wide. ***'She did what?*** On what evidence?'

'Blood on his shoes. His own, by the way.'

He puffed wind into his cheeks, then let it go. 'She can't hold him, that's ridiculous. Anyway, Tracey's managed to get hold of ***that thing*** ….' He twisted his head around for potential earwiggers. ***'You know, the thing we spoke about before in the pub.'***

'Ah, yes, we remember ***the thing.'***

'So, can I bring ***the thing*** round to yours? Maybe you could do ***that other thing*** you spoke of doing?'

'Ah, yes. I can do ***that other thing***. I should be back in an hour or two at the most. Don't suppose there's any news of Clarabelle?'

'That's ***yet another thing*** I was about to say. The answer is affirmative. You may see her very soon.'

'No ransom required, then?'

'No ransom. No worries. See you later.'

∞∞∞

Chapter 21 : Hoggy's Nicked

The cop station down town was positively Dickensian, with unattainably high ceilings and strictly low tolerance.

Hoggy stood in front of the custody officer's desk, scanning the windows anxiously for bars.

'Do you know why you've been arrested today, sir?' asked the officer, his pen poised over a grim-looking form.

'Maybe it's cuz that woman copper's gettin' a bit desperate.'

The officer peered over his horned rims with a frown. 'Let me ask the question more clearly. Did the arresting officer tell you ***why*** you were being arrested?'

Hoggy nodded. 'Aye, she did that.'

He ticked a box. 'Can I get your full name, sir?'

'Long as tha doesn't go off on one.'

'Why would I do that?'

'Tha won't believe me.'

'Why not? Are you the Boston strangler?'

'Nope. I is just plain Robin Banks.'

The officer put down his pen and closed his eyes. Pressing three fingers into his forehead he attempted to smooth out the furrows. 'Well, we'll leave that one blank for the moment, shall we, sir?' He picked up the pen again. 'Address?'

'God's country.'

'Right. ***"No fixed abode" it is then.*'** The officer waved his biro at Hoggy's clothing. 'Empty your pockets out onto the desk please, fella.'

From his jacket, Hoggy produced nine elastic bands, two pencils, a pack of cards and a tin-opener.

The officer made a list. 'Why do you carry a tin opener, may I ask?'

'To open tins.'

'What kind of tins?'

'Cat food tins.'

'You eat cat food?'

'No. Poorly hedgehogs do.'

'I see. Officer Chince, is this gentleman under the care of the mental health team?'

Chinless straightened up from a leaning position at the edge of the counter.

'Not that I'm aware, sarge.'

'Perhaps a referral may be in order?'

'I'll see to it, sarge.'

'Sorry to ask, sir, but that string holding up your trousers? I'll need to take that too.'

'Whaaat? My bloody kecks'll fall down.'

'We can get you a safety pin, hang on ….' The officer opened a drawer from beneath, taking out a massive pin with a shepherd hook's head on the end. 'Difficult to hang yourself with one of those, eh?'

Hoggy folded his arms and scowled. 'I's not happy with this. I has my dignity, tha knows.'

'You'll get everything back, fella. No-one's laughing at you here.'

Hoggy looked furtively around, then untied the knotted string in his trousers just as two school girls were brought in for shop-lifting. Twisting around as the swing doors opened, his trousers dropped to the floor. The subsequent screams reminded Hoggy that his underpants were still lying in a gutter where he lost them, somewhere along The Coast Road.

∞∞∞

Perched on a fully wound-up office chair in the very bowels of the library, Sylvie squinted at the microfiche reader's screen. Lights danced behind the images, like an old Buster Keaton movie but without any of the laughs. Already, she'd been through birth records for the year Charlie was born and several years either side of that. Charlie's birth parents were found as expected, Dorothy May Mountshaft, aged eighteen years and Ernest Winters, twenty seven. His occupation was listed as 'galley cook' while hers was 'shop girl.' By accident, Sylvie stumbled upon her own marriage listing to Ernest in 1936. The courtship had been brief, but purposeful. She tried not to dwell on the emotion of it all, but it wasn't easy. The memories were still very raw despite the time lapse and she knew she would take them with her to the grave.

She'd also found the death entry for the Mountshaft sisters' father from a 'garden accident,' and the stillbirth of an unnamed child to 'spinster' Eva Jane Shawcross in 1965. Feeling like an interloper, she took off her reading spectacles and rubbed her eyes. How much of this was any of her business? None, probably, but a murder investigation was bound to uncover secrets, relevant or otherwise. Her notebook lay open, and she knew she had to document ***all of her findings***.

As far as Ernie's other offspring were concerned, they weren't found in the six years of archives already searched. But Ruby was only twenty-seven years old, so it was logical that David, the boyfriend, was of a similar age. She'd need to make a stab at 1956 and later for him, and who-knows-where-else for any unknowns. This was going to take much longer than planned.

Meanwhile, Bobby searched newspaper archives at random. Without specific dates, nor access to his new spectacles, he followed the larger print items easier, hoping for a lucky break. Then he found a headline in The Evening Chronicle. The date was October, 1943. Normally, he would have skipped over such a news item, but the face of the boy alongside it was particularly upsetting and he had to read on.

'Unknown child abandoned in church grounds'

A child was found abandoned in the grounds of St Thomas's church in Newcastle-upon-Tyne on Sunday evening. The child is around 7-8 years of age and was wearing a blue shirt, dark trousers and grey

sleeveless pullover. He appears to be mute and unresponsive to questions. The boy is currently being cared for at a children's home in Houghton-le-Spring where other children who have lost parents in the conflict are being temporarily housed. Staff have named the boy, 'Pigeon' as he was surrounded with the birds when found. If anyone recognizes the child, please contact local council offices on the following telephone number …

'Sylvie, sweetums, take a look at this. It's heartbreaking,' he leaned in next her, keeping his voice low.

'Bobby, if it's another forty-year-old appeal for a missing dog, you've shown me three already, and I've one of my own already to feel depressed enough about, remember?'

'No, sweetums, it's a lost boy who couldn't tell anyone his name. It's even sadder than the dogs.'

'More sad, Bobs. Not sadder.'

'His sweater looks like the one you knitted for me last winter.'

'You mean the one you never wore?' Sylvie stretched sideways to look through his viewer and the colour drained from her face. 'Oh, no. Oh bloody hell, Bobs, that's my Charlie.'

'QUIET!' came a voice from the desk behind.

'How about we nip downstairs for a coffee, sweetums? Bobby whispered eventually, as she poured over the article.

Sylvie took a deep breath in and blew it out with a flubber. 'I need to find out what happened, Bobs.'

'Course you do, but coffee first ….then we make a proper plan.'

'Hmm …. Little girls' room first, Bobs. Bladder is sending S.O.S. signals.'

The Coffee Hub hadn't been open long, but it was going great guns with a lip-smacking muffin selection. Bobby set the tray down on the formica table-top while Sylvie sat on a brown plastic chair chewing a finger.

'Forty years, Bobby. How didn't I know something would go wrong?'

'Now listen to me, sweetums,' he said, seating himself. 'You're not to blame. Like you said, there was a war on. They probably just assumed his parents were bombed out or something. What happened to his street? ***Your old street?*** Is it still standing?'

'Yes, of course it is. I know that much. Maybe Norris knows something about the history of Saint Thomas's. If not, there must be records at that children's home in Houghton-le-Spring. If ***that's*** still standing.'

'Well if it's not, the records will be somewhere. Eat your muffin, it looks fabby.' Bobby took a mouthful of his and closed his eyes as he chewed, sending chocolate chips to warm themselves on his taste buds.

'We've a lot more work to do with those archives. A lot of years to trawl through,' said Sylvie.

'I'm willing and able. I've all the time in the world for you, sweetums. We'll get it done.'

She pondered for a moment. 'How the hell did Charlie stop speaking? Something bad must have happened.'

'Well .... ***he did lose you*** around the same time. That must have been pretty traumatic.'

'You say the nicest things at just the right time, Bobs.'

'That's why you love me. Now, are you gonna eat that cake? Mine's gone already.'

'The calories, Bobby. They're the little bastards that team up in your wardrobe and sew your clothes tighter. My wardrobe's infested with the little shits.'

Bobby took a big slurp from his coffee cup. 'Don't suppose you've got any space for a few of ***my things*** in your wardrobe?' He said, looking absently around the café.

Sylvie narrowed her eyes and frowned. 'I bloody knew it! That bin bag wasn't full of your laundry, was it?'

'Erm… no.' His eyeballs flitted nervously from side to side.

'So why did you let me take you back to the flat to drop them off?'

'Didn't want to show myself up, did I? Not in front of Hoggy, anyway.'

'You daft sod. Now we have to go back and get them.'

'Sorry. Can I have your cake?'

'No, you bloody well can't, Bobby Mason.' And with that, she attempted to stuff the whole thing inside her mouth, but just fell short of success.

∞∞∞

CHAPTER 22 : THE LINE-UP

Seymour Witless hit the swing doors with the flat of his hand and burst into the station with a face like thunder. The timing couldn't have been better, for D.S. Conway was standing behind reception checking over Hoggy's custody form with D.C. Chince. She looked up and her face dropped, but recovered in seconds.

'D.C.I. Witless, I thought you were on leave. To what do we owe this pleasure?'

'What have you got planned for my friend, Hoggy? Has he been questioned yet? Have you advised him he's entitled to free legal advice?'

Conway's mouth contorted into some kind of mild amusement, with a hint of Cruella De Ville, while a lone eyebrow showed an element of surprise.

'Everything's been done according to the book, have no fear of that.' She tore off her spectacles in an exaggerated gesture, poking one end between her lips.

'And has he accepted the offer?' asked Witless.

'He doesn't seem particular interested, so I'm taking that as a decline.'

'Not interested? Don't give me that. In his head he's still a juvenile. He needs to have these things explained to him. Give me that form …' Witless held out a hand across the counter, and she hesitated briefly before surrendering it.

He snatched it from her with a purposeful shake. 'It says here a referral is pending to the mental health team.'

'That's right. But referrals take time, and we need to get him processed quickly.'

'Quickly for what reason? Your reputation as the fastest collar in the north? Will there be a special gold badge issue in your honour? Is he in a bloody cell not knowing what the hell's going on?' Seymour shifted his weight from one foot to the other like he'd lost all sense of direction. 'I'm sitting in on the interview.' He glanced at his watch.

Conway shook her head. 'So many questions and demands, ***Seymour.*** But this case isn't any concern of yours, is it? So why don't you calm down, get yourself a cuppa at the corner café? Because we may be a while.' She turned away from him.

Seymour 's nostrils flared, his feet dithered some more, then he barged his way through the 'staff only' door and headed down to the cells. Opening each viewer window one by one, he finally found Hoggy kneeling on the floor of his cell, head bowed.

'***Our Father, whose heart's in Heaven,***

Harold be thy name

Thy kingdom's come

Thy grill be done …'

Hearing the viewer snap open, he raised his reddened eyes and forced a weary smile.

'Seymour? Tha's not forgotten me then?'

'As if! How could I forget my old mate? Have they told you what's gonna happen yet? Because they're telling me bugger all.'

'***She*** wanted to do me for indecent sposure, but the sarge said no, so that's summat at least.'

'Indecent bloody exposure? How the hell did that happen? Christ, the woman's unbelievable.'

Conway suddenly appeared in the corridor with D.C. Chince and a line of men dressed in Hoggy-type clothing following behind.

Seymour gaped. 'You're never doing a line-up! Who's the bloody witness?'

'Not now, Witless,' she hissed. 'You know I can't reveal that to a line-up of suspects. Why don't you just get lost and leave me to do my job? Open the cell, D.C. Chince.'

Chinless stepped forward with a bunch of keys. 'Scuse me, guv.' Witless stepped away from the door.

'Right, Hoggy, it's time,' Chinless announced through the viewer as he rattled the keys in the lock, one after the other. Witless shook his head. 'Use some bloody tact, Chince. And it's ***that key*** with the corresponding cell number.' He indicated with a forefinger.

Hoggy jumped to his feet. 'Time for what? I's never finished my prayers .... Seymour? You still there?'

'I'm here, Hoggy. Don't fret. The woman you spoke of earlier wants you to stand in a line with some other men until you've been looked at, then you can come back here and finish your prayers.'

Hoggy edged out of the cell with bloodshot eyes flitting up and down the corridor as the men, each carrying a number on a big yellow card, shuffled through into a wider passage. Chince shoved a number ten into Hoggy's hand, leading him by the arm to the end of the line as Witless looked on, powerless to intervene.

'Willst tha say thanks to the Sylvie missus for the shoes, Seymour? And say sorry I didn't get to use them for as long as I hoped.'

'Don't be talking like that, Hoggy. I'll get you out of here, I promise.'

'Can we have some quiet now, please,' said Chince, 'while a member of the public takes a look at you all. You might be asked to say something or do something, should the witness request it. But we'll take it one stage at a time.'

Sergeant Eccles appeared from another doorway with the bunion lady, who'd still not found any accommodating shoes judging by the pained expression. She hobbled slowly from the far end of the line, examining each face beneath the hat and each pair of feet, eventually arriving at Hoggy. She stared harder and longer at him than the others, while he kept his gaze fixed to the floor. Then without a word, she inched her way over to Conway with a look of pelvic pain and whispered something in her ear.

Conway stifled a grin. 'The witness requests that you all remove your footwear and stand in your bare feet.'

'Seymour?' Hoggy protested.

'Silence!' yelled Conway.

Sucking and slapping noises echoed down the hall as skin met with tiles and socks flew through the air. Bunion lady didn't even bother to walk the line again. She took one look at Hoggy's feet and had him condemned with another whisper in Conway's ear.

'Right, gents, you can all leave except number ten. Chince, take number ten back to the cell.' With that order, Conway retreated back to her office.

Hoggy watched the others reclaim their footwear as Witless came towards him.

'Put your shoes back on, Hoggy. You're no different to the others.'

'She says I am. I has to stay; they can go.' He shoved his feet back into the shoes.

'Sorry Hoggy, I'm gonna have to shoot off now. But I'll be back, and don't let her persuade you into signing anything.'

'Can't sign anythin' with this bloody hand.'

***'Let me see that** ….'* One glance at Hoggy's injured palm and Seymour dragged frustrated fingers through his comb over. 'Chinless!'

'Sir?'

'This man needs medical attention, and he needs it now.'

'I'll get the doc down here right away.'

'Well don't bloody forget.'

Chinless jangled his keys with a come-hither hand gesture, and Hoggy went quietly back to his cell.

Chapter 23 : The Gucci handbag

Bobby huffed at Sylvie's open wardrobe, despondent at the lack of storage space available to rehome his treasured belongings. ***But he had*** found some temporary amusement donning an accessory or two from Sylvie's special drawer.

The sound of clattering plates filtered through from the kitchen as Sylvie prepared boil-in-the-bag chicken madras with Pelaw* rice - as it was colloquially named.

'Are you in the mood for a poppadom, Bobby? Or there's a garlic naan we could share? Sorry I can't stretch to one each.'

'Half a naan bread would be lovely, sweetums. Don't have to worry about garlic anymore, being single and all.'

'Food's a trusty compensator when bad things happen. Until it makes you buy bigger pants. How about a drop of council pop?'

Bobby came through from the bedroom clutching a bottle of wine. 'Council pop? What's that?'

'Tap water, Bobs. Oh, what you got there?'

'This, sweetums, was mysteriously concealed inside my kung fu pyjamas.'

'You stole it, you mean?'

'Not stole, exactly. We were saving it for the big day. You know, the civil ceremony-come-wedding if the proposal ever gets through parliament. Which doesn't matter either way now, so ….'

'His loss is our gain,' said Sylvie, snipping the tops off the bags and pouring the contents onto plates. 'Corkscrew's in the drawer and glasses on the table if it's red. If it's white we may as well have the tap water.'

'Such a diva,' he said, uncorking the wine to a tapping sound coming from the door.

Seymour Witless stood on the step, with a guilt-ridden Chihuahua hooked under his arm.

'Oh, Clarabelle, I'm so glad you're back,' Sylvie gushed, snatching the dog from its delivering angel and smothering her with kisses. 'Seymour, come in and have a free sniff at the food. Where did you find her?'

'Tracey found her hanging round his local chippy,' he lied. 'She was after his battered sausage, I believe.'

'Oh, sweetheart, you must have been starving.' Clara's nose twitched as she was placed on the floor. 'Here, have some of my curry,' she said, handing her the lot.

'I've brought ***that thing,*** ' said Seymour, slipping a hand inside his coat and pulling out Ernie's Gucci handbag, partially wrapped in brown paper.

'Let me have a feel,' said Sylvie, taking the bag, '... and take a seat while I ***... oh yes, I can feel it*** ....hang on, just have to get my toolkit to unpick the seam.'

While he waited, Semour's gaze wandered to Bobby, shoveling curry into his mouth like he was feeding a dying furnace.

'What on earth is that on your head?' It took a while for Bobby to realize that something else other than the food before him required his attention. Fingers crept in a vertical direction until they made contact with Sylvie's brightly-coloured Indian headdress.

'Oh, I forgot about that. What do you think? Does it suit me? Would you like a try-on?'

Seymour responded with exaggerated disinterest. ***'No, I certainly do not.'***

Bobby shrugged, plunging a poppadom between his jaws. 'How about some wine? It's a posh one, none of your corner shop tat.'

Seymour rocked back and forth on the balls of his feet. 'I'll pass, thanks.'

Having licked Sylvie's plate clean, Clarabelle sat at Bobby's feet with an enthused wagging of her tail. But her silent plea was ignored and so the dog focused her attention on Seymour instead, standing determinedly rigid. But Clarabelle had become sufficiently acquainted to know what he kept in his coat pocket. Within seconds, his hard exterior began to melt. Casually, he slipped a hand into his pocket and took out a Rambo-sized treat. Clarabelle enthused even more.

'It is a key, Seymour.' Sylvie stood up from the sofa where she'd been working, holding up the metal object she'd freed from the fake Gucci lining. 'And I think I know where it fits.'

Bewilderment swept across Seymour's face as he watched her pad across to the mantel shelf. She twisted the clock that never ticked from front to back and tried the key in the lock. It turned with ease. Still chewing on the last piece of naan, Bobby's jaw slackened as he fixed his gaze on her movements. She slipped her hand inside the timepiece and pulled out a folded piece of paper. Disappointed eyes swept from the note to her partners-in-crime, then back again, and she read out loud just before Clarabelle snatched the treat from Seymour's fingers.

'Do your jewels hang low? Can you tie 'em in a bow?

Can you wrap 'em round your neck? Will you swing 'em to and fro?

Try to bounce 'em off the wall, where the sailor's alcohaul

Hides behind the secret door in the place along the shore.'

Seymour's eyes narrowed. 'Is there something you haven't told me about that clock, Miss Broadstairs? Does it …. belong to Ernest Winter's collection by any chance?'

Sylvie retraced her steps back to the sofa and sat uneasily, still staring at the note.

'This is so bizarre. Seymour, I didn't exactly tell you the truth about the last time I saw Ernie.'

'I see. Well would you like to enlighten me now?' He moved to an armchair, pinched his trousers at the knees the way men do, and sat down.

'He came to find me. It was a few years ago now. You see, we'd collected these clocks over the years, one by one. We loved the auctions and I particularly loved that clock. It's a George IV mantel clock, made around 1920.' Sylvie gazed up at the clock adoringly. 'Just look at the casing, it's beautiful.'

'I'm no connoisseur, but I'll take your word for it.'

'Yes, well, when I left him, I tried to take that clock with me like I tried to take my Charlie, but Ernie wouldn't let me have either. So when he turned up again offering me the thing, I wasn't gonna knock him back, was I?'

'Didn't you ask why the sudden change of heart?'

'I did, and he said he was running out of space or something. It was only after he left that I realized it must be broken, because it never worked after that and he hadn't left the key. But I just loved how it looked so it didn't matter that much. And I don't understand why he'd remove the mechanism. I mean .... it's completely empty inside.'

'Apart from that silly rhyme.'

Sylvie held out the note. 'This, Seymour, is a bawdy version of the lyrics to The Sailor's Hornpipe. He used to whistle that bloody tune all the time. It got on my flaming nerves.'

'Hang on a minute,' said Bobby. ***'You whistled that tune on stage*** the night Ruby got killed. Don't you remember?'

'Did I? No, I don't remember that. Was that in the second half? Did I say or do anything else?'

'Well, you strode around the stage with your hands behind your back …. Then you said something like, 'My flesh, my blood …. And you shouted MURDER really loud.'

'So that must have been Ernie speaking. ***Through me***. Don't you get it, Seymour? He was trying to tell us who killed him. What I don't understand, is what would be the purpose of setting a silly puzzle like this? And who was it meant for? Unless …'

'Ah! I may know the answer to that one,' Seymour said. 'According to the Medical Examiner, Ernie knew he was dying.'

'Of what? ***Oh, don't tell me***. It would have to be cirrhosis of the liver.'

'Apparently so.' Seymour scratched his head. 'But all this spirit message stuff is just beyond me. I can't fathom a rational explanation, and there has to be one.'

'How about this then, seeing as how we have no better idea?' said Sylvie. 'While we figure out the meaning to Ernie's silly conundrum, we need to find out who the rest of his blood relations are, still living, obviously. Because it's looking like one of his offspring has 'offed' him, and since David is already dead, we need to find Charlie next, and do a proper search for others. But I don't relish trawling through microfiche archives again, I can tell you.'

'I don't get why Ruby was killed at all, if the two killings are meant to be related. Why would one of Ernie's offspring want to kill Ruby?'

'Well, when Bobby and me were at the flat, we found a letter from one of those trace your ancestry businesses. David was searching for Ernie's offspring himself, looking for brothers and sisters. So what if he got that information? What if he met up with the killer? And what if Ruby knew who that person was?'

Bobby had almost finished the wine by now, and becoming rather animated.

'She'd have to be next in line, wouldn't she? And what if David's drug death wasn't accidental? Maybe he was deliberately killed with some dodgy gear?'

Seymour's eyebrows sprang skywards.

'Well, I suppose all of that's feasible, yes.'

'What if it's somebody local? There are parish records too. There'll be fewer of them, and they're written in actual books.'

'You're right, Bobs. So that's where we're going as soon as I've repaired Gucci's lining. And you'd better drink a gallon of water before we go, because I'm not dragging you around drunk.'

Chapter 24 : Norris is exposed.

In the reverend's private quarters, Norris lay back in the bath, pondering over the events of the the last few days. Prone to ear problems, he wore a bathing cap loaned by Daisy many months prior to protect his delicate hearing organs from flooding with water. The rubber flowers dotted at intervals around the cap's surface bothered him not one iota, since they'd never be seen by any other person but himself. Lowering his body deeper, the bubbles spun and swirled across the surface to 'Rock of Ages,' his personal choice of hymn for singing whenever he felt prone to troubled thoughts. Then strangely, despite the insulation provided by the rubber cap, he imagined a percussion section thundering away in the background, spurring him on to sing louder. However, when the accompaniment suddenly ceased and replaced itself by a female voice, he pulled himself up to a sitting position in such confusion that bath water lapped over the edge and ran across the floor in a tidal wave.

'I'm so sorry, Norris,' said Sylvie, covering her eyes pointlessly with wide open fingers. 'Daisy told me to give you a knock, but your singing must've made you deaf. I hadn't realized you'd such a powerful voice.'

Norris raised a soapy hand to indicate a bath towel, looped over a shiny brass rail on the wall. 'Pass me that towel, would you, Miss Broadstairs, ***please?'***

'Of course, Norris.'

He proceeded to drape said towel across his head in an attempt to hide his embarrassment, but the new look restored no dignity at all. Sylvie smirked.

'Well, now you just look like Queen Nefertiti on a bad hair day.'

'Can we dispense with the insults and just tell me why you're here, ***in my bathroom?'***

'Absolutely I can, Norris. Bobby and I are planning to bust Hoggy out of jail. But in order to do so, we need access to something you can provide, if you're willing.'

'If you mean that unexploded bomb they found in the church grounds, it was disabled and removed in 1975.'

'Damn. So it's plan B then. I was wondering … if we might take a look at the parish records?'

'What, you mean now?'

'Soon as, Norris. Just tell me where to look and you can finish your ablutions in peace.'

Norris slowly released a lung full of air. 'Oh, God, why didn't I read the terms and conditions for this stupid job before signing the contract? You know I can't just send you into the records room without a chaperone. There's personal information in there about people you know.'

'I understand, Norris,' Sylvie said, turning back to the door.'

'On the other hand ….'

'Yes?' She turned back again.

'Hoggy is a decent person who needs as much support as we can give him. Wait outside, and I'll be out in a minute.'

∞∞∞

The records room, as Norris called it, was in fact a dark but spacious cupboard attached to his office in the clergy house, with grinding door hinges and multiple mouse holes etched along the skirtings. Noise from the former was clearly used by inhabitants of the latter as a signal to scarper. Massive tomes lay side by side along drooping shelves, while smaller ones leaned against one another, cramming the walls on two sides. A tall pair of step ladders, draped in cobwebs stood in a corner.

Free of his bath, Norris had thrown on his cassock in record time but only fastened alternate buttons in his haste. Such was his dedication to duty.

Bobby shuddered as he entered the room.

'Is there a light switch?'

'Um, there is, but it has a tendency to deliver a lethal shock through the arm. However, there are torches and batteries,' he opened a desk drawer, 'in here, should you need them. What is it you're looking for may I ask? I may be able to put my hand on the appropriate register to save you the turmoil of going through the lot.'

'Oh, Norris, that would be a great help,' said Sylvie. 'Thanks so much. You know about Ernie Winters, the first murder victim, and coincidentally my husband?'

'I have since learned that fact, yes Miss Broadstairs.'

'And did you know that Dotty, Miss Mountshaft's sister had a son called Charlie, who Ernie and I raised until he was eight years old?'

'I did not know ***all of*** that.'

'Well, soon after Ernie and I parted, Charlie was found abandoned in St Thomas's church. But he couldn't speak and he was placed in an orphanage in Houghton-le-Spring. Bobby found a newspaper article and a photograph on the microfiche.'

Norris held his jaw in pensive mood, tapping a forefinger against his upper lip. 'I remember this! They assumed the parents had been either killed in a bombing or just abandoned him because they couldn't cope. He ended up at Hazel Street orphanage in Jarrow. I spoke to the bishop about it at the time.'

'Does this orphanage still exist, Norris? Is there a paper trail of where the children went?'

Norris began to walk up and down, which was all of three steps in either direction in such a tiny room.

'Hazel Street is long gone. There was terrible abuse exposed years after and someone set fire to the place. The records were distributed among church parishes. I have some of them here, but the books are fire damaged.'

'Where, Norris? Where are these books?'

Norris reached for the ladders. 'Bobby,' he said, 'would you mind doing the honours? I'm afraid I suffer from altitude sickness. If I climb up there, I fear I might vomit over you both.'

'Well, we wouldn't want that, Norris. Up you go, Bobs.'

Bobby made a point of crossing his arms. 'I do have a stomach full of all sorts myself, remember?'

Sylvie shot him a blank stare. 'The words 'self' and 'inflicted' come to mind…'

'Oh, alright!' he relented, shrugging off his best jacket. 'Just … take care of this. It's all you'll have to remember me by.'

Sylvie took the coat as Bobby took to the ladders.

'He's such a drama queen, Norris. Best plug your ears. ***He can get rather sweary on the red wine.'***

'Hmmm, I'll bear that in mind. You need to be over in that left-hand corner, Bobby,' Norris pointed, as Bobby dithered with the ladders between delicate hands.

'You mean over by that massive spider's web, don't you?'

'Yes, but Spidey's not home, so you should be fine.'

'That is such a comfort,' Bobby muttered to himself, climbing to the top. 'Ah, I think I see the books with the burnt edges. There are three. Which years do we want?'

'All of them, Bobs.'

'Fuck me.'

'What did you say?'

'I said, lucky me!'

∞∞∞

Six trips up the ladders later, and with two books each, the trio transferred the objects of their search to Norris's living room, where space was greater, light was brighter and tempers calmer. Mindful that they had no other name but 'Pigeon' to search for, and Bobby had a stomach full of wine, water and curry, it was a surprise when he suddenly shouted out from the fireside rug, 'I've bloody found him!'

Sylvie prayed he wasn't having drunken imaginings. 'What have you found, Bobs? Can you read it out? Because I'm buggered if I can get down there to peer over your shoulder,' she said from a very comfy armchair with a book, equal in weight to a hod of bricks resting on her lap.

'This entry is dated 14th. May 1947, so Charlie would be, how old?'

Sylvie did mental sums. 'Twelve, Bobby. So what does it SAY?'

'It actually says ***Charlie***.' He traced a forefinger across the entry. ***'Charlie Pigeon – D.O.B. in brackets – estimated 14th October 1935 …. discharged to adoptive parents Mary and George Mullins, 19 Alice Street, South Shields.'*** He lifted his head out of the book. 'Maybe he remembered his name after all. Or part of it, at least.'

Norris's eyes widened. 'But I know a Charlie Pigeon. He works in the ticket kiosk at the Gaumont cinema.'

'You mean he could still be living in South Shields?' Sylvie said.

'I believe he does. ***They do.'***

Sylvie and Bobby stared at Norris simultaneously. 'They? ***Who's they?'***

'Charlie and Eva …. Eva Shawcross.'

'You mean Eva Shawcross, the district nurse?'

'I do.'

'So … Charlie and Eva are boy and girlfriend?' said Sylvie. 'Living over the brush?'

Bobby sniggered. 'We don't use that terminology anymore, sweetums. Couples live together all the time these days.'

'I need to know if this woman is right for my Charlie. In fact I need to know ***everything about her.*** Do you remember, Bobby, when we were searching the microfiche?'

'How could I forget?'

'I found a stillbirth entry for Eva Shawcross. It was an accidental discovery, but I wrote it down anyways. Oh, what was the flaming date again?' She searched the walls for inspiration. Then blurted, 'Nineteen bloody sixty five! See, the old cogs are still turning.'

'And was Charlie Pigeon the father?' asked Bobby.

'Father unknown, it said. She was listed as ***'spinster.'***

'So probably not his child then.'

'Who knows? But in 1965 there was more of a stigma that went with illegitimate pregnancies. She may have just wanted to protect Charlie.'

'Why don't you just ask him?'

'Bobby, are you mad? So I take a casual stroll to the ticket office and say, "Hey Charlie, I know I buggered off and left you forty years ago, but I was just wondering if that baby Eva lost in 1965 was yours?" You crazy person.'

Norris tapped his forehead with two fingers. 'It ***must*** have been his child. They were an item before that, I'm sure.'

'How sure?'

'Back then, I went to the cinema every week. It was my guilty pleasure, if you like. Those black and white films were just wonderful. Still are.' His eyes turned wistful, lips turned up in the shape of a happy banana.

'And?'

'Oh sorry, yes, well …I remember Eva, must have been in her late teens, hanging round the ticket office fawning over Charlie lots of times. Saw them when they were walking out together, holding hands.'

'Do you know what the difference is in ages between them, Norris?'

'Oh, she's younger, I think. She was born in this parish. There's an entry for her birth somewhere in these books.'

'Don't suppose you know which? Norris?'

'Why don't we have a spot of tea, first? I can see it's going to be a long afternoon.'

CHAPTER 25 : HOGGY GETS A GRILLING

In a tiny consulting room somewhere down the back passage of the cop shop, Hoggy watched with fascination as the police doctor cleaned and dressed his hand.

'I doesn't have much to do with anythin' white, doc, and that bandage is a proper Bobby dazzler, i'n't it so?'

'It's the only colour we have, Hoggy. Just remember to keep it out of the shower or it'll never heal.'

'They has showers in here? Well, I'll be blowed. Last time I had one o' those was back in '69.'

The doc seemed unsurprised. 'They have a gym too. And I heard a whisper that's where they're taking you next. Oh, and there'll be a prescription waiting for your toe nail problem. And don't forget to remind officer Chince that you need to have a good dollop of cream applied three times a day.'

Cream? Was there to be a proper high tea with scones next? Maybe that was ***after*** the gym. Suspicion lingered in a gloomy corner of Hoggy's mind, what with all this sudden care for his welfare. He still wasn't sure why he had been arrested. If the Conway woman was about to fit him up for the murder of that Ruby girl, wouldn't they just lock him up and toss the key? Never mind patching him up first. No, this had to be tactics. A bit like leading a trusting lamb to the slaughter. Well, he was having none of it. He set his brain on full alert and determined to keep it there.

'Right, officer Chince, he's all yours,' said the doc as he tied the bandage at Hoggy's wrist, giving it a good luck pat.

'C'mon then, fella,' said Chinless. 'D.S. Conway wants you down the gym. How are you on the ropes?' He guffawed, but the humour completely missed its target.

∞∞∞

Conway stood in the corridor clutching a recording device and a thin cardboard file as she directed two boiler-suited men struggling inside the gymnasium with a large desk between them.

Another followed behind with a stack of plastic chairs.

'No, not in the middle for God's sake!' She wagged a finger in the far distance. 'Over by the window .... for the view.'

The men, sensing they were in the presence of someone with fearful powers, followed their instructions in silence, leaving her to find out for herself that the view she spoke of was that of police dogs taking shits in the yard.

The furniture arranged to her satisfaction, she indicated with a hand gesture for Chinless and Hoggy to enter, as the helping hands slunk from the room.

Conway placed her equipment on the desk. 'Right, let's get this done and dusted,' she said, waiting for a chair to magically slide out from under the table. Chinless obliged, and Hoggy sat opposite.

'Unfortunately, we're still waiting for forensic feedback on the shoes you discarded earlier, so I thought best we crack on with the interview.' She flipped open the file, hitting the record button on her stand-in machine.

'The date is Tuesday 5th September 1986. The time, 13.32 hrs. Present in the room are D.S. Conway and D.C. Chince conducting an interview with the suspect known as Mr. Hoggy, arrested today in connection with the murder of Ruby Porter.'

'Erm, missus, ***it's not Mister.***'

'I beg your pardon?'

'It's just Hoggy. Not Mister, missus.'

Conway dragged a palm down each side of her face, revealing the innards of her bottom eyelids. ***'I beg you so many pardons,*** Hoggy. Now can we just get on?'

'Where wouldst tha like me to start?' He stood up and removed his jacket. Conway's brows crinkled in anguish.

'How about at the beginning?'

He began to make his way across the room, pointing at the apparatus. 'Tha means this 'ere jumpy thing with handles on top? We used to call these 'orses. Stupid name if tha asks me.'

Chinless stood up. 'Hoggy,' he said, 'please sit down. You're here to be questioned, not exercised.'

'But tha said ....'

'Please, just sit down.'

Hoggy returned to his seat, disappointed to have his level of fitness dismissed just like that. He stared up at the ropes, even more confused than ever. Perhaps they planned to have him swinging by the neck, rather than the hands.

'For the tape, Mr. Hoggy…. ***Hoggy,*** has returned to his seat,' said Conway. 'Can you tell me where and when you sustained the injury to your hand?'

Hoggy showed his new bandage fondly. 'Oh this? Well, missus, you was there when I did this.'

'I was?'

'Tha was at the Broadstairs' caravan when I done it with the screwdriver. Not castin' any blame you understands, but you was doubtin' The Stranglers' lyrics, and I never gets those wrong. ***Not ever.'***

'Well, I didn't see that happen, so your explanation doesn't stack up I'm afraid.'

Chinless scribbled a note on the papers in front of him and Conway continued.

'Where were you on Friday, 1st September between the hours of 8 and 10 p.m?'

Hoggy looked up at the ropes again, scratching his head. He'd best get these answers right, because she must have them already written down.

'I was readin' a bit o' Shakespeare in the shed as it 'appens.'

Conway arched an eyebrow. 'Really? And I was herding bears in the south of France.'

'Well .... on ***thy*** wages, I imagine tha couldst do that ***every*** weekend.'

Conway looked desperately around the room. The man was driving her mad.

∞∞∞

Seymour Witless made his way back to the police station. Thankfully, no-one appeared to be manning the desk, and he continued through the building to his office. Outside the door, he paused. His name plate had been removed, and in its place was D.S. Conway's name embossed on a length of Dymo tape. It was unimpressive, but still it irked him. He went inside and found a space where his desk used to be, and the telephone had been demoted to the floor. He'd only just managed to close the door behind him before the phone suddenly rang and his guts leapt to his throat. He picked up the handset.

'Seymour Witless.'

'Ah, Shitless! Where the hell have you been?'

'Sir Hugo, I'm actually on leave on the moment. Is there something you wanted to speak to me about?'

'Well, I've had this blood tested on the shoes, but the request hasn't come from you .... It's from erm ..... hold on a mo.'

'D.S. Conway. She made the request, I believe.'

'That's the one, yes I have it here.'

'So, is the blood Ruby Porter's?'

'Of course it bloody well isn't! Completely different type all together. Quite a rare one in fact. Anyway, I'm faxing you a copy of the result now, and something else I must tell you about ***the real cause*** of Ruby's death, and I'm sorry to say I didn't spot this earlier.'

The fax machine by the window burst into life at that moment. It was slow and loud, and Seymour could barely hear what Sir Hugo was trying to tell him. Something about Ruby's eyeballs. He stuck a finger into one ear.

'Can you repeat that, Sir Hugo? Only louder?' He had to concentrate his full attention on what Sir Hugo said next, just as the door burst open and Craddock appeared, this time in full uniform, looking cross.

Witless spoke into the phone. 'I have to go, Sir Hugo.'

'Oh, righteo, I'll send the secondary report over as soon it's written up. Cheerio!'

'I ***thought*** I heard someone in here,' said Craddock. 'Go home, Witless, you're on leave. And what's more this room is unsafe.'

'Unsafe?'

'Conway said she could smell gas, so we're having it investigated.'

Seymour sniffed the air. 'I don't smell anything. Do you?'

'No, but we can't take any risks.'

'But there aren't any gas pipes in here. Where is Conway now?'

'She's in the gymnasium, interviewing a suspect.'

'The gymnasium? What's wrong with the interview rooms?'

Craddock raised a hand to his mouth and gave a tiny cough. 'They smell of gas too, apparently.'

'Well if that's true, perhaps the best course of action would be to evacuate the building.'

'I'm …. considering that.'

'Right. And while you're doing that, would you mind telling me which suspect is being interviewed? The one she brought in this morning?'

'***Some vagrant*** is my understanding.'

Seymour whipped across to the fax machine and tore off the print-out.

'I see. Well in that case, you'll have to excuse me, sir.' And with that, he swept past Craddock and out of the door.

∞∞∞

Peering through the swing doors, Seymour fought the urge to fly straight in there, scoop up his friend and take off through an open window to the Fortress of Solitude. But in the absence of super powers and a red cape, he'd just have to bluff his way through like he always did.

He observed, waiting for the right moment. Then Hoggy raised his injured palm and began to loosen the knot in his bandage. Conway made an unraveling movement with her hand while Hoggy watched her closely, imitating the same. This was the moment. Seymour threw open the doors and heads turned as he strode across the room towards the desk.

'Leave your dressing alone, Hoggy. Why are you taking it off?'

'Hoggy wanted to show us his injury, didn't you, Hoggy?' Conway said.

'No, missus, that's a lie. Tha asked me ***to prove*** I has one. That's not the same.'

'Why does he need to prove it? Do you imagine the police doc bandaged his hand for no reason?'

Conway traced a forefinger along the edge of her file.

'The possibility occurred to me that he'd sustained the injury in his cell. By his own hand.'

'And how would he have done that?'

'He had a safety pin. In his pants.'

'Would that be the safety pin ***given to him here,*** when he surrendered the string holding up his trousers?'

'That's correct,' she admitted with a painful squint.

Seymour shook his head. 'You have so much to learn, D.S. Conway. He glanced at the recording device. The red light was off. 'Why aren't you recording this interview?'

'To be fair,' said Hoggy, 'she did, up until we got to talkin' holidays, then her nostrils spread wide and she switched it arf.'

Conway grimaced, shuffling in her seat like she had a serious hemorrhoid problem while Chinless kept taking notes as instructed.

Seymour's bushy brows flipped upside down in puzzlement. 'I wonder why she would do a thing like that?' He took a chair from the stack and sat down next to Hoggy. 'Have they told you you're entitled to free legal advice, Hoggy?'

'Tha' means a lawyer, don't it? And I's done nuthin' wrong.'

'Lawyers are for innocents too, Hoggy. In fact ***they*** need them more than the guilty ones. D.S. Conway should have explained that, and since she didn't, I'm offering myself to sit in and support you.'

'Well, I is happy to have tha here, Seymour.'

'Good. So if D.S. Conway would flip that switch and record again, we can continue.'

Conway had no option but to resume recording. 'D.C.I. Witless has joined the interview at 14.20 hrs, in place of legal support for the suspect known as Hoggy.'

Witless corrected that statement.

'D.C.I. Witless ***officially*** joined the interview at 14.12 hrs, but the recording device had been switched off by D.S. Conway in the interim. Would you remind us, D.S. Conway, the purpose of this interview, and what it is in connection with?'

Conway inhaled, blinking slowly before answering.

'Mr. Hoggy ….. ***Hoggy, I beg your pardon,*** has been arrested in connection with the murder of Ruby Porter.'

'And is there evidence to support this arrest?'

'We're waiting for the lab results on Hoggy's shoes.'

'So this in an informal interview, and Hoggy can leave at any time until you get those results?'

'Well, ***he has*** been picked out of a line up by a witness,' she argued.

'A witness to what? Disposing of a pair of blood-stained shoes?'

'Blood that may belong to the murder victim, Ruby Porter.'

'And if it ***does not*** belong to Ruby Porter?'

'Then Hoggy is free to go.'

Witless slipped a hand inside his coat and pulled out the faxed copy of Sir Hugo's blood analysis. 'There's your lab result.' He tossed it down onto the desk and stood up. 'C'mon, Hoggy, we're leaving.' As she unfolded the paper, he helped Hoggy on with his jacket. 'And while I can understand the desire to have all trace of me eradicated from your space, D.S Conway, perhaps you'd find the common courtesy to ask permission before removing my nameplate and desk from my office. And as for your gas problem, the engineer has not detected any leak. He's sitting in his van outside right now, writing up his report to that effect. Turns out the drains need investigating.'

∞∞∞

Chapter 26 : An act of Sabotage

Sylvie faced two choices next morning. To force herself out of bed or risk drowning in dog saliva. The prodigal Chihuahua's tongue had been stuck on catch-up mode for thirty minutes, and even if she happened to survive from that, her bladder was about to release a second threat of the same nature. Dragging her feet to the bathroom, she just had time to peer into the mirror, a daily habit developed over the last thirty odd years, hoping the Oil of Ulay had lived up to its promise. Sadly, it had let her down yet again, so she took a pee, releasing a heavy sigh.

'Sylvie, sweetums? That you?' Bobby called from the dining table.

'No, it's Liberace, just popped in to give you a piano recital.' She rubbed the sleep from her eyes before condemning the thief. 'You're eating my bloody hot cross buns.'

'Found your secret stash. Have you tried them toasted with melted cheese and a banana on top?'

'Eurgh, what a gannet you are, Bobby Mason. Why can't you have a hangover like a normal person?'

'My liver, sweetums, is in its prime, that's why. Time enough for hangovers when I'm your age. There's tea in the pot.'

'Thank God you're good for summat.' She found herself a mug and poured the tea.

'Some secrets crawled out of the woodwork last night, huh?'

'I'm still reeling from it all.'

'Especially the Carolyn Carr exposé. That hit you hard, I could tell, sweetums.'

'How naïve was I? To be married to someone for eight years and not know that they had a secret child together.'

'So, where are we off today then, super sleuth?'

'Well, narrowing the suspects down the way we have, I want to concentrate on Ernie's cryptic rhyme. When I spoke to Seymour on the phone last night, we shared a few thoughts on what it might mean. I want to go back to the Shoreline. Persuade Prudence to let me look around.'

'Use your womanly wiles, you mean?'

'Oh God, I hope that's not necessary.'

'What makes you think you'll find anything at the Shoreline?'

Sylvie sat down at the table and pulled Ernie's note from her dressing gown pocket. 'Because it says here, *"**Do your jewels hang low? Can you tie 'em in a bow? Can You wrap 'em round your neck? Will you swing 'em to and fro?**"* Which most likely refers to ….'

'The missing diamond.'

'And then, ***"Try to bounce 'em off the wall, where the sailor's alcohaul***

Hides behind the secret door in the place along the shore." Which could mean?'

Bobby swallowed the last of his hot cross bun and shrugged. 'I … am clueless.'

'C'mon, Bobs, it's obvious! The place along the shore could mean The Shoreline? And we're looking for a secret door. And once we find that …'

'Bob's your uncle.'

'And Fanny's your aunt.'

∞∞∞

Clarabelle wasn't being left behind again. She lay on the back seat of the car, fully alert as Sylvie headed down to the Coast Road and Bobby sat in the passenger seat clutching an extra hot cross bun and a banana inside a brown paper bag.

'It won't be the same - ***cold,*** will it?' said Bobby.

'Probably not, Bobs. But if you don't want it, I'll take it off your hands.'

'Feeling peckish now, are we? I was starting to worry about you.'

'The appetite goes when the cogs are turning. Now there's an end in sight, I can feel the pressure lifting. Stomach's crying out for sustenance.' Sylvie glanced in her rear view mirror. 'Oh look, Bobby. Is that Seymour behind us?'

Bobby craned his neck. 'So it is. He's flashing his lights. I'll give him a wave. Hellooo Seymour. Is he following us?'

'Could be. Probably stuck for something to do, bless him.'

Approaching the turn, she gave the slightest touch to the brake pedal.

'That feels a bit odd.'

'What does, sweets?'

'Brakes feel a bit loose. More bloody expense, no doubt.'

Turning the car at the top of Marsden Bank, she changed gear to accommodate the downward slope and the vehicle suddenly sped out of control.

'Sweetums, the brake! Hit the bloody brake!'

Sylvie's foot flopped frantically up and down on the brake pedal. 'Bloody brakes have gone, Bobs! Shit!'

Clarabelle pawed at the side window and began to howl like a demented coyote.

Suddenly, Witless appeared alongside with window down, yelling, 'HANDBREAK TURN AT THE BOTTOM - STEER SHARP LEFT. QUICK AS YOU CAN!' Then just as suddenly, he dropped back behind her.

Blood drained from Sylvie's face; knuckles too, as she clung to the wheel in desperation, waiting for the perfect time.

'Three .... two .... one .... TURN!' Bobby shouted. Tyres screeched as she tugged on the handbrake and attempted a swerve onto the Coast Road, but instead veered across it diagonally, straight into the path of an oncoming Northern double-decker bus. Fortunately, both driver's brakes and reactions were in perfect working order, as was his potty mouth. Despite the car's speed having dropped dramatically, it mounted the pavement, continued across the grass verge, heading for the cliff-tops. Bobby farted, dropped his lunch and clung to the passenger seat instead.

'WE'RE GONNA DIE, SWEETUMS .... '

'Are we hellers-like Bobs,' said Sylvie, trying to steer as best she could, but the Metro had its own ideas. Bobby squeezed his eyes tight shut.

'I do love you sweetums .... You've been better than a real mam to me ... I want you to know that.'

'Shut up, Bobs. I'm trying to concentrate.'

At a mere two yards from the cliff edge, a sudden jolt stopped the car dead. Witless's Morris Minor stood proud, if a little bent with its nose pressed into the side of the Metro. Sylvie checked her passengers. Instinctively, Clarabelle had leapt to the other end of the seat while Bobby remained frozen to his.

'Open your eyes, Bobs. It's not quite Heaven, but it's the next best thing I reckon. Look at that view.'

Bobby prised them open, one at a time. Beyond the car bonnet, all he could see was a sheer drop.

'You're sick. You know that?'

Witless stepped out of the Morris, donning latex gloves as he approached the Metro.

'You two alright?' he asked.

Bobby opened his passenger door and staggered onto the grass verge closely followed by Clarabelle.

'We're okay, just a bit shaken up. How did you know to do that?'

'Something we learn in basic training. I'd like to take a look under the bonnet. Can you flip it open?'

Sylvie flipped the switch, unbuckled her belt and crawled across to Bobby's side to exit the vehicle.

'My lovely car. Can you fix it, Seymour?'

'I can't touch it. This is a case for C.S.I. and an R.P.V.E.'

'I've no idea what any of that means, but I've just W.E.T. myself.'

'I'll call someone. Get you checked over.'

'No, I'm fine. The Tena Lady's taking care of it.'

'Tena Lady? ***Who's the Tena Lady?'***

Bobby waved a dismissive hand. 'Don't ask.'

'Whatever. Anyway, I can tell just by looking that the brake fluid pipe's been deliberately pierced.

I knew something was wrong because your brake lights were on all the way down Lizard Lane. That's why I flashed you.'

Sylvie gave Bobby's arm a thump. 'And you were giving him a wave hello. Daft sod.'

'Did you hear anything odd during the night? Or early this morning?'

'I don't …. think so.' Sylvie straightened her hat. 'No, wait. Clarabelle did jump out of bed and bark a few times, but she does that a lot anyway. I didn't pay much attention to be honest.'

'Alright, well I'll radio it in and get someone to pick it up. Were you on your way to The Shoreline?'

Sylvie heaved a despondent sigh. 'We were. Just when I thought we were getting somewhere, this happens.'

'Well, ***my*** car's okay. It may need a few dents blowing out, but the engine's fine. I can wait in the car park while you talk to Prudence and have a snoop around. Until Conway chucks the towel in I can't get officially involved.'

'Seymour, I could kiss you!'

Seymour recoiled, headed back to his car for the radio, and safety.

∞∞∞

CHAPTER 27 : BACK TO THE SHORELINE

When Sylvie and Bobby turned up at the Shoreline, Prudence was sitting on the edge of the stage, dabbing her eyes with a hanky.

'Prudence? What is it, love?' Sylvie's words bounced off the walls of the empty hall and Prudence jumped. But the comforting sound of a familiar voice turned her frown upside down and she hitched herself down from the stage, landing with a resounding thunk and waddled up the aisle.

'Sylvie! And that lovely fiancée of yours. It's so good to see you.'

'And you. Have you lost weight?'

Prudence gave a coy smile. 'Oh, don't be silly. If only! I say, if you're after a gig, it'll have to be a freebie this Friday because the bailiffs may be coming in next week.'

'Surely it can't be that bad.'

'Been expecting it for a while, really. More clubs opening in the town centre, no-one's coming here anymore. We're doomed, I tell you.'

'The place ***is*** past its best, Pru. Not your fault of course. God knows what the council was thinking building a metal shed next to water. You can smell the neglect a mile downwind. But it's not over until….'

'…The fat lady sings, I know. Well I won't be prompting fate by doing that anytime soon. Maybe I'm being too much of a drama queen as usual.' She wiped her cheek with the heel of her hand and forced a smile. 'Would you like a drop of the hard stuff? At least a few of the optics are still up and working.'

'I won't, thanks Pru. How about you, Bobby?'

'Wouldn't mind a coffee if there's one going. And maybe a packet of salt 'n' vinegar?'

'Bobby!' Sylvie scolded. 'Actually, Pru, I was wondering if I could show Bobby the old dressing room I used all those years ago. He's been ***so interested*** to know everything about me, you know how it is.' She gave Bobby's shoulder an affectionate rub. 'Would you mind if I took him on a tour?'

'Of course not, Sylvie. Ernie used the same one, you know. In fact there may be one or two keepsakes you'd like to reclaim before they bulldoze the place. Do you want me to play escort? Or can you manage on your own while I make this coffee?'

'We'll just have a mosey around ourselves if that's okay.'

'It could even be romantic, couldn't it, sweetums?' said Bobby, complete with sarcasm.

Sylvie gave him an elbow poke to the ribs. 'We'll be back in a few minutes.' And off they scarpered.

Ernie's dressing room smelled of mould. A damp patch on the ceiling had dried then refreshed itself so many times it had morphed into the spitting image of Big Bird from Sesame Street. Nelson had apparently found his way back and lay in his basket with an exceedingly grumpy face. Bobby twitched his nose.

'Where the hell do we start?'

But Sylvie was already off, searching the dresser. 'Check that filing cabinet in the corner, can you, Bobs?'

Drawers and doors banged, their contents shuffled.

'Just paperwork, sweetums, an empty rum bottle and a jar that says ***tea money***. Oh, my God!'

'What, Bobs?'

'There's a bloody dildo in here!' He switched it on. It lit up, twirled a full 360 degrees and vibrated.

'For God's sake, Bobs. Put it back!'

Bobby huffed, but did as he was told.

Sylvie turned to the walls, strewn with posters from past acts. She ran her palms across them, feeling for the edge of a door she hoped she might be lucky enough to find.

'Copy me, Bobs. If you can feel anything at all.... investigate further.'

'Why don't we just tear all of these down? They're wrecked anyways.'

'Because we don't want Pru to know we're looking for anything in particular, ***that's why.'***

Bobby was having a good feel of The Hot Hunks when Sylvie began picking at the blue tack holding up one of Ernie's drag posters. He stopped as she peeled it from the wall. A carved wooden plaque sat behind it.

'What's that?' he said.

'That's a plaque of The Jolly Sailor, Bobs. Have you got a screwdriver?'

Bobby patted himself down. 'Oddly enough, I'm fresh out of manly tools, sweets.'

Sylvie opened her handbag and rooted around in the bottom. 'Sure I've got a nail file in here somewhere .... Aha!' She pulled out a small metal file. Slotting the broad end into one of the two screw heads she began turning. The first was stiff, but after a bit of momentum, both came out easily. She pulled gently on the loosened side, and hidden hinges on the opposite side allowed the 'door' to swing open.

Behind it was a small recess carved into the plaster, where a half bottle of Smirnov vodka stood on guard up front. Sylvie removed it, and behind was a clock mechanism with folded papers inside a polythene bag and a fist-sized tissue-wrapped object. Bobby watched open-mouthed, when suddenly there was a knock on the door.

'Are you two decent in there?' Prudence had clearly finished making the coffee.

Sylvie snatched both mechanism and object from their hiding place and closed the wooden 'door.'

'Hang on a minute, Pru. Bobby just has to make himself decent.'

Bobby's eyes popped with indignation, while his faux fiancée stuffed the items into her bag, snapped it shut and re-attached the poster to the wall just as Prudence cracked open the door. Bobby made a show of smoothing out his hair.

'What are you two like?' Prudence grinned. 'Are you coming out for coffee, or shall I bring it in?'

'We're right behind you, Prudence, just lead the way…'

∞∞∞

Witless peered closely at the collision damage to his left wing while he waited in the car park, wondering if Craddock would allow him to claim the cost on expenses. The Morris was, after all, a classic car, and his action could not have been avoided. It was surely worth a try, anyway. Clarabelle stared at him through the front passenger window with a doubtful face. What was it, he wondered, about animals and mind reading? They all had the ability, he was completely convinced.

It was then that Sylvie and Bobby came rushing out of the building, bickering as usual, this time over salt 'n' vinegar crisps, or rather the lack of them.

'Oh, Seymour, I'm so sorry about your car,' Sylvie empathized. 'But when you see what we've found, you'll know our lives were worth saving.'

'So, you ***did*** find something then?'

'Well, we haven't actually opened it yet, but it feels positive.'

'Sweetums, judging by Ernie's wicked sense of humour, it's more likely to be a lump of coal. Or even an intimate body part.' Bobby suggested.

Sylvie winced. ***'Now who's being disgusting?'***

'Shall we go somewhere more private for the great unveiling?' Seymour glanced around. 'You never know who might be watching.' He opened the rear passenger door. 'Hop inside. We can go to mine. Tracey's dog sitting again.'

∞∞∞

Seymour steered his precious car onto a wide open road in an old part of town. The gardens were sculpted with topiary carved hedges in the shape of ice cream swirls and unidentifiable rodents. Seymour's, however, was an unimaginative box shape. Rambo peered over the back of an armchair from the front downstairs window, nose pressed against the glass. And a tall, unshaven middle-aged man waited by the gate clutching a hold-all and smoking a cigarette.

'Oh, God, not him again.'

'Is that your brother, Seymour?' Sylvie asked. 'He's persistent, I'll give him that.'

Seymour climbed out of the car prepared for battle, followed by Bobby and Sylvie, her handbag slung over one arm, while Clarabelle snuggled beneath the other.

'I can't talk to you now, Frank. As you can see, I'm rather busy.'

'Well, when can you then?' said Frank, tossing down his cigarette and grinding it beneath his foot.

'This is a tidy street, Frank. Pick that up, if you don't mind.' The brothers couldn't have exchanged more filthy looks if they tried. After a four-second stand-off, Frank bent down, picked up his fag end and reluctantly shoved it inside his jacket pocket.

'Come back in an hour,' Seymour relented. '***I might*** be able to see you then.'

After a moment, Frank turned and headed away from the house, with a new, pronounced limp.

'Right then, team. Seems like I'm all yours. For a while, anyway.'

For one man and his dog living alone, the house was surprisingly tidy, though sparsely furnished. Rambo was banished to the kitchen for chastity reasons, while Clarabelle sat outside the door, whining every now and then, but listening always.

Seymour came back into the living room where the rest of the team sat patiently waiting. He moved over to the window and closed the curtains.

'Are we all ready?' he said.

'There should be a drum roll for this,' said Bobby.

Sylvie opened her handbag. 'I may swear ***if this is a bloody potato***.' She cupped her hand around the tissue-wrapped object and placed it on the coffee table in front of her. She took off the first layer. Then the second. 'It doesn't feel like a potato.'

'Coal, perhaps?' said Tracey.

'That's what I was thinking,' said Bobby.

'No coal dust,' said Sylvie. 'Can't be that.'

Witless stood up. 'Just whip the last layer off like a sticking plaster. I can't bear it any longer.'

'You do it then.' Sylvie tossed the thing across to Seymour. Unprepared, he let it bounce off his leg and roll across the floor, whereupon Clarabelle suddenly appeared from nowhere, snapped it up and ran up the stairs. Everyone rose to their feet and watched in horror. But it was too big for her tiny jaws. It bounced back down the staircase and landed on the mat by the front door. The final layer of tissue draped itself provocatively around the shoulders of the biggest diamond any of them had ever seen. It was an old European cut stone, faceted to perfection. Beads of light from the door panes danced across its many surfaces.

'That ***cannot*** be real,' said Sylvie. 'I bet the two of them planned this together all along. I mean, look at us all, plotting how much of a share we could all have, what we could spend the money on. They likely bought it down the market for a quid.'

Seymour picked it up. 'Whether it's genuine or not, we have to keep it somewhere safe until we hand it in.'

'This is all happening in the wrong order, sir,' said Tracey. 'We're meant to be solving the murders first. The discovery of this …. whatever it is, is secondary. And if we hand it in now, Conway will take the credit and we'll be warned off the case again. Might even be suspended.'

'You're right, Tracey. I can find a safe place to keep it until we fit all the pieces together.'

'We're almost there, Seymour. I can feel it in my water,' said Sylvie. 'You ***must*** come to the Saint Martin's gig tomorrow night. All the suspects are going to be there. I just have two more visits to make before then.'

'I thought you were barred from gigging at St Martin's?' said Tracey.

'Oh, it's not my gig. It's Mystic Mohawk's. My ***temporary*** replacement.'

'You ***hope*** temporary,' Bobby chipped in.

'Who are you visiting? And why?' Seymour waved his hands around as he spoke. 'Someone's already tried to kill you, Miss Broadstairs. I can't risk sending you off on your own.'

'There's one visit I ***must*** do alone. But you're welcome to be my chauffeur, if you like.'

∞∞∞

CHAPTER 28 : WHEN MOHAWK MET CRYSTAL

'The Food, the Bed and the Snugly' was not your average bed and breakfast stop, situated on yet another terrifyingly steep bank, according to Sylvie, as any bank would be thought of following her recent life-threatening experience. This time however, she'd taken the bus after calling ahead.

From the outside, there was clearly a western theme about the place befitting the name, with murals of Clint Eastwood and Lee van Cleef in the garb of their characters from the famous movie. On the wall behind reception was a sign saying, PLEASE HAND OVER YOUR GUNS TO THE DESK CLERK FOR SAFE KEEPING. In the case of it ***not being*** a tongue-in-cheek recommendation, Sylvie formed a fist around her keys with pointy bits protruding as a means of grossly inadequate defence.

She hit the bell on the counter. Within seconds, a leather waist-coated Randy Jones type from ***The Village People*** appeared in a cowboy hat, chewing gum and polishing a silver beer tankard.

'Howdy, ma'am, what can I get ya?'

Sylvie stifled a smirk. 'I've a meeting with one of your guests, ***Mystic Mohawk***. Can you let him know I'm here please?'

'Sure can do, ma'am,' said Randy picking up the telephone. 'Just grab yerself a seat,' he indicated, pointing the handset toward a nearby couch, 'and ah'll git him down here.'

Sylvie perched her bottom on the edge of the velveteen sofa. Having only spoken briefly to Mystic Mohawk on the phone, she'd found it difficult to assess what kind of person he was. On learning she was also a psychic, he had instantly adopted a more defensive tone. In her experience, this was indicative of a faker, though she could be wrong, and in the grand scheme of things, it didn't matter a jot.

Heavy footsteps shook the floor before he appeared at the foot of the staircase, dressed in a native American fringed jacket with greying hair plaits hanging over his shoulders, and a guarded expression across his face. After a few seconds of gazing, Sylvie began to laugh.

'It's never Stinky Simon, from Bessie Street Juniors?'

'Aw … get the hell out o' here! Sylvie Broadstairs, as I live and breathe.' He clasped both her hands as she came towards him. 'You still have those bright eyes and wicked smile, I see.'

'And you don't smell like a swamp anymore …. thank God.'

'You are relentless! Why didn't you tell me your real name? ***Crystal Gazer,*** indeed.'

'Well, look who's talking … Mystic flaming Mohawk. And what's with the American accent?'

'I've been living in the States for forty years. Retired and decided to come back home. Then I got bored and created this guy you see before you.' He spread out his arms. 'Whadya think?'

'Just …. fabby, I guess. I'm coming to see you tomorrow at St. Martins' and I can't tell you how pleased I am to find an old mate. I need to ask you a ***big*** favour.'

'Sure …. Let me get you a drink and we can catch up.'

∞∞∞

Sylvie left the meeting place with a satisfied smile on her face. At the bottom of the hill, Seymour waited in his battered Morris as arranged, starting up the engine as she came towards him.

'How was it?' he asked, as she climbed into the passenger seat.

'Much better than expected as it goes. Went to school with the fella many moons ago. What a turn up for the books. And my God, he could talk a glass eye to sleep.'

'And he's willing to go along with the plan tomorrow night?'

'He couldn't be more helpful, Seymour. I'm gobsmacked. By the way, what happened with Frank? Did he come back?'

'He did.'

'And?'

'He's on the sofa, just for tonight.'

'You big old softy. What happened to his leg?'

'Well, that's why I had to give him a second chance really. He says when he came round earlier, Rambo bit him. Hopefully they're burying the hatchet as we speak.'

'Did Tracey see it happen?'

'Not exactly, but Frank did try to barge his way in uninvited and Rambo's very protective, so it's possible.' Seymour released the hand brake. 'Anyway, where are we off to next?'

'The Gaumont cinema. This one might be a bit more tricky.'

Seymour drove off slowly.

'Maybe you should think about this a bit more, Miss Broadstairs. Charlie Pigeon could well be our man. And if he is, you can't be sure how he'll react to you turning up after all this time.'

'I know you're concerned, Seymour. But I can't believe I raised a killer.'

'But only for eight years. Beyond that, he's been through bad times. Could very well be a loose cannon. And here ***you are*** providing the gun powder.'

∞∞∞

It was early afternoon and Charlie Pigeon was just starting the late shift behind the counter at the Gaumont cinema. Afternoon screenings at the end of the long school summer holiday were pretty much pointless. Parents' money had run out and the kids were left to their own devices, indulging in cheaper pursuits such as pyromania and animal torment. In view of this decreased workload, Charlie's boss Mr. Lennox expected him to handle both sweet counter and ticket kiosk on his own. He also expected front line staff to be dressed formally at all times, and Charlie's outfit today was no exception, despite the tiny audience. The MacLeod tartan was the favourite of his two three-piece suits, stretching to four piece if you counted the matching bow tie. Although side burns had long since had their day, Charlie's cheeks were amply adorned, and he wore a slicked-back teddy boy quiff to rival Danny Zuco's from Grease.

Still not feeling quite himself after a recent bout of sickness, Charlie busied himself refilling empty counter spaces with Dime Bars, Opal Fruits, Marathons, and replenishing the fridge with cans of Lilt. And he did it quickly, before they changed all their names. Screening that afternoon was Herbie goes Bananas, but that wasn't quite Charlie's cup of tea. He preferred The Aristocats any day.

'Charlie? …. unload those cartons of John Players from the van before the kids break in and help themselves, will ya? There's a box of condoms for the machine in the gents as well.' Lennox tossed his keys down on the counter. 'Her indoors insists I don't strain meself before this weekend's dance marathon. ***Personally,*** a back strain would be divine in comparison.'

Charlie winced, as a sharp pain shot through his stomach. He snatched up the keys. 'Course, Mr. Lennox. Do you want the fags in the store room?'

Lennox checked the stock under the counter. 'Maybe one carton in here, the rest in the store. And by the way, put your goddam glasses on. I don't want you handing out packs of three instead of packs of ten.'

Charlie used the side exit, while Lennox wandered over to the double glass doors, idly polishing over a finger smudge with his apron just as Seymour cruised past in the Morris.

'Is that him?' asked Seymour.

'No, he's far too old. And bald. Norris says Charlie's a dapper dresser. He'd never greet the public in a pinny like that.'

'Where do you want me to park then?'

'Just pull up a few yards ahead. I need to devise a plan.'

Charlie opened up the van's rear doors. Lennox was right. The stock could easily be seen through the back windows. There were six cartons of cigarettes in all; awkward, but not too heavy to carry all at once. He stacked them on the pavement before securing the van. But as he did so, another shooting pain pierced his innards and he fell to his knees. Two young boys hanging around on the opposite corner had a quick exchange of words and one of them ran across.

'You all right, mister?' The boy's gaze swept from the ciggy cartons to the ailing man on his knees, then back to his mate waiting across the street.

Charlie threw up. 'Does it look like I'm all bloody right? Go get the boss …. from inside, will ya? Please?'

'What's it worth?'

'Oh, Christ! Aargh! I just need some bloody help! What do you want?'

'Giz one o' those, and I'll go get him.'

'Here …. take the bloody thing!'

The boy tossed a carton to his mate, now standing by. Then he pulled open the side door of the picture house and shouted, 'YER TEDDY BOY NEEDS AN AMBULANCE! HE'S DYING OUT HERE!' And with that he turned and ran away.

'You're having second thoughts, aren't you?' said Seymour. 'Look, there's no harm done. I can just take you back home.'

'What if I just go in and pose as a customer? Strike up a conversation that way?'

'Miss Broadstairs, it's a kids' matinée. And I haven't the slightest intention of posing as your grandson, nor as a fan of Herbie the ruddy talking car, or whatever madness it is he does.'

Suddenly, sirens cut through the chatter, and both heads turned as an ambulance pulled up outside the cinema. Lennox dragged open the heavy doors and let the paramedics inside.

'What the hell?' said Sylvie.

They watched as a stretcher was loaded into the ambulance carrying a dapper dresser with a wayward quiff.

'That's my Charlie,' said Sylvie. 'Follow that ambulance, Seymour!'

∞∞∞

Chapter 29 : Charlie's mystery illness & Royston's mystery girlfriend.

Seymour dropped Sylvie at the doors of Accident and Emergency while he found a parking space. A queue of three ambulances waited outside, and Sylvie hesitated, taking deep breaths in an effort to calm herself. Then she headed for the straggler at the end.

'Scuse me,' she said to the paramedic leaning against his vehicle, sucking on a matchstick. 'Is your patient Charlie Pigeon by any chance?'

A broad grin swept across his face.

'Nah, lady. This one's Roger Rabbit.' He cocked his head at the vehicle in front. 'Try the next one up. I think I can see some tail feathers sticking out the back.'

This wasn't the first time she'd been made an object of fun, and in normal circumstances she'd have come back with a suitable jibe. But this time she felt the red mist rising, and just as she was deciding whether to check inside the ambulance for herself or to swing at him with her handbag, Seymour's arm stretched across her shoulder clutching his badge.

'D.C.I. Witless. Who is the patient you're carrying please?'

The paramedic straightened himself up, plucked the matchstick from his mouth and coughed. 'Erm….one moment. I'll check with my colleague. ***Glenda! What's this patient's name again? The officer wants to know.***' Glenda checked.

'It's …. King …. Edward. I mean, ***Edward King, sir.***' Glenda's cheeks flushed. 'Sorry, the surname always comes first.'

'Thank you,' said Seymour, moving on to the ambulance in front with Sylvie shuffling after. 'This is difficult for you, I understand, Miss Broadstairs. I'm happy to handle these people. Try and relax.'

One of the rear doors of the next ambulance was already open and Sylvie couldn't resist a peek. 'It's him, Seymour. ***It's Charlie,***' she said.

'Just hang fire. We can do this according to procedure. Stay calm.'

At that point, a patient at the head of the queue was loaded into a wheelchair, taken inside and the vehicle moved away. Charlie's ambulance edged forward. He was now head of the queue. Sylvie took another peek inside. An oxygen mask swamped half of his face and his head was propped up on a pillow. He opened his eyes, and Sylvie quickly pulled her head back behind the door.

'This is torture, Seymour. I'm losing it.'

'Of course you're not. Once he's admitted, it should be plain sailing. He doesn't seem to be on his last legs anyway. Maybe it's just an asthma attack or something.'

Seymour poked his head around the open rear door, raising his badge at the paramedic seated beside the patient's trolley.

'Excuse me, I'm D.C.I. Witless. Is this patient Charlie Pigeon?'

'That's right. Can I help?' she said, stepping down onto the tarmac and partially closing the door for the sake of discretion.

'Can you tell me what the patient presented with, and if he's told you anything related to his condition?'

'He thinks … ' she looked around and lowered her voice. 'I mean … He presented with severe stomach pains and vomiting. Also breathlessness.

But he suffers from anxiety and takes medication for that. So it could just be a severe panic attack.' She looked along the line and responded with a hand signal to her partner up ahead. 'Anyway, he's going in now. Speak to reception. They'll inform the staff that you're waiting for information.'

She climbed back on board and rolled Charlie's bed from the back of the vehicle. With her partner in assistance, they dropped the legs on the stretcher and wheeled the patient past Sylvie. For a brief moment, their eyes met, but in his gaze, Sylvie spotted no recollection at all.

∞∞∞

Meanwhile, on Chillbottle Road, D.C. Richard Tracey bounded along the path and up the steps to his father's house clutching grease-stained brown paper bags in both hands. Placing them on the top step, he fumbled in his jacket pocket for a key just as Royston's nosy neighbour, Betty Bristow, swung open her front door. Strands of foil-wrapped hair stood rigid, each at ninety degrees from her scalp. With narrowed eyes and puckered lips, she crossed both arms across her chest.

'You might want to ring the bell first,' she said, nodding at the door bell in question. 'So as to warn him, like.'

'Hello, Mrs. Bristow. And why should I need to warn him?'

'He's entertaining a lady friend.' Betty Bristow raised a disapproving chin. 'This is the second day, and I haven't seen her leave yet.'

'I see. Well I should think after two days he might welcome the interruption.' He pushed his key into the lock. 'Having your hair done, I see?'

'He's losin' his marbles you know. Shouldn't be left on his own.'

'I do my best, Mrs. Bristow. But thanks for the heads up,' he said, retrieving the bags and stepping over the threshold.

'Dad? It's me. Hope you're decent,' he announced louder than usual, nudging the front door closed with his foot.'

'Aye, son. We're just in here,' answered Royston. The Archers' theme tune played on the radio, so that was usual for the time of day.

Tracey pushed open the living room door, peering around it at first. His view was side-on, with Royston sitting on the sofa next to a female figure dressed in clothes he recognized as his mother's. The checked green skirt and purple sweater he remembered from one of her last Christmases. Only the party hat was missing.

'Hello. Um, are you going to introduce me, Dad?' The figure didn't move.

'This is Lucinda,' said Royston. 'She's going to be staying for a bit.' He patted Lucinda's knee as he spoke. 'Come in, lad and say hello. Don't stand there behind the door.'

Tracey took a few cautionary steps inside the room. He felt the warm grease seeping through the food bags as he clutched them tighter. Slowly, his jaw dropped.

'Dad, where did you get … ***Lucinda*** from?'

'Old Bob down the road said he wasn't using her anymore, and I could have her. ***Almost naked she was*** when he brought her round, so I had to find her some of your mother's bits to wear. Lucky I kept some. She's a looker, don't you think?'

'Dad …. you do realize, this is an inflatable doll?'

'Get away with yer! Of course I bloody realize. I'm not gaga yet, thanks very much. I just miss your mother, that's all. No harm in having a bit of company, is there? And the clothes still smell of moth balls.' He sniffed her to demonstrate. 'Tis a comforting smell, don't you think?' Royston switched his attention to the bags in Tracey's hands. 'What have you brought us?'

'Us? I've brought ***you*** some Chinese. I'm not giving Lucinda a plate. I don't care what you say.'

'Take no notice, Lucinda. He'll come around.' Royston raised an eyebrow at his son and frowned. 'Well don't just stand there. Stick it on a plate.'

Reluctantly, Tracey retreated to the kitchen.

'And bring two forks…'

∞∞∞

After a twenty minute wait in A & E for news of Charlie, Seymour took himself off for a stroll. The hospital was like a rabbit's warren, each corridor marked with a coloured line, and he imagined by following the brown one, it might lead to a coffee vending machine. Turning his fifth corner into more hopelessness, he almost collided with Staff Nurse Brenda Cole clutching a clipboard next to her ample bosom.

'Whoah!' he said, grabbing both her forearms impulsively, then, just as quickly releasing his grip. 'Nurse Cole. This ***is*** a coincidence, obviously. Erm, what are you up to?' His cheeks reddened.

'Sure, I'm at my work, Inspector,' she answered, flashing more eyeball than usual, with a slight tilt to one side of her mouth which could have been mistaken for a smirk.

'Of course you are.' He gave a tiny laugh. 'I'm just here with a friend. Giving a lift, you know.'

'I see. What a good Samaritan you are then.'

'Could I ask you…?' he began. But nothing else came.

'Could you ask me what, Inspector?'

'C… Could I ask you where a fella might get a cup of coffee?'

Brenda flipped a shoulder back in the direction she'd come from and pointed a perfectly manicured finger. 'Sure, there's a machine just around the next corner. It only takes fifty pences though mind.'

'Oh, I've a pocket full of those, no worries.' He patted his trousers and a crackle sounded from the radio in his pocket, ***'L.B. to Yankee Papa 69.'***

'Now there's an offer you can't refuse…' her eyes grew wider. 'Well, I'd best get down to A & E with these forms.' She gave a brief wink and started on her way again.

Seymour silenced the radio.

'I … erm…' he began again.

'Yes?'

'I wondered if you'd like to accompany me to a psychic show tomorrow evening?'

'A psychic show?'

'It's um … silly idea, naw, forget it.'

'Okay.' She turned and was gone.

Now, was that okay she would? Or okay, forget it? He rubbed his forehead to bring the answer, then decided a coffee might help.

On his return to the waiting area with the drinks, Sylvie was gone. He took a few steps towards reception, but there was a queue. He doubled back but kept walking, until he found himself in a corridor of treatment bays, peering through gaps in the badly hung curtains. Sylvie's voice was easily recognizable, and he could hear it quite clearly behind the washed out curtains of bay number 4.

'You mean they actually stole a whole carton of cigarettes, while you were lying ill on the pavement?'

'They actually did. I've seen them before, hanging around, trying to nick sweets. Chased them a few times.'

'I just despair. Really I do.'

'And Lennox will take them off my wages, you can bet on it.'

'Whhaaat? Unbelievable! Maybe I should have a word.'

'That's very nice of you, Mrs. Smith, but you're not my mother.'

Sylvie laughed. Rather too forcefully. 'Oh, that's just me, being protective. Can't help myself sometimes. Well, it's been lovely meeting you, Charlie, and hearing your story. Will they be admitting you, do you think?'

'The doc said he wants to do some tests so I may be in here a couple of days. They've already had an armful of the red stuff, and they want me to swallow a hose pipe with a camera on the end, which I can't say I'm looking forward to, but I suppose if it gets to the bottom of this stomach trouble I've been having, it'll be worth it.'

'Oh dear, well if you need someone to hold your hand ….(shuffling noise) … here's my …. number. Maybe I'll see you again sometime. Take care, won't you?'

That was Seymour's cue to distance himself. He almost skipped back to the end of the corridor as the curtain parted and Sylvie emerged.

'And who might Mrs. Smith be?' asked Seymour, as Sylvie took a coffee from his hand.

'I might have known you'd be earwigging. ***Mrs. Smith,*** is a hospital visitor, employed by the Women's Voluntary Institute. Her photo's pinned on the notice board with a dozen others. Turns out I'm her spitting image.' She plucked the lid from the plastic cup, took a sip and grimaced. 'That's … warm and wet, anyway.'

'Really, the security in this place is diabolical. I don't suppose anyone asked for I.D.?'

Sylvie fumbled inside her bag. 'Well, if they had, I'd have shown them this.' She held out her pensioner's bus pass, complete with photo.

Seymour rolled his eyes. 'That's ridiculous. No-one would be fooled by that.'

'Well, Charlie was. Turns out his eyesight is crap, like his father's.'

'Miss Broadstairs, ***you do know*** that posing as a registered member of the voluntary services is an act of fraud?'

'Well if you're gonna arrest me, can you wait until after tomorrow night? I can't miss that performance. ***You*** can't miss that performance either.'

'I'll need to know exactly what he told you, chapter and verse.'

'Of course, Seymour. But let's have our coffee first.'

Nurse Brenda Cole suddenly reappeared at Seymour's side with a folded piece of paper in her hand.

'Inspector, if that invitation was for real, give me a call. She pressed the note in his hand, winked again, and with a swivel of the hips, she turned and went about her business.

'Oohoo, Seymour, you've pulled there, no messing. So is she coming tomorrow night?'

He stared after her. 'Looks like it.'

'Excellent! The whole motley crew of suspects.'

But Seymour was still distracted.

'Earth to Seymour….' Sylvie said.

'Did you see which doctor attended Charlie? I need to speak with him.'

With Seymour out of the way, Sylvie remembered the folded papers she'd claimed as her own, buried inside the polythene cover of the clock mechanism. She lifted the flap of her handbag, fumbled around inside and pulled out two separate papers, one wrapped inside the other. The inner document was yellowing and delicate. She opened it with care. It was a certificate of provenance for the stone, with the country and date of origin, purity, etc. The outer paper was a drawn up legal agreement between two parties, overseen and registered by a local solicitor. As she held up the papers, a smaller piece of notepaper fell out from between.

'Farewell, my sweet little Sylv. I knew you'd solve it - Ernie xxx'

Short and to the point, as always.

Chapter 30 : Brothers at War

Later that day, Seymour reached home with a throbbing head full of practical theories engaged in open warfare with his own silly romantic notions. All he wanted was to empty his mind with the help of some brainless television, a quick fry up and a beer.

Live radio coverage of the 4.30 from Chepstow galloped through the house as he stepped across the threshold, with a pervading pong of chicken teriyaki invading his nostrils. He slung his raincoat over a hook on the wall and marched up the hallway. The sight of Rambo greeting him with tail end swinging made him crouch to reciprocate with a double ear tickle, and he softened.

'Hello, old boy. What you been up to today? Bite anymore legs? Because I wouldn't scold you at all. You'd be saving me the bother.' He groaned as he stood upright, kicked off his shoes and padded into the kitchen. Rambo became very excited as Seymour checked his empty food dish on the floor. He retrieved it, filled it with tap water and the dog wolfed it down in seconds. He checked in the fridge, then opened the tinned food cupboard. Closing it with a sigh, he padded through to the living room. Frank lay full length along the sofa, big toes poking out from holey socks. Aluminium food trays with congealed remnants of a stolen supper sat on the coffee table with scrunched up balls of yellow-stained kitchen roll. And the worst crime of all – a half drunk bottle of Old Glen Fiddich whiskey with the screw cap nowhere to be seen.

'Frank! Where's the bloody top for the whiskey? ***How dare you*** open it.'

'Oh, it's you,' said Frank. 'Don't start on me, I've had a rough day.'

'A rough day? Aw diddums, did your horse lose?'

'Not just one, sadly. Five of them on an accumulator. Still, tomorrow's another day.' He yawned, extending both arms. Seymour silenced the radio.

'Why did she chuck you out, Frank? Was it the gambling or the fact you've been a bloody waster all your life?'

'All of the above, I reckon. See? You can't drag me down any further. I'm at rock bottom.'

'Well boo bloody hoo. I want you out of here tomorrow. And get this mess cleared up. You didn't even feed the dog did you?'

'I gave him half a poppadom and he loved it. No need to thank me. Anyway, once we sell that diamond you've got stashed away in the freezer, we'll be quids in.'

'You what? You went snooping around in my freezer?'

'Needed ice .... for the whiskey. What did you expect?'

'That stone is police evidence. What have you done with it?'

'Calm down, Seymour. You'll give yourself a heart attack. And I don't fancy spending all night in A & E with you.'

'WHERE IS IT, FRANK?'

Frank held up his palms. 'I put it back. I did!'

Seymour wagged a forefinger, 'you better bloody had!' He stormed off to the kitchen. The freezer door slammed and he returned.

Saying nothing, he began grabbing at Frank's trouser legs, gathering the fabric up to his knees.

'What the hell are you doing, brother? I told you I put it back.'

'Rambo didn't bite you at all, did he? There's not a mark anywhere.'

'***Not there*** …. it's near the top end …'

'Show me then.'

'I'm not letting you see my goolies.' Frank straightened the legs of his trousers, giving them a good tug at the hem for emphasis.

'I knew it was a mistake letting you kip here. I mean it, Frank. You're out of here by eight a.m. in the morning. Go pack your stuff.'

'But I've got nowhere to go.'

'Tell it to someone who gives a shite. Not me.'

Seymour stomped up the stairs to his bedroom, closed the door and scanned the room. Over by the bed, he lifted the rug, prised out a loose section of floorboard, took the stone from his pocket and laid it inside the hole. Replacing everything, he went back downstairs to make supper.

∞∞∞

CHAPTER 31 : AN UNEXPECTED HITCH

It was early morning back at the caravan and Bobby's second attempt at the same yoga pose was about to fail as Sylvie returned from her dog walk. Crashing into the sofa, he stayed where he landed, face down and motionless. Clarabelle, having completed two laps of the football field already, was in no mood for an obstacle course. Wearily, she stepped onto, then over his limp body, made her way to the kitchen and sat patiently by her water dish. Sylvie followed in the same fashion.

'While you're down there, Bobs, can you check under the sofa for the remote? Those lycra shorts are very fetching, by the way.'

'You're all heart, you know that?' came his muffled response.

'Don't go giving yourself a hernia before tonight, will you? I shall need your presence,' she shouted from the kitchen. Bobby groaned to a sitting position.

'Does that mean I have today to myself?'

'Unless you fancy taking my clock down to Neyves and get the mechanism put back in for me?'

'If I have time, but dog-sitting Clarabelle is a full-time job, as you know.'

'Hmmm, well if you can I'd be that grateful I might not chuck you out in the morning.'

'Wow. No pressure then.'

'Seymour's calling for me in an hour to see some dealer. That should be interesting. And just to warn you, Clarabelle's been looking a bit peaky since she came home.'

'***Dealer?*** Are you buying or selling?'

'Not drugs, you pillock. Antiques .... gems. ***One particular gem*** to be precise. Fancy some toast?'

Half way through breakfast, there was a soft tapping at the van door, and Sylvie got up from the table.

'You know, Bobby, it's like they do it on purpose. Seymour said nine o'clock and it's only just gone eight.'

She opened the door still clutching her toast, and Carolyn Carr swept into the room.

'Thank God you're home!' she said.

'Where the hell else would I be? It's the middle of the night, woman. ***And come in ... why don't you?'***

'Sweetums, do you want me to leave?' asked Bobby.

'Don't you dare, Bobs, you're fine where you are.'

'I need to buy up your complete stock. It's urgent,' said Carolyn.

'My complete stock? ***Of what?*** My collection of Des O'Connor albums?'

'Des O'Connor? ***Of course not.'***

'It's Led Zeppelin, isn't it? I can see you as a head banger.' She bit into the toast, tearing it viciously from her teeth.

'What's wrong with you? Are you on something?'

'Huh! Listen to the pot calling the kettle. Had any more children lately?'

Carolyn lowered her gaze. 'Oh. So you know.'

'It only took me forty two years to find out. Now sit down, tell me the whole story, and I might think about getting you what you want.'

∞∞∞

Seymour Witless woke later than usual with a bad taste in his mouth to see Rambo standing expectantly by the bedroom door. A tiny whimper escaped from the dog's throat.

'Okay, boy, I'm coming. Just give me a minute,' he said, groping his way out of bed.

Having seized the remainder of his precious whiskey the night before and determined to keep it close, what better way than to drink it? Or so he thought. In his intoxicated sleep he had not heard his brother leave, but no trace of him was left behind, only the door key on the eiderdown and a pair of scruffy socks lying discarded on the floor. Frank was not usually this amenable, but Seymour wasn't in the mood for fathoming it all out. His mouth felt like the bottom of a bird cage and he craved carbohydrate. Retrieving the disgusting socks between finger and thumb, he plodded downstairs to the kitchen and poured milk onto a massive bowl of cornflakes. Not even pausing to sit down, he shoveled cereal into his mouth, staring blankly through the kitchen window. Why had Frank gone without anymore argy bargy? It was most odd. Then suddenly, he dumped the cereal dish into the sink and took the stairs two at a time back to his room. Grasping at the bedside rug he tossed it aside and lifted the loose piece of floorboard.

'Shit! Shit! Bloody Twatface!'

The diamond was gone.

∞∞∞

Meanwhile, back at the caravan site, Nelson the cat had reclaimed his self-appointed role as defender of the sacred wine in the hollow beneath Sylvie's living quarters. He swung out his claws and hissed like a Tasmanian devil, forcing Hudson the chauffeur to retrieve a pair of gauntlets from the boot of the Daimler in an effort to save what was left of his arms. The warbling witch became more impatient by the minute watching from the passenger seat. She poked out her head from the side window.

'I say, why don't you get Mister Qualified out here? Didn't you say he was a lion tamer, to boot?' She guffawed, then snorted. Sylvie tossed an appropriate glare in her direction.

Just as Hudson was about to throw in the towel, Witless's Morris Minor turned from the main road into the caravan park.

'Ah, thank heavens … the cavalry's arrived,' Carolyn said, craning her neck, tortoise fashion.

Witless stepped out of the car followed by an exuberant Rambo, hips gyrating at the mere sight of Clarabelle.

'Good morning, Inspector,' Carolyn continued. 'Is this lucky timing, or did one of the neighbours report a crisis?'

'Neither, Ms. Carr. I have an appointment with Miss Broadstairs as it happens. But I can see your problem. And I may know how to solve it.'

Hudson was glad to get up off his knees and straighten his back. He removed the gauntlets.

'I would suggest you wear these, Inspector, before you wade in for the kill.' He looked around randomly at the caravans. 'Maybe I should knock on some doors. Someone here must have a cattle prod.'

'Oh, why didn't I think of that, Hudson?' said Sylvie. 'I keep a spare one myself in the back room. Just like all us country bumpkins around here.'

'There'll be no need for anything like that.' Witless opened the passenger door and pulled out a pack of pork scratchings from the glove box. Both dogs were instantly alerted as he opened the wrapper. He placed the packet on the ground just three feet from the wine stash, and Nelson sprang from the hole as both dogs joined the free-for-all.

Hudson wasted no time. He had the wine in the boot and was back in the driver's seat within seconds.

'Bye bye, Inspector. Call me sometime…' Carolyn waved and blew a kiss, as the Daimler sped around, heading for the exit.

'I'm afraid I have some bad news, Miss Broadstairs,' said Seymour.

'Come inside and tell me. Next door's net curtains are beginning to twitch.'

Bobby retreated to Sylvie's bedroom to change out of his exercise gear while Seymour broke the news.

'So what do you plan to do?' said Sylvie.

Seymour gasped in frustration. 'I thought … maybe do a circuit of the jewellers in town? Second hand dealers too. See if anyone's asked for a valuation.'

'Surely Frank wouldn't be able to sell something like that in a hurry. No-one would have the balls to take it off his hands. If it's authentic, of course. Maybe you should tell Craddock.'

'That would mean dropping myself in it, as well a Frank.'

'Any idea where he might be headed? After the dealer shops anyway.'

'There aren't any other family members. And if he had any close friends he wouldn't have come to me for somewhere to stay. He doesn't have any money to get far.'

'Then he's got to be close by. When he finds he can't sell the diamond, he's likely to be back, tail between his legs. You don't have to tell Craddock yet. Not about the stone, anyway. But you will need him on side at the right moment.'

Seymour headed for the door. 'That makes sense. I'd best get going, maybe call in and have a word with Craddock first, then see if I can find a trail. Will I see you at the show tonight?'

'No doubt about it.'

∞∞∞

CHAPTER 32 : PREPARATIONS ARE UNDERWAY

Daisy Harbottle dragged an apron over her head and hastily tied the sash around her waist. Snatching a brief glance at the clock on the wall, she turned to the pantry, flinging both doors wide.

'Flour …. Sugar …. eggs, butter, milk …' she muttered, plonking each item onto the work bench in turn. 'Cheese? Cheese? No ruddy cheese! ***Norris? We've got no ruddy cheese!'***

Norris sat at the table in the foyer, totting up the figures in the church hall's accounts ledger. He threw down his pen, scraped back his chair and made his way to the kitchen.

'Jesus Christmas!' Daisy shouted, as Hoggy sprang up suddenly from the floor on the other side of the serving counter dangling a field mouse by the tail.

'And here's the thief tha's lookin' for Daisy.' The mouse wriggled all four limbs in protest.

'Oh … no, no, NO! I can't bear mice….. take it away!'

'What on earth?' Norris asked, as he marched into the room.

'I's just found this field mouse, Norris. And Daisy's missin' some cheese.'

'Hoggy! Will you just GET IT OUTTA HERE?' Daisy yelled, snatching up a soup ladle.

'Where did you find it, exactly?' said Norris, as Daisy came out from behind the serving hatch wielding her utensil.

'Behind yon tables …. Just over….***Bloody hells bells, Daisy Harbottle.'*** Hoggy spun around and ran for the exit, rodent in hand with Daisy giving chase, just as a short-legged fearsome woman in a pillbox hat entered the foyer. She carried the deadliest weapon – a government- issue clipboard. Both Hoggy and Daisy froze in mid flight and Madam Pillbox's jaw gaped.

'What in the name of …..and who might you be?' she addressed the question to both.

'Well, missus, that depends on who ***you is,'*** said Hoggy.

Madam Pillbox raised her lanyard for identification. 'Cressida Plum. Senior social worker. I'm looking for Daisy Harbottle.'

Daisy lowered her weapon along with her voice. 'That's me. What is it? Is it Arthur? Has something happened?'

'Mrs. Harbottle, I've been trying to get you at home, but you're never there.'

'Well you've got me now. So go ahead, tell me your worst.'

'We're trying to arrange a date for Mr. Harbottle to be discharged from Senior Moments care home. The thing is, are you capable of looking after him?'

Daisy attempted to conceal the ladle behind her back.

'Of course I am! The only reason I'm here so much is because he's not there. Once he's home he'll have my undivided attention.'

Pillbox gave Daisy a quick once over from head to foot. 'Well let's hope so. Mr. Harbottle should be home by ten tomorrow morning. We'll be making unannounced visits thereafter. Just to make sure he's still alive, you understand.' She turned to leave when Daisy stopped her.

'Might I ask .... Why the sudden change of heart?'

'No change of heart, Mrs. Harbottle. As it happens, the other care home residents just couldn't take any more of him.' After two seconds of stunned silence, she turned and left the building.

'Daisy, that's wonderful news.' Norris's supportive words brought trembles to Daisy's bottom lip and Hoggy took her arm with his spare hand and led her to the nearest chair.

'Oh, Daisy, just sit thaself down and I'll make tha some tea.'

'No, you bloody won't,' she said, tearfully. 'Not until you take that goddamn mouse miles from here and go find Nelson. He's needed.'

∞∞∞

Meanwhile, back at police head quarters, Seymour Witless emerged from Craddock's office with a smug smile spreading across his face as he made his way up the corridor. Reaching the door of his own office, he picked at the sticky edge of D.S. Judy Conway's name strip on the wooden surface until it came away easily between finger and thumb. Rolling it into a ball, he opened the catch on a nearby window and flicked the thing outside in the yard. He checked inside the room. His desk was back in place and everything was as he'd left it. Closing the door again, he made for the car park.

Rambo lifted bloodshot eyes but not his head from the back seat of the Morris as Seymour slipped into the driver's seat and adjusted the rear view mirror.

'Turn that frown upside down, my old mate. How do you fancy playing detective for the day?' He started the car and headed for the prime source of second hand goods in South Shields – Frederick Street.

Even for a childless man, Seymour could guess that schools had opened that day for the start of autumn term, not only by the lack of children out and about, but the joy on adults' faces reclaiming the streets.

Parking up, Seymour raised the flap of his coat pocket, peered inside and grimaced. With forefinger and thumb he pulled out one of Frank's stinky socks and held it to Rambo's nose. The dog sniffed, then sneezed, spraying a layer of snot over the sock and the car's leather upholstery.

'For God's sake, Rambo ….' Dropping the sock, he snatched the dog's lead and squirmed his way out of the vehicle. The dog leapt out onto the pavement and sniffed the air. Seymour barely had time to lock the car before being dragged along the street towards The Old Curiosity Shop and a whiff of chips and vinegar. It was difficult to know which aroma was attracting Rambo the most, but Seymour's compulsion to find his brother drove him on.

The shop door chimed as he nudged it open and a black cat raised its head from a lounging position on top of a walnut dresser. The proprietor's t-shirted belly rested on a glass counter next to a half-eaten portion of pie and chips. His black shiny waistcoat hung either side of the paunch with no hope of meeting in the middle and he sported a moustache littered with pastry crumbs.

'No dogs allowed in here mate,' he said, mouth half full.

Seymour held up his badge. 'D.C.I. Seymour Witless. I need to ask one or two questions if I may.'

The man grinned. 'You havin' a laugh? You can buy those badges across the road, two quid a pop. Did you get yours from Old George then?'

Seymour's eyes rolled. 'I can assure you …. ***this is the real thing***. And Old George, whomever he is had best be careful about selling anymore of those badges, otherwise he can be arrested for fraudulent practices.'

The pie eater looked doubtful, but shrugged his shoulders and popped a chip between bristly lips.

'Alright, but if your dog kicks off, my Lucifer will have him by the bollocks before he can scarper. Just so's you know.'

'This dog is actually quite fond of cats. Mind you, he couldn't eat a whole one.'

Seymour's attempt at humour missed its mark, and the pie eater responded with an icy glare. Seymour cleared his throat.

'Have you by any chance had a male customer, approximately six feet tall, forty years old this morning trying to flog a gemstone of any kind? He may not have been wearing any socks.'

The pie eater lifted his gaze skyward and a forefinger to his chin. Then shook his head.

'Naw, the fella I saw had some jazzy socks as it happens. Only noticed 'cause his trousers were too short. Yes, if I remember rightly the socks had Fred Flintstone's ugly mug on them.'

'The bastard!'

The pie eater's face ceased chewing and offered a look of disapproval. 'No swearing allowed in here either, Mister D.C.I. or whatever your name is. That's two of my rules broken already. Keep goin' and you might make a hat trick.'

'So, ***bollocks*** doesn't count as a swear word, in your book of rules then?'

'Bollocks? ***Who said bollocks?'***

Seymour gave his second eye roll. 'What ***colour*** were these trousers?'

'Sort of a sage green with turn-ups. You're not gonna swear again are ya?'

'Aargh! No, not yet. What was he selling?'

'Well,' he said, in between chewing and swallowing. 'He claimed it was a diamond. Should have seen the size of the flaming thing. Must've taken me for a complete plonker.'

'So you didn't buy it then?'

'I ***certainly*** did not.'

'Did you see which way he went?'

'Across the road and down the other side I think.'

'How long ago?'

'Maybe twenty minutes. Now if you don't mind, my dinner's gettin' cold.'

Seymour headed off to the shops over the road, peering inside each one in the absence of any further surge of enthusiasm from Rambo. As he reached the end, he glanced back across the road where he spotted a familiar figure lurking in the doorway of the Eureka pub. Without hesitation, he made his way to the other side.

'Miss Broadstairs? What are you doing skulking around here?'

'Shush, Seymour - Carolyn Carr is entertaining your brother in that café a few doors up.'

Seymour sighed. 'How come you're always one step ahead of me?'

Sylvie tapped the side of her nose. 'Because, Inspector, ***I have a nose for murder.***'

'You can't mean you suspect Frank now?'

'Of course not you daft beggar. Why, do you?'

'Ms. Carr then?'

'Well, I'm starting to wonder now how this little rendezvous ties into everything else.'

'Be honest. You ***want*** her to be involved, don't you?'

Sylvie threw him a sidelong grimace. '***Everyone's*** involved, Seymour … right up until the bitter end. Now stop prattling on and get in there.'

'Actually, I will, if you hold onto Rambo here.' Slapping the lead into her hand, he marched up to the café and went inside without a pause.

The pair didn't notice him right away. They sat opposite one another in a red vinyl booth halfway up the shop. She twirled a glass of something red with bubbles by the stem as it rested on the table between them. Frank had his back to the door, head bobbing about the way it tended to do when in full bullshit flow. Then Carolyn looked up.

'Inspector!' she announced to the whole clientele. Hostile faces turned to look. 'Do come and join us. How lovely to see you.'

Seymour didn't need asking twice. He slid himself along the bench, up close to his brother and eyeballed Frank's lower half. Carolyn stood up and took her purse from her bag. 'What can I get you? A tea? Coffee?'

'A coffee would be delightful, Ms. Carr, thank you,' he said, covering his anger with a smile. She reciprocated with a toothy one of her own and moved across to the serving counter.

'Those are my trousers, Twatface….' He muttered from a corner of his mouth. 'And the socks were a birthday gift from my D.C. you absolute arsehole.'

Frank inhaled deeply through his nose. 'What was I supposed to do? I'm skint, Seymour. And homeless, thanks to you.'

'Thanks to ...? Oh, you take the sodding biscuit you do. Your situation is entirely of your own making .... So don't you dare put this on me. What have you done with the stone?' He glanced across at Carolyn. 'Have you given it to her? How do you know her, anyway?'

Frank smirked. 'How do I know her? ***Everyone*** knows Carolyn bloody Carr. We don't all live under a rock like you, Seymour.'

Carolyn returned to the booth with a mug of brown-looking liquid and placed it on the table.

'There you go, Inspector. Get yer chops round that, as they say in these parts.' She sat herself down, clearly delighted to be entertaining two men at once with her knowledge of the local lingo. 'I suppose you two have introduced yourselves?'

Seymour looked suspiciously from one to the other.

'Introduced one another? Oh, yes. Shall we compare stories? How do you know um, what did you say your name was again? Mister?' Seymour gave his brother a wide-eyed stare.

Carolyn looked amused. 'His name is Frank. He answered my ad.'

'Your ad?'

'Yes, Inspector. I lost something a while ago which is rather valuable to me. I placed an ad in the newsagent's and offered a reward. Frank kindly gave me a call.'

Frank stared blankly at his shoes, with no input to the conversation.

'Well that figures,' said Seymour, offering his own sidelong sneer. 'So has ***Frank*** helped you recover the item, Ms. Carr?'

'Not yet. But he says he knows where it might be. Just getting hold of it might take a bit more work.'

'Right. And by ***more work*** does Frank mean the job will require ***more money?'***

'We haven't actually got that far in the conversation, Inspector.'

'Can I ask .... How much reward are you offering for this lost item, Ms. Carr?'

'A thousand pounds, Inspector.'

'Goodness. The item must mean a lot to you.'

'Oh, it absolutely does, Inspector. I can't begin to tell you.' Carolyn craned her neck in the direction of the door. 'Oh, goodness, there's Hudson waving to me from outside. Maybe he needs change for the meter. Would you two excuse me for a moment?' She got up and tottered her way to the exit.

Seymour strained to contain himself until she was out of earshot.

'If you don't hand the bloody thing over right now … I swear I'll slip the cuffs on you right before her eyes …. ***right here in the ruddy shop**.*'

'You wouldn't do that. I'm your brother for chrissakes…'

'Just try me!' Seymour held out his hand under the table. Frank glanced behind him. Carolyn was still talking with Hudson in the doorway. Reluctantly, he slipped a hand into his inside pocket, and placed the stone in Seymour's outstretched palm. Seymour quickly concealed it inside his own coat, got up and made his way to the exit.

'Oh, Inspector, are you dashing?'

'Always, Ms. Carr. ***Don't give that one any money, will you?'*** He flicked his head in Frank's general direction. 'He's well known to us lot down at the nick. Nice to have seen you, anyway. Thanks for the coffee and I hope your item is returned very soon.'

'Why, thank you. Goodbye Inspector.'

Sylvie tugged desperately on Rambo's lead as he sniffed the nether regions of every passer-by in a skirt. Her fisherman's hat lay skewed upon her head and her cheeks were an embarrassing shade of pink.

'Thank gawd you're back, Seymour. Some sleaze ball offered me a fiver for a quickie round the back of the pub.'

Seymour seemed distracted but Sylvie continued.

'And … he wouldn't even up his offer.'

'Sorry about that, Miss Broadstairs,' he answered, taking the lead from her hand. 'Can I give you a lift anywhere?'

'Only if you're gonna spill. ***What happened?'*** she said, following him to his car.

'I have the item,' he said, patting his inside pocket.

'That's bloody marvelous. See what an asset I am? And what about the warbling witch?'

'I'll tell you in the car. But first we need to get this rock valued. See just how much two murders …. plus two more attempted ones are worth to someone.'

∞∞∞

CHAPTER 33 : GIG NUMBER TWO

D.C. Richard Tracey came out of his father's lavatory and skipped downstairs to the sound of the cistern flushing. Peering into the hall mirror, he licked a forefinger to smooth out both eyebrows. Then he straightened his tie and checked all three pockets of his new sports jacket with a gentle pat.

'You need toilet rolls, Dad. Remind me next time I go to Tesco's,' he said.

Royston hobbled out of the living room in an old but comfy cardigan over a white polo shirt he wore only for special occasions.

'You stink like a hooer's handbag. What the hell have you been spraying on yerself, yer great nancy?'

Richard Tracey huffed. 'You won't spoil tonight, Dad. We're gonna have a nice time. My boss is coming, so ***please*** be good.'

'Of course I'll be good. Can't say the same for Lucinda though.'

'What? Oh, Dad, ***you can't take bloody Lucinda***. She's a house doll. We agreed, remember?'

Royston gave an impatient shake of the head. 'She won't be a bit of bother. If you're that embarrassed, you can sit in the row behind, can't you?'

∞∞∞

As doubtful about the whole evening as he was now, Richard Tracy felt marginally pleased to find the church hall's car park occupied by only two other vehicles.

'Right, Dad, this will have to be an organized operation. You do understand?'

'Anything you say, son.'

'So, the plan is … Lucinda links arms with both of us on the way in. That baseball cap on her head will cover her face partially, and the scarf is doing its bit too. Once inside, you go on ahead of me and

I'll pay for an extra ticket at the desk. But I've no idea how you'll cope at half time when you have to take her into the gents for a pee.'

Royston's indignant face blazed.

'Take her into the gents? I can't do that. ***You'll*** just have to look after her.'

'Oh no you don't, Dad. You wanted to bring her. She's your responsibility.'

'I won't need the gents anyway. It'll be fine.'

Richard cocked an eyebrow. 'You wanna bet a tenner?'

'Shut up and let's get out of this bloody car before the place fills up even more.'

Inside the foyer, and luckily for Lucinda, Hoggy had been temporarily upgraded to ticket master for the evening. Norris had loaned him a British Railways cap complete with badge from lost property as a bribe, and Hoggy sat proudly behind the desk which he'd dragged to a more central position, indicating his new-found authority.

Daisy flapped about nervously, flitting from room to room. She burst her way through to the foyer, shoving Hoggy's spread-eagled legs out of the way to reach the desk drawers.

'Daisy Harbottle, what's tha doin'? I is tryin' to work here!'

'Oh, ***work*** is it? You want to try ***my job***,' she said, rifling through a bottom drawer. 'Have you seen a box of matches in here?'

'Aw, has bloody pilot light gone out again? Just use meecrowave. It'll be fine.'

'You have no idea, do you? One ***meecrowave*** is no bloody good for thirty five punters, now is it?'

Royston hovered with Lucinda half in, half outside the entrance with his son peering over the top of their heads. Richard watched Hoggy bend to open another drawer of the desk and shoved his father gently from behind.

'Quick, Dad. Get yourself inside. If you're stopped, just jab a thumb in my direction. I've got the tickets and the money. Pretend you're gaga. That shouldn't be difficult.'

'Quick? You're bloody delusional. I just had a knee transplant, remember?'

Royston made a shuffle-style surge forwards with Lucinda's pink, toeless feet skimming across the floor next to him. From the corner of her eye, Daisy did a double take, just as Richard Tracey presented himself in front of the desk brandishing two entrance tickets and a five pound note.

'Good evening! My father has just taken my mother inside – she's a little unsteady on her feet, so here are the tickets, plus payment for one extra, if you please. ***My fine fella.***'

Hoggy pulled his head out of the drawer and beamed at Tracey's compliment. No-one had ever referred to him as a ***fine fella*** of any sort, and he knew he'd remember it always.

'Why thank tha, kind sir!' He tipped his cap, and Tracey attempted to rush off.

'Hold on a minute, sir….' Hoggy insisted. And Tracey looked terrified. Royston and Lucinda appeared to have escaped into the main hall unnoticed, so what was the bother?

'Tha needs some change, sir.' Hoggy jingled some coins about in the cash drawer.

'No need for that, fella. You keep it. You're doing a great job.' And with that, he hurried off in pursuit of his family.

'That's awfully strange, Hoggy,' Daisy said.

'What, leavin' a tip? Not strange at all, Daisy Harbottle. Stick with me and we'll make a few bob tonight.'

'Not the tip. That woman with no toes. And no bloody shoes. Most suspicious.'

'Don't be daft. She might have toelio, like me. Tha's worryin' for nowt …. this is all about Arthur comin' home tomorrow. Tha' knows it'll all be fine

… and there's yer matches.' He plonked a box of Swan Vestas into her hand. She rattled the box in his face and spun around, heading back to the kitchen.

∞∞∞

Back at the caravan, Clarabelle had barely moved from her basket all day. Having tried her with all the usual treats, Bobby had moved onto the forbidden ones from the snacks cupboard, without success.

'Come on, Clara. Mummy will not be happy if we don't make it there tonight now, will she?' Clarabelle gave him and the cheese puff a brief sidelong glance, whimpered, then closed her eyes once again. Bobby sighed, returned the snack to its bag and glanced at his watch.

'The vet's will be closed by now.'

Clarabelle gave a throaty growl at the sound of the ***vet's*** word, and covered her nose with a paw.

'Oh, bugger. What can we do then?' He reached across to his jacket and took a little black book from the pocket, flicking through the pages. 'Now, that could be an idea, Clara. Shall we phone my pal Dan, the medical man? He works late on Wednesdays …. '

Clarabelle removed the paw from her face and gave Bobby a suspicious look as he picked up the telephone.

'Good evening. Extension 2456 please. Yes, I'll hold.'

∞∞∞

Twenty minutes later, Bobby alighted from the Economic bus and crossed over towards Harton General. Clarabelle curled herself into a tiny ball beneath his coat, and he felt her tremble against his chest. Reaching a back entrance to the Diagnostic Centre, he nudged the door with one knee and stepped cautiously across the threshold. Dan the medical man appeared at the end of the corridor, beckoning wildly, and Bobby darted towards him.

'You know I'll get the sack if anyone finds out, Bobby? Quickly, this way.' Dan swiveled around with white coat billowing and marched along the blue line towards Radiography with Bobby scampering behind. Passing a uniformed policeman guarding a private room, Dan acknowledged with a brief nod without stopping.

'What's going on there?' asked Bobby from a safe distance.

'No-one tells us lot anything .... There's been a watch on that room since yesterday.'

'So… it could be a prisoner having treatment?'

'Or .... a victim under protection. So you can see how awkward it was getting you in here. I had to tell him you were an urgent case.'

'If there's anything I can do for you in return, you only have to say…'

Turning several corners, they reached a door marked **Ultrasound suite 1** and Dan led the way inside.

'Stick her on the bed, mate,' he said, grabbing a bottle of gel.

Clarabelle lay on her side watching wide-eyed as Dan squirted gel onto her belly. Then he picked up the scanning wand and touched it against the dog's skin. All eyes, including the dog's were fixed on the monitor as it lit up with a fuzzy black and white image.

'Bloody hell, what's that?' said Bobby.

'Shush,' said Dan. 'Watch … and listen.'

∞∞∞

Back in the cloakroom at St. Martin's, Sylvie perched on the lumpy old couch with a sense of impending doom. To compliment Mystic Mohawk's American Indian costume, she wore the same feathered head dress and Oxfam outfit from the last gig. But she'd left the pink trainers behind for a pair of Hiawatha-style moccasins.

'I can't think where Bobby's got to,' she said, staring at the clock for the umpteenth time in the last half hour. 'Hope nothing's happened.'

Stinky Simon, the Mystic Mohawk, drained his coffee cup, stood up and grimaced.

'Lordy, that's strong. Gets the old adrenaline goin' though, that's for sure.'

'My adrenal glands are shot to hell these days, Stinky. Caffeine can't do a thing for them.'

'How many are out there, Sylv, last time you looked?'

'Just about full, Stinky. Witless is wearing a dickie bow, sat next to his fancy piece from the hospital. She scrubs up better than I thought. The warbling witch has brought an orthopedic cushion to sit on. It serves two purposes, of course. Haemorrhoid relief for one, and for another, to annoy the folks behind by making herself four inches taller. Then there's Dick Tracey's dad. He's snuggled up to a limp-looking woman wrapped up for winter.'

'You don't miss a trick, do ya? You sure that's all?' Stinky laughed.

'No, actually the district nurse, Eva Shawcross has come on her own despite having bought two tickets. Unless the other is for her medical bag, which goes everywhere with her.' Sylvie smirked.

'And why is that so funny?'

She waved a dismissive hand. 'Oh, that's a personal thing…'

'Do you even know how this will turn out? I'm about to go out there and do my bit. You sure this is gonna go to plan? If not, I may have to improvise.'

'Let's just see how it goes, and if you have to improvise, I trust you. I'll be right behind the curtain. And no, I don't really know if it'll turn out alright. I'm hoping for a bit of spiritual guidance as far as that's concerned.'

The expected tap on the door sounded, made by Daisy this time.

'Your five minute call, Mystic.'

Stinky reached out a hand to Sylvie.

'C'mon then. I want you right behind me. And keep your head down.'

∞∞∞

From backstage, Sylvie watched the professional at work, feeling rather exposed without her earpiece and Bobby's supportive voice which normally came with it. Norris, who had appointed himself lights technician for the evening, sidled across to where she was standing.

'I'm most disappointed to see you backstage, Miss Broadstairs. Why aren't you sitting in the audience?'

'Because I'm learning, Norris, which is best done from back here. ***You know this.***'

Norris's frantic jowls flapped with disapproval. 'Well I hope you have no intention of getting onto that stage …. The bishop would not be happy.'

'Norris, pleasuring the bishop is my ultimate goal in life. Surely you know this? I'm just observing.'

Norris lingered momentarily with a scowl, then started back to his lights control panel.

A silent grin worked its way across Sylvie's face as he walked away, and she continued her observation.

Stinky worked quite differently. With an old-school-type microphone in one hand and its trailing cable in the other, he moved with confidence around the stage. A two-seater sofa and an armchair placed centre stage invited audience members to partake beneath a banner, emblazoned with Mystic Mohawk's brand name stretched across the back curtain.

'I know what y'all are thinkin'- who the hell is this oddball in fancy dress and what's he doin' here?

Well, truth is, I was a Sand Dancer too, who deserted camp. But now I'm back to reconnect with old friends even though many of 'em have passed now – but that don't have to get in the way. And I'm guessin' most of y'all believe that too or you wouldn't be here tonight. So that's what I'm gonna try to do for you. To reconnect.'

Stinky strolled to one end of the stage then back again, flicking the microphone's cable from his path as he scanned the audience.

'I have a sweet little old lady here with silver hair.... She's lookin' to connect with her son .... Last name begins with a 'W'? Is this familiar to anyone?'

Brenda Cole turned her eyes on Seymour Witless in the seat next to her. Seymour flicked his gaze sideways for just a second to meet hers, then back to the stage. But Stinky spotted it and moved to the corresponding zone. Raising his cable-holding hand, he pointed a finger at Witless.

'I'm feeling it could be you, sir, in the bow tie. Am I right? Has your mother passed?'

Seymour hesitated, and Brenda nudged his arm gently.

'May … maybe, yes.'

Stinky rubbed his chest and twisted his face. 'I'm getting pains in the upper body .... Tell me, was it a heart problem she had?'

Seymour cleared his throat. This was the last thing he needed.

'Not heart, no.'

'But .... upper body? Respiratory perhaps? A lung problem?'

'That's correct.'

Nurse Brenda reached out for his hand and he willingly offered his own in return.

'She wants to say how proud she is of you .... And not to worry, because the pain has all gone now. She's having the best time and ... what's that? Okay, so she wants to let you know she approves of the lady friend and sends both of you her love. Always.'

There was a gentle eruption of applause from the audience that lasted around ten seconds, and Sylvie wished she'd brought her note book. Then she felt something brush past her leg, but when she looked down, there was nothing.

'Was that stuff true, what he said?' Nurse Brenda whispered in Seymour's ear.

Seymour leaned in. 'Only the lung disease part. But mother's hair was black. And the bit about sending love and bein' proud? .... She'd need a personality transplant to say something like that.'

Stinky kept on pacing …. and scanning. Until he fixed his gaze on Royston, then he stopped.

'I'm being drawn to you, sir, in the white shirt.' He pointed once again.

'Oh, God, no…' muttered Richard Tracey. ***'Dad, you'll have to go deaf. He might leave you alone then.'***

Royston fired a warning glare at his son and waited for more revelations.

'Is your lady friend having some health issues sir? I only ask because it's a little warm in here and she's wearing a lot of outdoor clothing. What's her name?'

'Her name's Lucinda. And she'd like you to bugger off and leave her be,' Royston shouted.

Richard Tracey covered his eyes with one hand and lowered himself in the seat.

Stinky raised a palm in submission.

'Hey, that's fine …. I may just have had a message for her, that's all,' he said, beginning to move away to the other side of the stage.

Sylvie felt the brush against her leg again, but this time she spotted Nelson the cat on the wander.

'WHAT MESSAGE?' Royston shouted, and Stinky turned back.

'Well, if the two of you would like to come up here, I could do a personal reading?' He stretched out an arm, indicating the empty sofa.

'Don't you sodding dare, Dad!' Richard Tracey muttered. But Royston's bottom hovered in mid air above his seat, ready to make a move. Richard leaned across and grabbed hold of his father's trouser leg. ***'Sit down, for God's sake.'***

Royston pulled away from his son's grip and his trouser button flew off. Abandoning his walking stick Lazarus-style, he shuffled down the aisle grasping Lucinda by the waist. As he got to the steps, Nelson strolled on stage from behind a curtain with a lifeless mouse between his lips. Some of the audience began to chuckle, but Stinky seemed unaware. He held out a hand for Royston to ascend.

'Up you come, young man … and Lucinda.'

Royston mounted the steps, dragging Lucinda alongside and Stinky helped the couple onto the sofa as the stage lights dimmed for effect. But as Stinky headed to the armchair, Nelson landed there first and Stinky backed away. His eyes began to roll as he clutched at his chest.

'C …. Cats! I'm allergic …. Can't … brea … breathe ….'

Nurse Brenda began to rise from her seat. ***'Should I go up there and help do you think?'***

Seymour placed a hand on her arm. 'Hang fire there, Brenda. Could be part of the act.'

'Oh dear.' She sat back down.

Stinky was on his knees by now, with head bowed, struggling to draw breath. Sylvie ran onto the stage, shooing Nelson away and dashing to Stinky's assistance. Then suddenly, Eva Shawcross was beside her, kneeling on the floor fumbling inside her medical bag.

'Inhaler .... I have an inhaler here somewhere,' she said, as Stinky's breathing seemed to regulate itself as quickly as it had faltered.

'No need .... I .... I'm okay now .... Now the cat has gone .... I'll be fine.' Regaining his feet, he helped a puzzled Eva to hers. Gazing into her eyes for several seconds, he took a step back. 'Forgive me, ma'am, but I believe I have a spirit with me who wishes to convey something to you.'

Eva recoiled. 'Really? Well perhaps we should do this in private. I have no wish to ...'

'Ma'am, this entity is accompanied by another .... Both are new to the spirit world and have limited strength to convey their message. I would strongly advise you not to dismiss their presence at this time.' Stinky offered the empty armchair to Eva with a wave of his hand. Hesitantly, she lowered herself into it.

Royston shuffled on the sofa. 'And what about us, Chief ruddy Mohawk? Lucinda and me … we were here first.'

'Sure, no worries …. I'll get to you sir, I promise,' Stinky said, now fully composed, he turned back to the audience. 'But my guest joining me on the stage right now is the wonderful psychic Crystal Gazer, and she is the one chosen by the spirits to deliver this important message.'

Steam was about to burst forth from Norris's ears as he continued to fume behind the curtain. Curiosity had compelled Daisy and Hoggy to join him.

'I'll be having strong words about this with Miss Broadstairs,' said Norris.

'Aw, c'mon Norris. What else could she do?' Daisy reasoned. 'Anyways, a bit of drama is always good for publicity.'

'Publicity?' Norris looked horrified. 'No, we have to keep this quiet. Thank God the Gazette didn't send anyone.'

'But they did, Norris,' said Hoggy. 'That camera fella's standin' at t' back. Look, you can see him. And in t' back row …. See those three men sittin' in overcoats? They's coppers.'

'How on earth can you tell?'

'Cuz they flashed their badges at me at t' desk. Some folk will do owt to get in for nowt.'

Sylvie took the microphone from Stinky and nodded with humility to the crowd.

'Why, thank you, Mystic. It's a pleasure to assist you here tonight. These two spirits are telling me all kinds of things.' She stared into the distance and shook her head. 'I'm just hesitating because it's important I get this right.'

'As you may all know, there are two unsolved murders that happened right here in this town in the last few days. The first, a local drag queen by the name of Ernie Winters was pushed down the fire escape of the Shoreline Club.'

'We knew him by another name,' said Royston, with a chuckle.

'Do you want to tell the audience his stage name, Mister Tracey?'

'Ophelia Ass. Hee hee!'

'That's right. So then, having survived the fall, Ernie was taken to hospital where the murderer finished him off with a dose of Nembuthal. The police found his flat had been burgled that same evening. This man was related to me by marriage. Following that, a grand niece of mine, Ruby Porter was injected with a huge shot of insulin at one of my gigs right here in this room. The district nurse, Eva Shawcross came to her aid, just as she came to my friend Mystic's aid, moments ago. Such diligence must be praised.' Sylvie gave a nod to Eva, who dismissed it with a shy smile.

Royston raised a finger. 'She's a good lass, is Eva. Can't praise her enough.'

'Indeed,' said Sylvie. 'But to continue with the story …. My caravan was turned over on Sunday night, and the brakes on my car were tampered with two nights ago.'

The audience gasped.

'My assistant Bobby and me, we were lucky to escape with our lives thanks to the prompt action of D.C.I. Seymour Witless.' Sylvie gave another nod of gratitude in Seymour's direction, upon which he lowered his head as the audience turned towards him.

Royston grunted, shuffling once again in his seat.

'What's this? An awards ceremony? Where are the trophies then? Bring on the nibbles.'

Sylvie smiled, and continued.

'…. And it turns out all of these incidents were connected. We have Carolyn Carr, the warbling ….

erm, the singer, sitting in the audience with you all now.'

Carolyn turned her toothy smile on the crowd surrounding her, waving a white-gloved hand as Sylvie continued.

'In 1939, the Maharajah of Bapoda took a fancy to Ms. Carr - gave her a whopping great diamond as a token of his love. She kept it hidden away, until she met my husband Ernie and they began a very long affair. She entrusted him with the stone. More fool her, because it went missing. So you see, the murderer wasn't just intent on eliminating family members at random, they were cherry picking potential heirs to this thousand carat rock which has yet to be authenticated.'

'YOU'VE FOUND IT?' squealed Carolyn from the audience.

'That's .... what I'm being told,' answered Sylvie.

'By whom? I need to know where my diamond is. TELL ME NOW!'

Stinky raised both palms. 'Please ma'am, I'm sure that information will come to you. I beg you, be patient.'

Carolyn scowled. 'This is insufferable!' But she appeared to be pacified for the moment.

'So, knowing the murders are all about who inherits, it was important to find Ernie's beneficiaries, including all of his illegitimate children.

'But that doesn't make sense!' Carolyn said. 'The diamond wasn't Ernie's to bequeath, it was mine. He stole it from me.'

'Well, that's not quite true, Ms. Carr. Your signature is held on a document drawn up by Ernie's solicitor, gifting the diamond to him. It was witnessed by two people in December 1951.'

'Poppy cock! I'd never sign away such a valuable thing like that.'

'Well, ***you did***. And someone else was also present at the signing of this document. Although just a child at the time.'

'I don't remember this at all. It's complete nonsense!'

'The child was yours and Ernie's. So now, we have two potential murderers. Yourself and your child.'

'Surely you can't think it was me? I mean, for heaven's sake ....'

'Well, if not you .... there's only one other. That sweet eleven year old you took with you that day to sign over the diamond thirty two years ago.

This was a dilemma D.C.I. Witless and myself struggled with, which one of you could it be? There were one or two clues. The access to drugs for one thing, but that's not unfamiliar territory to either of you, is it Ms. Carr?'

Carolyn stood up. 'I don't have to sit here listening to this nonsense.' She turned to leave, but then a flash went off as Max Wade from the Gazette snapped her full frontal with his Pentax. She made a u-turn and sat back down.

'Where the hell did he come from?' Seymour muttered to Brenda.

'Are we gonna be on the telly?' said Royston, giving Lucinda's forearm a squeeze.

'I certainly hope not, Mister Tracey,' said Sylvie.

'Well, get on with it then! Which one of them is it? We can bring the gallows up on stage. Have it all done and dusted by supper.'

'As I was saying,' Sylvie went on. 'The second clue, and most important as far as I was concerned, was the smell left behind in my toilet after I was burgled.'

'Hee hee! This just gets better 'n' better!'

Richard Tracey, sitting as low in his seat as possible, was now wondering how he could sneak out of the building and then perhaps onto a flight for Outer Mongolia.

'The smell troubled me for a while. But then I remembered you, Eva Shawcross, District Nurse, passing me on the Coast Road on a horse, just an hour or so before my place was burgled.' Sylvie gave Eva a narrow-eyed stare.

'So? I spend time at the stables at weekends. Where's the crime in that?'

'She does,' said Royston. 'But I must admit, that smell's a bit of a passion killer, Eva. That poor fella of yours …'

'The smell in my toilet,' Sylvie continued, '… and you ***were*** in my toilet that night, because the wall cabinet had been searched and my pills were on the floor – ***the smell was hay***. D.C.I. Witless said it reminded him of a tortoise he had as a child – his tortoise slept on hay, hibernated in hay. I knew it had to be you.'

Eva scoffed, reaching down for her medical bag, still lying open on the floor. 'This is silly. Didn't you just say you suspected Ms. Carr's child, the eleven-year-old who witnessed this so-called signing over of the diamond?' She tugged gently on the bag, bringing it closer.

'That's right, Eva Shawcross. And that child was you. We found your birth entry in parish records. Your mother's birth name is Carolyn

Shawcross, changed when she became famous to Carolyn Carr. And your father was Ernie Winters.'

Still clutching Lucinda at his side, Royston stood up from the sofa. 'Eva? Is this true? You're the bloody murderer? My God! To think I've exposed every part of my body to this woman. She might have killed me!'

'Of course it's not me, you stupid man. This is all circumstantial. I'm being set up here.' Eva's hand hovered over the open bag.

Sylvie remained calm. 'Well of course, there's always the third victim …. Charlie Pigeon, who you decided to bump off when he couldn't be the man you wanted him to be…'

'What utter nonsense. Charlie's my partner. Why would I ***bump him off***, as you call it?'

'Because you discovered ***he was in fact your half brother***, yet another of Ernie's beneficiaries. But you decided not to tell him. He'd already lost a chunk of his memory from wartime trauma. All the odds were in your favour to claim Ernie's inheritance for yourself. You made Charlie go along with the whole charade of being a couple, didn't you, Eva?'

'I have no idea what you're talking about. We ***are*** a couple.'

'He's gay, isn't he Eva? You even pressured him into having a child together, but sadly, the child didn't live. You blamed him, didn't you? And when the idea of getting the diamond all for yourself entered your head, what would be the point of keeping him around?'

Eva's face became contorted. 'You bitch!' she said, throwing herself at Sylvie, swinging an arm backwards with something clasped in her hand. Royston came between them, using Lucinda as a shield. The syringe went straight into Lucinda's chest, and a loud farting noise echoed across the hall as her life-giving air escaped in a rush. Stinky grabbed Eva from behind, squeezing the syringe from her hand. It dropped to the floor as Witless and Tracey leapt onto the stage, grabbing an arm each, with two undercover cops closely behind.

'Get off me!' she screamed. 'I'm innocent. It was her! My so-called bloody mother. I hate her ….. and I hate you!' She spat the words in Sylvie's direction.

'Let's get her out of here, fellas,' said Witless.

As they shunted Eva away, Royston stood motionless, still supporting his deflated girlfriend with an arm around her middle.

*'**She killed my Lucinda,**'* he said.

Sylvie turned to the audience and shrugged. 'Well, that was a show and a half, folks. Tune in next week for more shocking revelations.'

∞∞∞

Out in the car park, Chinless and Conway stepped out of a police car just as Eva was being escorted through the church hall's doors by two burly coppers, with Witless and Tracey close behind.

'Late as usual!' said Witless. 'I suppose you want to take this one off our hands, now we've done all the hard work for you.'

Behind Conway's car, Craddock stepped out of his with another officer.

'No, Witless. Conway will not be taking credit for this one. We'll take the suspect back to the cells for you, there's no reason why you should have your evening interrupted. And I want to see you back on the job in the morning. Conway and Chince can deal with statements from those inside. That should keep the pair of them out of trouble. For now.'

∞∞∞

Chapter 34 : Winding up

Back inside the building, the unofficial murder team were having a catch-up in Reception. Norris, having forgiven Sylvie for the impromptu appearance on stage, poured communal wine into plastic cups from dusty green bottles while Daisy handed out home-baked scones, minus the cheese this time. Sylvie took a plate from her, slipping a roll of notes into Daisy's apron pocket as she did so.

'What the divil?' said Daisy.

'I sold your special brew, Daisy. Hope you don't mind.'

'No, not at all. Glad it's off my hands to be honest. What with the place swarming with rozzers.' She gave her pocket an appreciative pat. 'Thank you.'

'I heard Arthur's coming home. That must be a relief.'

'Well, let's wait and see. I've never known such peace while he's been away. Oops that just slipped out. Must get on. See you later.'

Sylvie found Nurse Brenda Cole sitting with Stinky and drew up a chair.

'That was a bit much, having your date ruined like that. All my fault, it was unforgivable.'

Brenda cocked an eyebrow. 'Well, it had to be done. And I'm sure Seymour was glad to get the whole thing wound up so quickly. A grand performance, by the way.'

'Couldn't have done it without Stinky. He played a blinder.'

'Stinky?'

'Oh, that's me, ma'am, otherwise known as Mystic Mohawk, otherwise known as Simon. Pleased to meet ya,' said Stinky, planting a kiss on her hand.

'Don't get any ideas about Brenda, Stinky, she's already taken.'

Richard Tracey came through from the foyer, followed by Seymour Witless.

'Miss Broadstairs, have you seen my dad?'

Sylvie grabbed Tracey's sleeve and drew him closer.

'He took Lucinda with him to the Gent's. He may be needing some comfort for his loss. ***Also, his trousers are falling down.*** Here …. take this.' She reached inside her bag and took out a safety pin.

'Thanks, I'll get him sorted out. Aw, hell. What am I supposed to say to him?'

'Tell him time heals; that there's a drink with his name on it out here; that you'll get him a dog. Anything. And if none of that works …. ***you may have to buy him another Lucinda.'***

'Anything but another Lucinda. Right. Wish me luck.' And off he went.

'Ah, there you are,' said Seymour, approaching now with Hoggy in tow.

'Here I am, Seymour. So are you ready to take me dancing then?' said Brenda, with a sly wink in Sylvie's direction.

'Dancing? With these feet? You might regret that.'

'Oh, pull up a chair then and have a drink. I was just telling Sylvie ***how grateful you were for tonight.'***

While Seymour hesitated, Hoggy grabbed two chairs.

'Seymour is very grateful, missus. He's just about to express his gratitude in pork scratchings all round, isn't you Seymour?'

'I is. I mean ***I am,*** Hoggy. Just let me take the weight off these weary feet for a minute,' he said, plonking his bum on a chair.

The next person to burst into the room was Bobby, with Charlie Pigeon following behind.

'***Almighty shite!'*** Sylvie muttered, rising from her seat. 'They let you out already, Charlie?'

'Well, when a gallstones patient turns up needing a bed, what's a fella to do?'

'Pull up a seat. We have a lot to catch up on.' Sylvie's grin could not have spread any further across her face. 'And you, young man,' she said, poking a finger into Bobby's shoulder, 'You were right about Ruby still being alive before Eva planted the lips on her.'

'I knew it! So what was the actual cause of death?'

'Asphyxiation. Eva didn't give her the kiss of life. She smothered her.'

'Blimey. What a night I've missed. Though it wasn't completely wasted.'

'How so?'

'Well, your Charlie seems like a nice bloke. We were getting on like a house on fire out there in the car park. Weren't we, Charlie?'

'We certainly were, Bobby.'

'Oh dear. I see trouble ahead .... Anyway, you need to tell me where the hell you've been all day, Bobs,' she said with another shoulder prod.

Clarabelle poked her tiny face out of Bobby's coat and licked her hand.

'Oh, Clara, ***you're alive.'***

'She's been a little off her food today. Whimpering too.'

'I see. So you just thought you'd not tell me any of this in case it spoiled my performance tonight? How considerate.'

'Kind of ... but ***I have*** been trying to find out what's wrong with her.'

Sylvie's brows crinkled. 'And how have you been doing that? What's wrong with her?'

Bobby leaned in and whispered something in her ear. Her face fell into a horrified grimace.

'But ...' Bobby continued, 'I took your clock to the repair shop and you can pick it up on Friday.'

'Oh, that's just fabby, Bobs.'

'So, you're not gonna chuck me out then?' His question was left hanging on Sylvie's uncommitted stare.

'You know, Miss Broadstairs,' said Seymour, 'you were lucky to come out of that performance tonight unscathed.'

'Whatever do you mean?'

'Well … for one thing, you should have maybe waited until the diamond had been valued. Your performance may have been all the more impressive if you'd had that information.'

'Why? Do you know how much it's worth?'

'I do.'

'Well are you gonna tell me?'

Seymour took a swig of wine from his cup. 'Absolutely bugger all.'

'You're kidding me?'

'Nope. And if it was valued before signing it over to Ernie, which it would have had to be, then he's had you all for fools.'

'You mean … he had it copied? ***After*** the valuation?' Bobby said.

Seymour shrugged. 'Well that's the only explanation I can think of.'

'But what about the certificate of provenance?'

'It was a copy too, but a good one. Lightly sand-papered along the folds, painted with tea stains. If he sold the original diamond, then the certificate would go with it.'

'Flaming typical,' Sylvie scowled. 'And if he wasn't already murdered, I might just murder him myself.'

'And another thing. The pills that Charlie took for his anxiety had indeed been tampered with. But we haven't had those results back from the lab yet.'

'But that doesn't matter now, does it? Eva will still be convicted for the other two murders.'

'Yes, she will. It was just risky to suggest he was the third victim at this moment in time.'

'Well, maybe you'll keep me better informed next time.'

'Next time? I doubt there'll be a next time,' he scoffed.

'You don't get rid of me that easily, Seymour. We're part of the same family now.'

Seymour picked up his drink again. 'I don't know where you get your ideas from, Miss Broadstairs, but that's the most unlikely thing I ever heard.'

'Well, hear this, Seymour. Your Rambo has got my Clarabelle up the sodding duff.

'Listen up, everyone .... raise your plastic cups for a toast .... Seymour and I .... We're about to be grandparents ..... to a litter of very odd-looking pups.'

'Congratulations!' said everyone.

∞∞∞

END

NOTE FROM THE AUTHOR & ACKNOWLEDGEMENTS

Thank you for choosing to read ***A Nose for Murder***. As a second novel, it would mean a lot if you could leave an honest review on Amazon, Goodreads, etc.

This book is dedicated to the slings and arrows that fuelled my determination; lockdowns and shielding which supplied the time, and my incredible daughter who gave me encouragement.

Thanks also to the Writing Community of Twitter, in particular James Pierse who contributed much needed support and many laughs.

Chapter 23

Starred references (*) : Pelaw is a residential area in Gateshead, U.K.

OTHER BOOKS BY M.S. SAXON

Cheese on wheels : a recipe for Trouble, starring Bubble and Squeak

A children's collection of cartoon illustrated rhyming jokes and limericks.

Dinner's in the dog and other sod's law stories, starring Bubble & Squeak.

Book 1 in the series. A collection of cartoon illustrated, rhyming jokes & stories for ADULTS.

Dinner's in the dog. Again!

Book 2 in the series. A further collection of cartoon illustrated rhyming jokes & stories for ADULTS.

A Nose for Murder – M.S. Saxon

The Purple Dolphin

Women's crime fiction novel.

A critical parent with alcohol issues, a parrot with an underwear fetish, death threats in the post. Catherine's life is stuck on a treadmill and something needs to change.

1960's - 1990's North East England

Contemporary women's crime fiction novel following two rival families. The Grimshaws are market traders, the Morettis - known criminals with a grudge. Catherine is left holding things together when brother Steven is incarcerated, her mother becomes mentally ill and her father arranges his own exit.
Steven has his own personal war to fight behind bars, while Catherine goes sleuthing to find her missing nephew. Along the way she uncovers hidden family secrets, the chance of a whole new future, and dare she hope, even romance? But it's a rocky path to climb. And just who is her real father?

∞∞∞

If you would like to receive an email about new book releases & offers from this author, please send your name and a current email address to: info@mssaxonbooks.co.uk

Printed in Great Britain
by Amazon

28275674R00234